THE CALLING OF
ELIZABETH COURTLAND

by Colleen Reece

Flip over for another great novel!
HONOR BOUND

Barbour Books
164 Mill Street
P.O. Box 1219
Westwood, New Jersey 07675

Typesetting By
Typetronix, Inc., Cape Coral, FL

89   90   91   92   93   5   4   3   2   1

THE CALLING OF
ELIZABETH COURTLAND

"Miss Betty, your mama says for you to come down right now!" The freckled face of the serving maid in neat gray uniform looked worried. "The carriages are coming, and Mr. Prescott's glarin' at his watch and watchin' the stairs. All the people are —" she broke off sharply. "Miss Betty, whatever is the matter?"

Elizabeth Courtland whirled from the dressing table. Her white skirts billowing about her made her look like some heavenly creature. "Abbie, have you ever been in love?"

The maid's eyes reflected her shock. "In love! Me?"

"Yes, you."

"Of course not, Miss Betty. Who'd look at the likes of me?"

Elizabeth cocked her head to one side. "Oh, I don't know. You are well put together and have shiny hair and blue eyes. A man could do worse."

Abbie just stared, then roused herself. "You'd better come. All those folks waitin' for your engagement to be announced. Your papa's goin' to be up here after you if you don't get downstairs."

"Let them wait!" The imperious head crowned with sweeping dark hair was in sharp contrast to the creamy white shoulders and snowy lace dress. "It's *my* engagement party, isn't it? I'll go down if and when I feel like it. I may not go at all."

"Miss Betty!"

"What's wrong, Abbie? Shocked because I'm in no hurry? Why should I be? I've been practically engaged ever since I was born." She waved a haughty hand toward the newspaper clipping on the dressing table, mocking its contents.

HOUSES OF COURTLAND AND
WETHERELL TO BE JOINED
*In the most lavish ball of its kind
ever to be held in Grand Rapids
Miss Elizabeth Courtland's
engagement will be announced to
Mr. Prescott Wetherell.*

She dropped to the bed, appraising the Wetherell's best guest room. "Hah! What choice did *I* ever have in the matter?"

1

Concern for her mistress replaced Abbie's anxiety over getting her downstairs. "But Mr. Prescott just about worships you, Miss Betty! He'll give you everything you want and let you do just as you please. He's even letting me go with you to your new home just because I've always been your maid. Aren't you happy?"

At the risk of crushing her gown, Elizabeth sprang from the bed defiantly. "Why should I be? Prescott is — Prescott. As for having my own way, haven't I always?" She did not wait for a reply. "Too bad I didn't have a passel of brothers and sisters to look after. I've never had anything but my own way."

"You'll have children of your own to look after."

"Children? You must be out of your mind. Having children ruins your figure and makes you unfit for dancing."

"Yes, ma'am. But children have a way of comin' when you're married."

"Then I just won't get married!"

"Miss Betty!"

"I mean it, Abbie. I won't be tied down with children, even if nurses do look after them. It's bad enough marrying Prescott, who's dull as dishwater, but at least we can travel. He says he'll take me anywhere I want to go."

Abbie's freckles stood out at her own daring as she asked, "Miss Betty, don't you love Mr. Prescott?"

"Love Prescott Wetherell?" There was honest surprise in Elizabeth's voice. "Why should I? We've grown up together, and I'm fond of him. He's the most suitable match. Why should he want more than that?" She turned back to Abbie. "What do you know about it, anyway? You said you'd never been in love."

Abbie's face was sober. "Before my mother died she taught me never to marry a man I didn't love with all my heart. She said it was a sin to marry without love."

"Sin!" Betty broke into peals of laughter. "The only sin in this world is not doing as you please."

"Elizabeth, your guests are waiting." Mrs. Courtland's icy voice from the doorway broke into the conversation. "Abbie, I told you to send her down. Why we should have to have this engagement ball here instead of in our own home, I'll never know."

Betty chose to ignore the oft-heard complaint. "You know Prescott's mother." She linked her arm in her own mother's. "Why bother? If I'm to marry Prescott Wetherell, why not just elope?"

"That's enough from you, Elizabeth. I must say I'll be glad when you're married and safe. I'm tired of your odd remarks and wild ways. The gossip columns refer to you as 'Madcap Betty.' That's all a nice girl needs — to get herself tagged as wild. It's fortunate Prescott is so understanding."

Halfway to the top of the stairs, Abbie close behind, Betty stopped. "Mother." There was an unaccustomed tremor in her voice. "Did you love Papa when you were married? Before the ceremony, I mean?"

"Elizabeth!" Her well-padded mother drew back in horror. "What a thing to ask! No nice girl ever loves the man she marries before the wedding. Love comes afterward. It would not be dignified to have such feelings until you were married. Only a wanton would admit to it, and as for discussing —" Her voice trailed off in suggestive cadence, matching perfectly her raised eyebrows.

"That's funny. Some people think it's a sin to marry without love."

Betty cast a mischievous eye toward the frightened Abbie, but her mother cut her off. "We won't discuss it further."

"Here she comes!" A hundred pair of eyes turned toward the curving staircase into the ballroom. In a moment Betty forgot her rebellion. A tiny pulse beat in her throat. All those faces upturned, admiring her! Carefully she descended, walking as she had been taught, tiny steps in her silver slippers, swishing her train behind her in an aura of beauty.

There were Mr. and Mrs. Wetherell, dour and grim, determined to show the world that no Courtland would get ahead of them, even if she was marrying their son. There were the Ashleys and the Beaumonts and the Fosters and all the other cream of Grand Rapids society. At last her eyes singled out Prescott. After her talk with Abbie, Betty had secretly hoped he would suddenly become devastatingly handsome, mysterious, exciting. She bit her lip. He was the same Prescott she had always known — sandy haired, good-natured, smiling at her slow progress.

Betty's eyes widened. *Who is the stranger standing next to Prescott?* His hair was as dark as her own. Was that a challenge in the laughing dark eyes behind the admiration she could see from the light of a hundred candles and gas lamps? A stain of color covered her cheeks. How exciting! A new man — and evidently unattached. No belle with carefully curled hair stood next to him. What fun!

Betty came to earth with a thud. What good did it do for that handsome stranger to appear? It was her party, her engagement party.

So what? The imp of mischief that had earned her the nickname "Madcap Betty" snapped its leash. She was not married yet. Another spurt of color highlighted her already beautiful face. The stranger was too choice a prize to let slip away to some other girl.

"Elizabeth, my dear." Prescott stepped to the foot of the staircase and offered his arm. A spontaneous burst of applause interrupted her surveillance of the visitor. Bother! Why did all those people have to be there?

"May I present my good friend Daniel Spencer?" Prescott smiled at the stranger. "Dan, my fiancee, Miss Elizabeth Courtland."

Why did she feel like this? Betty's hand was swallowed in the strong grip of the stranger's. Was it mockery in the dark eyes as he murmured, "Miss Courtland"?

"Mr. Spencer." How ridiculous! Following all the courteous formalities when she longed to ask who he was and where he came from. Suddenly Betty wanted to know everything there was to know about this disturbing man. Her plans were thwarted by the arrival of her mother.

"Really, Elizabeth, Prescott! You are holding up the receiving line." Her glance set Daniel Spencer down as totally insignificant. "Come."

"My apologies, Mrs. Courtland." Prescott turned Betty around, but not before she caught the amused glance that Daniel Spencer gave them. Her blood boiled. He *was* laughing at her!

"Elizabeth." Her mother's whisper recalled her to the present. "Will you stop gaping at that man and stand here where you belong? Your father and I have gone to a great deal of expense to launch you as Prescott's bride. You might at least act as if you are enjoying it instead of acting like an open-mouthed fool, staring as if you had never seen a minister before!"

"Minister!" Betty stopped in mid-stride. "Mr. Spencer is a minister?"

Prescott's eyes twinkled. "Oh, yes. He's just ready to leave for the far West. He has quite an interesting story. I hope you can hear it before he goes."

Something inside Betty froze. A minister. How could a man like that be a minister? Weren't they all dreadfully self-righteous and old? Or in poor health? She stole another glance at Daniel Spencer. He was bronze — in sharp contrast to Prescott and the other men in the room. She caught his fleeting smile as he saw her looking his way. How dare he look like that! Impetuously, denying the answering thrill in her heart, she turned to Prescott with her most charming smile. Let Daniel Spencer see she had no interest in him!

Only once did Betty drop her assumed gaiety to casually ask, "What is a minister doing at a ball? I thought they were all too goody-goody to come to an event like this."

Prescott was too well-bred to show surprise at her question. "We met at college and became good friends. He said balls weren't in his line, but I insisted that he meet you. He finally gave in and came."

"How soon did you say he was leaving?"

"In a few weeks."

Someone came up, interrupting their conversation, but Betty pondered. So Daniel Spencer would be in Grand Rapids for a few weeks. Could she see him? She would like to make him fall in love with her, then turn him down hard as punishment for laughing at her.

Why did he seem to have the power to make her feel like a giddy butterfly? Was it his profession? He probably disapproved of her and all her friends. It was remarkable he did not stand up and tell them they were all sinners the way that uncle of Lydia Beaumont had done at her ball. Of course he was hurried out, but it had been terribly embarrassing. Yet she saw no accusation in the dark eyes following her as she danced and flirted, only that maddening amusement.

In the midst of the ball Betty suddenly wished it was over. Why wear herself out pretending to have a good time when she was not enjoying herself at all? What was wrong with her, anyway? Was it the prospect of spending the rest of her life with Prescott Wetherell? Yet she had always known it was to be. Why should it bother her now, unless it was because the engagement party made it seem so final.

Worst of all, why did Abbie's freckled face and solemn words, "a sin to marry without love," float between Betty and her partners? She cast a scornful glance to the corner where Daniel Spencer was evidently telling a story to a group who had gathered around him. He had not danced, but then he would not, being a minister. Would he think it was a sin to marry without love? Probably. What did he know of love?

Betty was not prepared for the sharp pain that threatened to smother her and caused her partner to exclaim, "Are you all right, Miss Courtland?"

She wrenched her thoughts back to him. "Quite all right, Mr. Foster. I often catch my breath like that." Her dark eyes dared him to defy her unusual statement. Tired of him, tired of the ball, she dropped her eyelashes to make dark crescents on her flushed cheeks. "I think I'd like to sit down for a moment." She paused and calculated distance. "Perhaps over there?" She indicated a settee close enough to hear Daniel Spencer, yet far enough away so she would not rouse his suspicions, but before they could reach their chosen destination a fanfair of trumpets sounded. Prescott walked toward her.

For one moment of sheer panic Elizabeth Courtland considered fleeing through the open window into the garden, refusing to have her engagement announced. Another glance into the cool, dark eyes of the unexpected guest firmed her control. She took Prescott's arm, walked to the small dais, and mounted. Her mother beamed. Her father harrumphed and then said, "I am happy to announce the official engagement of my daughter Elizabeth to Prescott Wetherell. I present to you the bridal couple."

Betty could feel chains dropping over her, nailing her to the floor. Yet even as they dropped, she rebelled. She would not be parceled off to Prescott Wetherell before ever having really lived. So what if she had turned twenty and nice girls were married long before then? That did not mean *she* had to be.

She opened her mouth to deny the engagement — and saw Prescott looking down at her, gentle, smiling. She slowly closed her mouth. She could not hurt and humiliate him there in his own home. She would wait and tell him when he drove her to the Courtland mansion when the ball was over. Yet guilt sent red flags of color into her otherwise startlingly white face as she bowed her head and accepted the storm of congratulations following the announcement.

"Elizabeth." Prescott hurried to her side when she came down in her long evening wrap. "Mother has had a spell and needs me. I won't be able to drive you home."

Betty's heart sank. That meant another day at least before she could tell him she had changed her mind about marrying him. "I can go with Mama and Papa."

Prescott looked worried. "They've already gone."

"Allow me." Both turned to meet Daniel Spencer's steady gaze. "I will be happy to drive Miss Courtland home."

Betty's heart leaped wildly, but she managed to protest, "Really, Mr. Spencer, that won't be necessary. I am sure Prescott can get away long enough to drive me to my home."

"It's no trouble, Miss Courtland. Prescott, your mother is calling." The inflexible mouth settled the issue.

"Thanks, Dan. Take good care of her; she's precious cargo." Prescott gripped Betty's hands, then ran lightly up the stairs.

Betty did not speak as Daniel Spencer led her to a covered carriage and tucked her inside. Swinging easily into place he took the reins. "Which way?"

"Left." Before Betty could hold them back, hot words burst out. "You don't approve of me, do you?"

"Really, Miss Courtland. I hardly know you."

The same amusement she had seen in his eyes all evening colored his voice and infuriated her. In her best Courtland manner she accused haughtily, "I know you don't. I could see it all evening. Just why don't you like me?" He started to reply, but she forestalled him. "Remember, you are a minister. You need not lie to be polite."

"I never lie, Miss Courtland." His voice was colder than the icy breath of Lake Michigan when she had visited it once in winter. "You are a beautiful girl. You are also thoroughly spoiled — and you do not love Prescott Wetherell in the way you should in order to be his wife."

"Nice girls learn to love their husbands after marriage, Mr. Spencer," she told him primly.

"Rubbish!" She could see his hands tighten on the reins as he turned slightly toward her in the early morning dimness. "It is a crime to marry without love."

"You and Abbie!"

"Abbie?"

"My maid. She seems to be quite an authority on love. She told me much the same thing before I came down tonight." Betty bit her lip. Why had she revealed Abbie's words to this man?

"She is a wise maid. Too bad you didn't listen better."

"What right do you have to speak to me like this, Mr. Spencer?"

"The right of a man called by God to teach foolish children something of His will in their lives."

"You consider me a child?" The ominous note in her voice should have warned him.

It did not even slow him down. "Certainly. A petted child who is of no earthly use except to look pretty. Tell me, Miss Courtland, can you bake a loaf of bread such as your cook bakes? Can you make a dress such as your seamstress makes? Can you even make a bed, or dry a dish, or keep your clothing in order, as I'm sure your little maid Abbie now does? If something happened that you had to provide for yourself and keep from starving — could you do it?"

"You are impertinent, sir!"

He suddenly sounded weary. "No, I am realistic. I see you girls who have not been given a chance to learn anything important in life and —"

"Important! I can ride and dance and play the piano and —"

"And flirt and starve to death if your life depended on your own skills!"

"No one has ever talked to me like this!"

"Then isn't it time someone did? I'll be gone in a few weeks. Shall I tell you what it will be like where I am going?" He did not wait for her answer — probably would not have heard if she had spoken it, Betty realized.

"I am going to a town out West called Pioneer. It is carved from the heart of a great forest by men who are as rugged as the trees they cut to make homes for their families. There are seven saloons. There is one small grocery store. There is a railroad into town and enough children for a one-room school. Could you teach eight grades in one room, Miss Courtland, as the brave little teacher does? Could you hoe corn and plant beans and wash your own clothing on a scrub board with water you had hauled from a creek?"

"I could if I had to. I never will have to."

"Ah, yes." Betty caught the mirth in his voice. "If you had to. I doubt it, Miss Courtland. Perhaps I shouldn't blame you too much. I am sure your parents have encouraged you to fritter away your life and eventually marry Prescott Wetherell and raise daughters just as useless as yourself. Well, let me tell you this, Miss Elizabeth Courtland. You have never lived. You will never live or love until you find the place in this world God created for you to fill, and then fill it with all your strength."

Betty could hardly keep from striking him. "And you think that place is *not* as Prescott Wetherell's wife! Could it be that you are simply jealous, Mr. Spencer? Jealous of Prescott and his wealth and position?" She warmed to her subject, hands clenched in her lap. "If you could trade places with Prescott, wouldn't you do so — and gladly?"

"Never!" The vehement word rang in the still night.

He reined in the horses and turned to her. "Nothing on earth could induce me to live the indolent life you and your friends live — even Prescott. I had hopes for him in college. He would have made a brilliant lawyer. It was all he ever wanted to do."

Betty gasped.

"You didn't know that, did you, Miss Courtland? There are a lot of things you don't know about Prescott. He gave up his plans because his selfish, petted mother, who once was just like you, demanded he come home and be with her during her 'spells.' The only thing wrong with Prescott Wetherell's mother is her temper. If she had to fend for herself and would let her son be a man, she would find those 'spells' strangely absent."

"Why didn't Prescott break free, if he wanted it so badly?" There were disbelief and shock in her voice.

"Why don't you break free of the useless life you lead?"

"I, sir, am a lady." She drew herself up, angry at herself for listening to him for so long.

Daniel started the horses once more. His voice was colorless, his impassioned words cooled to ice. "That may be, Miss Courtland, but I pray the day will come when God will allow you to forget the lady part and become a real woman."

Betty was stung more than ever before in her life, shaken by his words. "I suppose you could teach me to be a real woman."

"I could." His jawline was hard. "But frankly, I don't want the job. When I find a wife it will be one who can be a helpmate and companion, not someone to be waited on and pampered. Why, you couldn't even be the fit mother of a child, Miss Courtland."

"Sir!"

"If I shock you it is because I mean to do just that. Name one qualification you have for motherhood, for the daring challenge of raising a human being to be more than you yourself are." He broke off. "Is this your home?"

Betty nodded wordlessly, unable to get anything past the gigantic mound in her throat. Finally she said, "If you believed me so worthless, why did you come to the ball to meet me?"

He helped her from the carriage and stood facing her in the pale light. "I came because I was curious. Curious about a society girl with enough spirit to be called 'Madcap Betty.' Perhaps I thought she would be more than the typical belle — with warmth and humor and love for Prescott."

"*And?*" The single word nearly choked her.

"I found a spoiled child. One who will never make Prescott happy or be happy herself." His words were grave, almost sad.

Betty struggled with tears as the mansion door opened; the impassive butler stared woodenly ahead. Every invective she could dredge up to hurt this man who had been judge and jury, tried and condemned her, damming up behind her frozen lips.

"Good night, Miss Courtland. No, good morning."

A tip of that hat, a spring to the carriage, and he was gone, leaving a shaken Betty Courtland peering after him into the dawn of a new and unwelcome day.

"How dare he?" Betty paced the floor of her own room, white skirts trailing. She had swept up the staircase so like the one in the Wetherell mansion she had descended in triumph earlier that evening but with such a difference. So she was a spoiled child? She would show him. But how?

For hours she walked, heedless of servants arising, a new day in full swing. Her anger grew, at herself as well as at Daniel Spencer. How could she have allowed him to speak so, condemning her and others like her? Why should she care what he thought — the country dolt? He would go to his precious town of Pioneer and she would never have to hear of him again.

But before he goes, I will repay him. I will entrap him, make him fall in love with me, then throw in his face how different we are by parroting his exact words to me! An unpleasant smile marred the classic features, turned the blue eyes almost to black. She dropped to the dressing table bench and stared at her misty reflection.

Suppose — suppose I should marry him, then run off and leave him! Her face glowed at the plan. She sprang to her feet and ran to the window, throwing wide the curtains. "I'll do it! I'll even marry him — then have the time of my life when I tell him I'm getting a divorce! A minister with a divorce. That should ruin him forever!"

A perplexed frown crossed her face. "I wonder where I should begin?" She paced the carpeted floor again. "Perhaps I could play the part of a penitent — pretend I really took to heart what he said. I wonder if I could learn to cook?" She shuddered. "Horrors!" Yet a moment later her chin was set. "I'll do it if I have to. I'll get even with Daniel Spencer if it's the last thing I do."

Betty slumped to a big chair, suddenly drained. The night of dancing followed by Daniel's indictment and her determination had left her exhausted. But there was no time to waste in sleeping. He would only be in Grand Rapids a little while. She must not waste any of that time.

Imperiously she rang her bell to summon Abbie. The maid responded with wide eyes. "Miss Betty, you're still in your ball gown. Didn't you go to bed?"

"Never mind that. Get me some breakfast up here on a tray. Then get out my driving clothes. I have a call to make."

"At nine o'clock in the morning?" Abbie's voice oozed disapproval.

"Oh, bother, Abbie. Do as I say! I'm going to see how Mrs. Wetherell is after her spell last night." For one moment the eyes of the two girls met in perfect understanding. Mrs. Wetherell's 'spells' were known to both of them — an excuse to keep Prescott close at hand.

"Yes, ma'am."

In an incredibly short time Abbie was back. Betty stuffed a little breakfast in her mouth, dressing as she ate. Through a mouthful she mumbled, "Have Sam bring the small carriage around with Beauty. I'll drive myself."

"Miss Betty, your mama ain't goin' to like it."

"So?" Again her level glance quieted Abbie. She even laughed and waved good-bye to the still disapproving figure as she lifted the reins and drove down the avenue she had traveled the night before in company with Daniel Spencer. The clear morning and fresh air whipped color into her face. She had taken the first step. Now if things would only work out as she hoped at the Wetherells.

They did. The Wetherell butler was quite surprised to see Miss Courtland at such an early hour, especially after a ball. "Why, why, Miz Wetherell isn't up. I'll get Mr. Prescott." He scuttled away, nearly upsetting a vase of flowers in his hurry, muttering to himself, "Callers. Nine o'clock in the morning. That woman must be up to something!"

"Betty, my dear," Prescott's face was alight with surprise.

"I just came to see how your mother is."

Prescott's smile faded. "Not so well. She seems to have overtaxed her strength at our engagement ball. She plans to spend the day in bed." He looked at Betty apologetically. "I'm afraid I'll have to stay around. She gets so upset if she calls and I'm not here."

Without thinking Betty asked, "Prescott, is that why you gave up the study of law?"

He froze in place. It was a long moment before he answered. "Yes, Elizabeth. She was so against it —"

Betty's anger at Mrs. Wetherell mixed with contempt for Prescott. "I think you should do what you feel is right."

"It's all right." He managed a crooked smile. "Just knowing we'll be married will make up for it." His laugh was shaky. "Who wants to spend all their time in a stuffy court, anyway?"

Now was the time to tell him she was not planning to marry him. Betty could not do it. Instead she said, "I'd hoped you would be free to drive in the country with me. I've been promising our old cook to stop by for weeks, and today's such a beautiful day. Mama would have fits if I went by myself." She managed just the right amount of wistfulness.

"I'm sorry, Betty," he took both her hands. "I just can't." His face brightened. "Say, why can't Dan go with you? He's top company. Didn't you get along capitally with him last night on the way home?" Carried away by his own enthusiasm Prescott rang for the butler. "Ask Mr. Dan to come in here, will you please?"

Betty felt like a hypocrite as she protested, "Oh, don't bother, Prescott. I'm sure Mr. Spencer has other plans. I can put off going until another day."

"Don't be silly. He'll be delighted to go. Not much fun for him hanging around here."

"Good morning, Prescott, Miss Courtland." There was nothing in Daniel Spencer's voice to show he had ever said anything more to Miss Courtland than a formal hello. Betty's eyes took in every detail. He was even more striking in worn clothing than he had been in formal garb. There was something outdoorsy in the careless way his shirt was open at the neck.

"Elizabeth had plans to pay a visit to her old cook out in the country to-day, and I can't go," Prescott explained. "I suggested you would accompany her."

"Delighted, of course." His eyes bored into Betty. Did he wonder why Betty would have any interest in a cook? Betty's ruse became reality. She *would* visit the cook.

"I tried to tell Prescott the visit could wait." She lifted innocent eyes toward Daniel Spencer, knowing full well how she looked with the shaft of sunlight streaming through the draperies to highlight her. "He thought you might enjoy seeing some of our countryside while you were here, and as he isn't free —" she lifted one shoulder daintily.

She was rewarded by a flash of humor mixed with admiration. "I am sure I will enjoy seeing — the countryside."

"Very well." She turned back to Prescott to hide her confusion. Somehow she had not fooled Daniel Spencer at all. It would take all the skill she had to convince him of her sincerity. "Good-bye, Prescott." She gazed up at him fondly, still aware of Dan's eyes on her. "Give your mother my sympathy."

Daniel Spencer did not speak until they were in the light carriage and well on their way out of the city. "Miss Courtland, you didn't really appear on the Wetherell doorstep at nine in the morning to see how Mrs. Wetherell was, did you?"

Betty decided to drop her pose, at least for the time being. "No, Mr. Spencer, I came to see if I could inveigle you into a drive with me." She caught his involuntary slowing of the horses and added rapidly, "I wanted to tell you I spent several hours after you left taking inventory of myself. You were right. I really have not been good for anything important in life until now." A passing breeze stirred one long lock of raven hair. "I also wanted to ask you —" The tremble in her voice was real. "Do you think I could change? Could I become the woman you said God wanted me to be?" She felt, rather than saw, his suspicious glance and hurried on. "I didn't sleep at all. I felt I had to see you."

"I see, Miss Courtland." He hesitated. "Am I to understand then that the casual words of a stranger could so affect you?"

"Casual!" Betty repeated. "You accused, tried, and convicted me all in the space of minutes."

"I know." His grasp of the reins tightened. "I believe I was very rude. I had no right to come into your life and speak so."

Betty leaned forward, eyes on the road they traveled. "I am glad you came into my life, Mr. Spencer. You will never know just what it meant to me." It was the truth, she knew. Under lowered lashes she saw him turn toward her and played her trump card. "You said God had a plan for every person's life. How do I find what it is in my life?"

Just ahead and off the road stood a big oak. Toward it Daniel guided Beauty until she stood quietly beneath the leafy branches. "Miss Courtland, if you are sincere, if you desire to change your life, there is no reason you cannot do so. God stands ready to accept you. When you take the first steps toward Him, He does the rest in receiving you."

Betty shivered in spite of herself. What was she getting herself into? She took refuge in a question. "Mr. Spencer, tell me. How did a man such as you, who went to college with Prescott, decide to become a minister?"

"It's a long story." Yet he looked at her wistfully.

"We have the whole day." Her smile encouraged him to spring from the carriage and throw a blanket on the ground under the big tree. Helping her down, he stood before her, his face lifted to the sky. Was he *praying?* What if he were praying for *her?* The next moment he dropped to the blanket beside her.

"Miss Courtland, from the time I was small I knew someday God would ask me to serve Him." His solemn voice sent shivers up Betty's spine.

"My father was a minister. We always had enough to eat and wear but never any luxuries. Yet I remember the faces of those who loved him. Wherever we were sent, he left a trail of hope. He worked with doctors, often bringing comfort when medicine failed. It was my father who introduced me to Jesus Christ." Betty knew she had been forgotten, and a pang of envy filled her. What a different childhood he had known! If only her family had been close like that.

"I must have been about seven when he started taking me with him on some of his calls. He had fought in the Civil War, and when he came home he wanted no more fighting. He would spend the rest of his life fighting a different battle.

"I will never forget the day a man he had worked with to help find a better life reverted to his old ways and took his own life. My father's brow was furrowed. Young as I was, I realized what a blow it had been. I asked, 'Father, isn't it like losing a battle?' He always compared the fight for men's souls to the fight for men's freedom.

"He looked at me for a full minute before he said, 'Son, losing the battle isn't so important. Winning the war is.' I believe at that moment I knew I was to follow in my father's footsteps. He insisted that I get schooling, be better prepared to meet some of the modern questions and indifference than he had been. I finished college and was assigned to a small church in Kansas. Then my real call came — to build my own church for God in a place that desperately needs it."

Betty found moisture on her hands. Had it slid from brimming eyes at the touching story? "Why didn't you take a real church, one in a huge city where there are hundreds of people who need you?" Neither noticed the absence of hostility between them.

"I considered it. I even had an opportunity for a church right here in Grand Rapids." He named a large church she knew well.

"Daniel." The unaccustomed name felt strange on her lips. "Could you still have that church?"

"Yes. But I will not take it."

"Why not?" Hot color stung her cheeks. "Don't you think there are people here in Grand Rapids who could benefit by what you have to offer? You could have money and prestige and make a name for yourself."

"The name I make must be for my God, not for myself."

Betty was silenced. Yet her agile mind seized on another facet. "You have education. You could reach the cultured. What need do people such as those in your town of Pioneer have for such education? Does your God want all your training wasted?"

"The loggers in Pioneer need God's message as well as the elite in Grand Rapids."

"But someone else could go there! Someone who isn't so well-prepared, someone who couldn't handle the church here. Why, with your friendship with Prescott Wetherell, all the best people would attend your church. You could reach ten or a hundred times as many people as will ever respond in that dump out West."

"The gospel of Jesus Christ is for all, Miss Courtland. I do not need the Wetherell backing in order to present my Lord."

Betty stared. "Then you really will throw away a chance like that, just because of your pride in what you believe? Aren't you being self-righteous?"

She was prepared for anything except what happened. Daniel Spencer laughed until the leaves above them shook. "Self-righteous! My dear Miss Courtland, have you any idea what a snob you really are?" He was off again, his gales of laughter sweeping through the clear morning air.

"Really!" Betty jumped to her feet but tripped over the hem of her long skirt. He caught her, for one moment holding her while she regained her footing. The touch of his strong hands unnerved her. Angrily she jerked free. How could she respond to such a boor?

"You are a fanatic, Mr. Spencer. No one in his right mind would make the choice you are making. And while we are on the subject, I am not your dear Miss Courtland. I belong to Prescott Wetherell."

"Do you, Miss Courtland?" There was a disturbing gleam in his dark eyes. "I think not. You belong to only one."

"Who? Not you, I dare say," she flouted him, a sarcastic smile touching her lips. "You wouldn't be crazy enough to believe that."

"Not at all. You could never belong to me."

In spite of her fury something inside hurt at his words. "Then just whom are you referring to?"

"God."

"God! *I?* I am not even sure a God exists. How could I belong to Him?" She saw she had overplayed her role. Where had the assurance that she could fake an interest and wind him around her finger gone? "I mean," she added hastily, "I've never known anyone who could show me there really was a God. Perhaps you could do that?"

"I wish I could!" His vehemence startled her. "I wish I could show you how precious you are to that God you say may not exist. You think it is chance you were born in beauty and luxury? No. It is part of God's plan, as surely as those trees and flowers are part of it." He waved across open fields to clumps of trees surrounded with blossoms. "How can you look at all that beauty and not see God's hand!"

"Why, it's always been there," she faltered, unsure of herself against his strength. "Ever since I can remember, it's always been there."

"And before your remembrance? Before your parents and their parents? What then?"

Betty put her head in her hands. "It tires me to think of it. Why not just have a good time in life? Why spend it by thinking deep and solemn thoughts? Your God makes long faces. I've seen them, the holier-than-thous who sneer at me when I ride by. Even if there is a God, what would I have to do with Him?"

"Miss Courtland, will you sit down again, please? I think you might like to hear a story about a great woman."

Betty eyed him distrustfully, then reseated herself. What woman would he speak of, some paragon he planned to marry? She pushed back a twinge at the idea and regarded him with unfriendly eyes. "Perhaps you had better make your story short, Mr. Spencer. I really do have other things to do today."

If he caught the bald contradiction from her earlier statement he ignored it. Leaning against the tree trunk, hands clasped behind his head, Daniel Spencer seemed part of the outdoor world itself. Betty resented the effect he had on her. Why should her heart pound at his nearness, the resonant note in his deep voice?

"You say you think God makes long faces. The most beautiful woman I ever knew didn't find God that way at all."

Betty drew in a sharp breath, nails biting into her clenched hands. So it was true. He would parade the virtues of some distant fiancee before her, showing by comparison how wicked and inadequate she was. She stared stonily at Beauty as he began.

"She never had much, but everywhere she went people loved her. Fretful children stilled under her hand. Old people smiled, and young people laughed when she came. Her home was open to all. There was music and fun — not balls and luncheons and teas such as you need to survive, but the joy of living. She worked twelve hours a day gardening, mending, sewing, cooking — yet found time to watch every sunset, hear every bird song, see every early spring flower. She taught others to do the same.

"Jesus Christ walked with her. Whether she sat mending stockings or was picking berries for jelly and jam, God was there. She saw Him in every cloud. Do you know why, Miss Courtland? Because first of all, she had Him in her heart. They called her 'Mrs. Minister' instead of by her name. The ministry she gave equalled, if not surpassed, what her husband was able to do. You asked me what God wanted in your life. If you could ever become half the woman Mrs. Minister was, you would be the happiest, most loved person on earth.''

Mrs. Minister. In a flash Betty knew. The woman he spoke of must be his wife. But he had said *was*.

"You said *was*. Isn't she living?'' The words forced themselves through her tight throat. Why did she care? Why did she, Elizabeth Courtland, hold her breath waiting for his answer?

"No. She died as she lived — gloriously. The last thing she ever said was, 'I'll be waiting for you all — with Jesus.' ''

"And she changed your life, made you willing to go out to that place, Pioneer, to live in squalor and dust and crudeness?''

Daniel Spencer seemed to have moved a thousand miles away. "Yes, Miss Courtland. Because of her, I am not only willing to go — I am eager.''

Betty's lips felt still. Nothing on earth could have held back the question. "She — Mrs. Minister was your wife?''

Blank dismay greeted her comment. "Of course not, Miss Courtland. I am not married. Mrs. Minister was my mother.''

"Your *mother?*" Relief washed through Betty, leaving her furious with herself. Why should she care that Daniel Spencer's ideal was not a former wife?

"Certainly, Miss Courtland. She followed my father wherever he was sent. She could make a home of the simplest surroundings. I wish you could have known her."

"She probably wouldn't have liked me," Betty blurted. She was shocked at her own frankness. "She wouldn't have approved of me."

"She would have liked you."

But not approved. The unspoken words hung in the air between them. Betty dropped her head forward so her hair would hide the flush in her face. It was nothing to her that Daniel Spencer's ideal woman would have despised her for the way she lived. Defiantly she stood, ignoring the churning emotions inside that had been triggered by his story.

"I believe we had better go, Mr. Spencer. Thank you for the story." There was nothing in the colorless words to show the impact that same story had made on her.

"Very well, Miss Courtland." Good heavens, could the man read her mind? Stiffly she accepted his offer of help, but once in the carriage she kept silent. The day that had started so joyously was spoiled. She could not even think of a subject of conversation.

"It's very kind of you to go to all this trouble to visit your old cook." Was there disbelief in his voice? Betty controlled her feelings enough to reply, "I was always fond of her," and suddenly realized it was true. She who had treated servants as servants and nothing else, with the exception of Abbie, realized she *had* missed Emma since the cook grew too old to work for the family.

The cottage they finally reached was tiny but immaculate. Was it much like the home Daniel's mother would have created from such a building? Neatly planted flowers broke the earth on each side of a little walk. White curtains floated at the miniature windows. The whole house was not much bigger than Betty's bedroom, but there was a good smell of stew in a kettle in the fireplace.

"Why, Miss Betty," Emma's crone-like face burst into a sunburst of wrinkles. "How nice of you to come! You said you would, but I'd about

given up hope.'' She glanced approvingly at Daniel looming in the doorway behind Betty. "And is this your young man? I heard you had become
engaged.''

Betty turned fiery red but was saved by Daniel's deep reply. "Sorry, I'm
not the one. Prescott was busy so I took his place.''

"Well, now, that's kind. Won't you sit down?'' She crossed to her kettle
and stirred the contents. "I was just about ready to have a wee bit of stew.
You'll join me?'' There was nothing in her manner to indicate any difference
in station. Betty marveled. Was that what happened when one was independent of others? Mrs. Minister would have greeted guests in much the same
way, Betty knew with a flash of insight. Could she herself ever —?

"I'd love some.'' Betty shut off her train of thought and flashed a smile.
"Mr. Spencer, no one makes stew like Emma.''

"I can tell that by the smell.'' The look he gave the old lady endeared
him to Betty. "Let me lift the kettle from the hook for you.''

"Thank you, laddie.'' Emma ladled steaming stew into plates Betty
recognized as having been discarded from her own household. There were
a few chips from the edges, but they were still beautiful. What would it be
like to exist on hand-me-downs? The quick glance around the cottage
showed nearly all the furnishings had originally been Courtland possessions. Yet there was something in the room that was not to be found in the
mansion where Betty lived. Was it — peace? She scoffed at the idea. What
could this old retired cook have that she would want?

"We'll just have a word o' prayer.'' Emma bowed her head, and Betty
stared. "Father, we thank Thee for this food and these friends. Bless both.
Amen.''

Betty's spoon struck the edge of her bowl as she raised it, fingers trembling. How disgusting, getting upset over an old woman's prayer! There
were always prayers at the Courtland table mumbled, it was true, but a formal grace by the head of the household. Yet Emma's prayer had been
almost like a petition to a friend. From under her lowered lashes Betty
caught Daniel's quick glance toward her. That would be right along his
line.

"Do come back, Miss Betty, and you too, sir.'' Their white-haired
hostess waved from the doorway as they climbed into the carriage for the
long trip home.

"Good-bye, Emma, and thanks.'' Betty was still waving when they
rounded the corner by the fence and drove out of sight.

"She's certainly a wonderful person, isn't she?''

Betty answered soberly, "Yes, she is. I felt closer to her today than all the time she worked for us." Her fingers played with her purse. "I wonder why?"

"In your home you were mistress and servant. In her home you were equals."

"Equal? Myself and a servant?" Betty could not hold back her indignation.

"I beg your pardon, Miss Courtland." Was there mockery in his careful apology? "I should not have called you equals. Your friend Emma has something you do not have, so really you are not equal at all."

"And pray tell what might that be?" Betty's jaw was set as she hurled the question at him.

"She has the joy of knowing that she is in exactly the right place in this world, the one God prepared for her."

"Why, you — you —"

Daniel laughed softly as if enjoying it. "I probably am whatever you choose to call me, but I still hold that Emma is a far wiser and happier person than you are, Miss Elizabeth 'Madcap Betty' Courtland!"

If the conversation had languished before, it suffered sudden death at that moment. "I really don't care to discuss it." Icicles tinkled in Betty's retort. She folded her hands in her lap and turned her head away to hide the vexation swelling from the tip of her toes to her all-betraying eyes.

It did not daunt him. To her amazement he started whistling, of all things! How could he whistle after insulting her the way he had? Perhaps she was being too hard on him; he was just a country lout. Yet he had gone to the same college as Prescott. It was not lack of manners but poor manners that caused him to plague her.

"Will your parents be concerned over your absence?"

"Why should they? I do as I please."

"Amen to that!" His wide grin was enough to drive her insane. For one moment she considered throwing her small purse straight at his head. No, she would not give him the satisfaction of knowing how he had scored. Instead she maintained her glowering silence until they reached the edge of the city.

"Go straight to the Wetherells. Perhaps Prescott will be free to drive me home," she ordered, deliberately using the same tone she would have used to her coachman.

"Certainly not, Miss Courtland. I couldn't allow such a thing. If Prescott was not free this morning, he will not be free now. I will drive you home and walk back."

"Walk! It is miles!"

"So it is." Behind his mild surprise lay more laughter, stinging Betty anew.

"I insist you go to the Wetherells!"

"Sorry. If you choose to drive there yourself when I have gone, that is your affair."

Was there ever such an infuriating clod? Betty counted to ten. "Very well." The cauldron of anger threatened to erupt. "If you insist on being a fool, I won't stop you."

"You couldn't anyway," he gently reminded. "You see, Miss Courtland, I am also in the habit of doing — what I think is right."

When they reached her home Abbie was on the porch, her face as disapproving in the early evening gloom as it had been that morning. "Your mama wants you right away." The ominous note in her voice raised the corners of Daniel Spencer's lips in another grin and sent a quick pang through Betty. She would be in for it; that was obvious. And for what? She had made no headway at all in her plan to entrap Daniel with her charms.

As a last-minute maneuver she abruptly did an about-face. "Mr. Spencer, I did appreciate your escorting me. I also —" She swallowed the word *enjoyed* as too much even for him to accept. "I found your stories quite enlightening. I hope you will call, perhaps tomorrow?" There! She had left the way open.

"If Prescott is not able to come and wishes me to do so, I will call." He turned back toward the carriage. "Shall I take Beauty to the stable before letting your fiance know you are safely home?" There was just the slightest shade of emphasis on *fiance*.

"Of course not," she snapped. "My man will do that." Without even a good-bye she turned haughtily and swept through the door Abbie held open. The insufferable prig, reminding her she was engaged to Prescott!

"You'd better see your mama," Abbie reminded. Betty whirled on her. "I'll see her after I've bathed and changed. I don't know why I went anyway — out in that dusty country just to see Emma. Get out my yellow gown, Abbie, and stop that chattering.

Mrs. Courtland's anger strangely rolled off Betty. She merely stared at her mother, listening to the accusations of impropriety. "Riding the whole day with a man you barely know! If Prescott couldn't take you as his affianced wife, then you knew better than to go off with that — that preacher!"

"He was perfectly proper." Betty yawned daintily, covering her mouth with her fingers.

"It doesn't matter. What will people say?"

"Who cares?" Betty's languor vanished. "I'm tired of living where it is according to what 'they say' and 'they think.' Mother, have you ever done one single thing in your life without wondering how 'they' will react?"

Mrs. Courtland snorted. "I certainly hope not! Pleasing society is the most important thing in life."

"Is it?" Betty's thoughts were upon an oak tree, blue sky, and flowers surrounding a strong man who gazed at them. "What about pleasing God?"

"God!" It was Mrs. Courtland's turn to stare. "That is positively blasphemous, Elizabeth, to speak of God in that familiar way." She rose magnificently and walked toward the door. "I suggest you do some serious thinking about what you have done this day and be ready to apologize to Prescott when you next see him." The door banged shut behind her, leaving Betty feeling again as if a prison door had closed her in.

The fresh air should have made Betty sleepy. It did not. She paced the floor as she had done the night before, memories churning. In vain she flayed herself for caring what Daniel Spencer thought. When she finally did prepare for bed and turn out her light, it was to find his face floating in the darkness. Sometime later another face seemed to join him — the face of a woman, laughing, with workworn hands. Betty knew it must be Mrs. Minister, the one who had found God not formidable but a companion.

A vague and fleeting wish crossed Betty's heart, too slight to register more than an imprint. Would Mrs. Minister really have disapproved, or would she have seen something — it was too nebulous. At last Betty slept.

Sunlight streamed through her curtains when Betty awoke. She stretched deliciously, at peace with the world — until the sharp pressure of the ring Prescott had placed on her finger brought her back to reality with a thud. She had to break her engagement — today. Daniel Spencer might be odious, but he had been right about one thing. She did not love Prescott. She had sensed it when she spoke to Abbie. It had been confirmed at the actual announcing of her engagement.

Sluggishly she slid from bed, impatiently calling, "Come in," to the knock on her door. Abbie's curly head appeared. Her capable hands carried a tray. She set it on a bedside table and threw wide the drapes, letting in even more sunlight.

"Good mornin', Miss Betty." Abbie uncovered plates. "Fresh berries and cream. Hot toast. An egg, just the way you like it." She poured cream into the coffee. "Anything else?"

"Yes — no — Abbie, stop rushing off so soon. Sit down, and talk while I eat."

Abbie's eyes sparkled. It was not often her mistress requested such a thing. Usually after being up late the night before Betty was in no mood to talk with anyone, let alone her maid.

"Was Mama really upset yesterday?"

Abbie's lips turned down. *"Was she!* First she asked where you'd gone at the ungodly hour of nine. Then she waited lunch for you until the souffle fell. She finally sent Sam over to the Wetherells to find out when you'd be home. She wasn't very happy when Prescott sent word you'd gone into the country with that Mr. Spencer."

"I see."

Abbie leaned forward, confidential. "I reckon she's afraid of what Miz Wetherell might think."

"I reckon she is," Betty mimicked, suddenly losing her appetite. Must she always be bound by convention, by what others expected? "Take it away, Abbie. I'm not hungry."

"But you've scarcely eaten a bite!"

"Take it away, I tell you. I don't want it. Then come back and help me dress."

When Abbie returned, it was with a scowl on her face. "He's here."

"Who's here? Prescott? I can't see him. I'm not ready for the day."

"Not Prescott. Him." She jerked a thumb toward the open window. Betty threw a robe over her gown and ran to the window.

"Daniel Spencer!"

"In a carriage, even. Looks like Mr. Prescott's carriage. What's he doin' here?" she demanded sourly.

"How should I know? Help me get dressed, Abbie."

"Why don't I just tell him to go away?"

"No!"

Abbie's face showed growing understanding. "So that's the way of it. You're interested in him — after all Mr. Prescott's done for you."

"Don't be ridiculous!" Betty managed a scornful laugh. "He's Mr. Prescott's guest, a preacher. I have to be courteous to him."

"Don't much look like a preacher in that rig. Looks more like someone comin' to court."

Betty was furious. So that was what came of being friendly with servants. "It's none of your business, Abbie. Fasten my dress."

"Yes, ma'am." But Abbie's look of gloom reflected in the mirror, and Betty refused to meet it. Some of the anger from the day before had faded. All Betty could think of was that Daniel Spencer was downstairs.

"Yes?" Her voice was cool when she entered the library. He stood in front of the great fireplace, cold now. She was struck by his height, even more than when she had seen him before.

"Prescott asked me to come. His mother is feeling no better, and he said you had had plans for luncheon and a musicale that would need an escort."

Betty had completely forgotten her plans for the day. Now she hastily consulted her mental engagement book. "Oh, yes, at the Beaumonts'. It really wasn't necessary for you to come, Mr. Spencer."

"Prescott thought it was, and as his guest —" He shrugged his shoulders indifferently, setting Betty simmering again. "So this is where you live."

"Obviously." She watched him survey the room, seeing it through his eyes instead of her own. The choice furniture, priceless rugs and drapes, the formal elegance of beautifully bound but little read books. Did he recognize their rarity, the first editions?

"Well?" She could not refrain from asking.

"It is tasteful, of course. Do you ever have a fire?"

"When it is chilly. I'm afraid I really don't spend much time in here." Her light laugh hung in the semi-gloom.

"I thought not."

"I suppose you prefer that one-room shack of Emma's." *He certainly has the talent for bringing out the worst in me.*

"I do." He crossed to a shelf, removed one of Scott's works, opened it. "Hm. Doesn't look as if it is used often." He replaced it and turned back to her. "I like to see books read and reread. We never had many, but they were always tattered from being loved. I used to dig out an old favorite on a rainy day. It was like a visit to a friend."

"Remarkable. But I suppose those in poverty must find some outlet for their leisure moments." Betty knew she sounded like the snob he thought she was but could not resist the dig.

"There are many kinds of poverty, Miss Courtland, not just financial. I find poverty of the mind and soul the hardest to understand."

Betty could not trust herself to speak. She swept toward the door and tossed over her shoulder, "I'll be ready to leave for the luncheon at twelve sharp. I hate to be kept waiting."

"So do I."

Betty ran across the marble floor and up the great staircase to her own room. Flushed, ruffled, she sped to the window and watched him leisurely stroll out to his carriage. Evidently he had not waited for Sam to let him out the massive front doors. She saw him stop and deliberately look over the entire estate, then caught the shrug of his shoulders as he climbed into the carriage and lifted the reins. His back was as straight as the chairs in the dining room as he drove away.

There was another argument with her mother before Betty escaped to the luncheon. It started when Mrs. Courtland marched in to see why Betty was not ready and why Prescott had sent "that man" in his place. "You're not wearing that, I hope!" She frowned at the gauzy yellow dress. "That's the first of your trousseau frocks."

"It's mine. I'll wear it when I please."

"Elizabeth, you are a wicked, unnatural child. Take that dress off, and put on one of your old ones."

"I will not!" The fire in Betty's eyes matched that in her mother's. "I said I'd marry Prescott to please you, but I'm not married yet! I'll wear what I please, when I please, and with whom I please. And I wish you'd stop referring to Mr. Spencer as 'that man.' You know his name perfectly well. Do you also know that he's been offered the pastorate of the biggest church in Grand Rapids?"

"Well!" Mrs. Courtland's shock was complete. "I would never have suspected it. Perhaps there is more to this young man than one would suppose. I will have to cultivate his acquaintance. After all, he is a friend of Prescott's and —"

"He isn't taking the position." Betty took wicked delight in the way her mother's face fell. "He's going out West just like he'd planned and build some dinky church in some dump of a town where he'll have loggers and birds and squirrels for a congregation."

"I forbid you to go anywhere with him, Elizabeth! If he is doing that, he must be insane!" She bustled further into the room. "Or worse, he is a fanatic. You can't be too careful about him. He may hypnotize you, and you'll be wanting to go off with him!"

"He wouldn't take me if I wanted to go." Betty regretted her thrust as soon as she made it. "That is, can you imagine me wanting to ever be a minister's wife? Heaven help the minister who married me!" She pushed past her mother toward the top of the stairs.

"But Betty, you mustn't go with this man to the luncheon. What will people say?"

"I really don't care." Betty raced downstairs in her yellow dress to where Daniel Spencer waited, chiding herself for her unreasonable excitement, but unable to still her leaping heart.

"You're in love with her, aren't you, Dan?" The words were infinitely sad but held no accusation.

Daniel Spencer whirled toward Prescott. He opened his lips to utter a denial, but only produced a hoarse laugh. Finally he said, "Can you imagine a match between 'Madcap Betty' and myself?"

"I not only can, I do." Prescott faced him squarely, eyes steady. "Don't try and apologize, old friend. I've known since we were children that Elizabeth did not love me the way a woman should love." His voice faltered a bit. "I hoped in time she would learn."

"She will! She has to." Daniel paced the floor of the Wetherell library. "She couldn't find a better man anywhere, or one who would cherish her the way you would do. As for me —" Suddenly strength flowed into his determined face. "I have to be honest with you, Prescott. The first time I saw Elizabeth Courtland something struck me — the way she held her head like a proud, wild thing. When I found she was to be betrothed to you something in me died before it had been fully born. As I learned to know what a selfish person she is, I rejoiced. Nothing could ever come of my first feeling."

"Yet you love her."

"Love? Or is it simply attraction for what I know I can never have?" Daniel's smile was crooked.

"She is interested in you, Dan."

"Certainly she is. Isn't she interested in any man who won't fall and worship at her feet?"

Prescott ignored the bitterness. "I have never seen Betty as she has been since you came. She laughed and told me frankly you disapproved of her in every way. Yet behind the laughter I saw tears of hurt."

"You are imagining things!" Even as he denied the possibility, Daniel's heart took an uncontrolled leap. "I ask you again, can you imagine Miss Courtland working alongside me as any helpmate would have to do? Living in semipoverty? Bearing my children?" His laugh was harsh. "She could never do it."

"I think you underrate Betty. She has never had the chance to show what she could do under stress. She's been dandled and petted and just about ruined by permissive parents who never denied her anything she wanted."

26

"You are championing your fiancee as a fit companion for me?" The incredulity in Daniel's voice sent a wave of red to Prescott's hairline.

"You think I would go ahead and marry Betty, knowing her heart is not mine?" Prescott stared at this friend. "I have known all along she did not love me, although she is fond of me. It took seeing her look at you to expose the truth. I want no woman who cannot look at me in that same way."

Wordlessly Daniel held out his hand to be seized in a mighty grip and said, "I will go away. I know that I will find peace in doing my heavenly Father's will. She is young. It is a passing fancy, even if it should be as you say, which I doubt. I think she is merely intrigued because I don't bow down to her wishes." He ignored the protest in his friend's face. "She will see you as the man you are." For a moment his face twisted in agony. "Prescott, most men would hate me. It takes great love for a friend to accept what you have just done."

"Why should I hate you? If it hadn't been you, perhaps it would have been another man — after we were married." The somberness of Prescott's voice cut into Daniel like knife blades.

"I would stake my life that once she marries she will be true."

"If she marries the right man." Prescott's quiet statement sounded in Daniel's ears like a death knell. "It will never be me." Before Daniel could reply Prescott deliberately changed the subject. "The opening at the church has not yet been filled. It isn't too late for you to change your mind and accept it. Why don't you think about it some more?"

"God has called me to Pioneer."

"Perhaps. Yet how do you know He isn't calling you here to Grand Rapids first? You believe this God of yours directs those who trust Him. How do you know your coming here at this particular time isn't for a reason? How do you know Betty isn't meant to be your companion? With her finances and your ability to preach, you could build this church to gigantic proportions. Perhaps God knows that. Perhaps this whole thing has been planned."

Daniel's shoulders slumped. "I have thought of it — often — especially since I met Betty." He sounded tired. "Prescott, I want you to know that I have fought against this strange attraction, this spell she seems to have woven about me. You know the only times we've been together have been when you were unavailable. Each time the unsuitableness of anything ever coming about between us has been thrust home to me sharply, even if it hadn't been for you! She is absolutely heathen. She believes in nothing except her own pleasure. Can you imagine her ever becoming a 'Mrs. Minister' as my own mother was?"

"I still believe you are seeing only the surface. Underneath all the society whims and fashions, Elizabeth has depths that are as yet unexplored." Prescott stood abruptly. "Will you consider what I have said?"

"How can I help it?" The cry burst from Daniel's lips without warning. "It would be better for me to go away tonight and leave this temptation. Surely that is what it is, the last great temptation before I enter the work I have been called to do."

"Perhaps not. Perhaps it is something far different." Prescott halted in the doorway, his face lined and suddenly old. "I am breaking the engagement with Elizabeth tonight. You must decide what you want to do, what you must do. But it will not change my decision." Suddenly he looked young again, younger than Daniel had seen him since college days. "I have already arranged to finish my studies and become the lawyer I have wanted to be since I was small."

"Thank God for that!" Again the two men gripped hands. "But what about your mother?"

A gleam came into Prescott's eyes. "I believe that when she knows Elizabeth and I are not getting married and coming to live here, she will find she isn't so ill as she thinks.

"By the way, Dan, whether you decide to take the Grand Rapids church or not, they would like you to preach before you have to leave. I told them I was sure you could fill the pulpit this coming Sunday."

"I don't know whether to bless you as a friend or tell you to get thee behind me, Satan," Daniel warned. "You seem quite able to arrange my life." He joined Prescott in the hall. "I hope when you think this over you won't regret it. How will Miss Courtland take it when you tell her?"

"You needn't worry. She'll think it was her idea." A curious look crept into his face. "Actually it is. I'll give her an opening by telling her I'd like to postpone the wedding since I want to get into law."

"You think she'll accept that?"

Prescott turned sober. "She will have to." Steel infused his voice. "Now that I've made my decision, I wonder that I didn't do it long ago. Funny thing, somehow I feel freer than I have in a long time." He flexed his arms in a sweeping motion. "I can hardly wait to get into a different atmosphere, one where I can work. Even Elizabeth and the prospect of travel with her couldn't quite drown the dreams I had to bury because of Mother." He was halfway up the stairs before he turned back, lit by a kindly sunbeam from the skylight above. "As for hating you —" He lifted his hands helplessly. "No regrets, Dan." He disappeared from sight, leaving Daniel standing at the foot of the stairs wishing desperately he could cry.

Slowly Daniel made his way into the garden, swallowing the lump that persisted at the gallantry of Prescott Wetherell, a prince among men. But it did not solve his own problem. It only compounded it. If Prescott had been angry, it would have been easier. He could have packed and gone, leaving part of his heart and many regrets. But not now. He had to face what might lie ahead.

Can Prescott be right? After all my plans, being so sure God wants me in Pioneer, can God be using Elizabeth Courtland as an influence to keep me in Grand Rapids? In spite of himself his whole body thrilled with remembrance of her beauty. *What if she can be led to the Lord? What a wife she would make!* A tide of red swept into his face. *What right have I to consider such a woman? Betty would never be the choice God has for me. She couldn't be. She is shallow, selfish, spoiled. Yet haven't other shallow, selfish, spoiled people turned over their lives to the Lord and gone on to become noted servants?*

"Nonsense!" He viciously thrust his toe against a rock, sending it flying, relieving some of his frustration. "She couldn't be part of God's plan in my life!" Yet the words of his friend had sunk deep.

Just ahead lay a green bower, private, encased by hanging vines and weeping trees. He had spent time there when he first came to the Wetherells. Now he automatically parted the curtaining branches and stepped inside. There was a carpet of green, bordered with flowers, a small bench. Unerringly he headed for it, dropped to his knees, and buried his head in his hands. His Gethsemane had come.

"Oh, Lord, this girl is everything against You. Why did I have to meet her? Why did I ever come here — to disturb Prescott's life?" The low cry seemed to stay on the ground. "Are You there? Is it possible Prescott could be right? Are You telling me to change direction, to accept this church at least for a time?"

Hours later Daniel Spencer rose from his knees. He had received no change of orders from his Commanding Officer. He would preach as Prescott had arranged, then leave for Pioneer immediately. Betty Courtland would remain. She was not for him. Yet deep inside his soul was the cry, *Help her, God, to find Christ — and happiness — even though it can never be with me.*

"Mr. Prescott's downstairs." This time Abbie's face was lit with smiles. "Says he won't keep you long but needs to see you."

"How tiresome!" Betty stuck her foot into her slipper and pushed back her hair. "It's almost dinner time. Why should he come now?"

"It wasn't my place to ask," Abbie said primly. "But he's waitin' for you in the little sittin' room."

"Oh, Abbie, why didn't you show him into the library?"

The maid's face set in stubborn lines. "He asked to go into the sittin' room. Said when you came down he didn't want to be disturbed."

Was it fear that shot through Betty? It must be very important for him to come at that hour. How could he get away from his mother? Her lip curled, her confidence returning. Probably some trivial matter about the wedding. She tightened her fingers into fists. Very well. It was the perfect opportunity. She would tell him she no longer wished to be engaged.

She did not get the chance.

"Sit down please, Elizabeth." Betty looked at him in surprise. Seldom did he take such a solemn tone when addressing her. The usual good-natured Prescott seemed eclipsed by a stranger. Whatever had happened? Was Daniel — her heart lodged in her throat.

"Nothing has happened to — anyone?"

"Yes, Elizabeth. Something important has happened."

Betty narrowed her eyes as he continued.

"I have decided after all to pursue the career in law I have wanted for so long. I realize that will upset your plans, especially about the wedding. If you choose to break the engagement, I will understand."

It was the last thing she expected. She could only stare. She could hear the clock ticking away seconds in their noisy rhythm before she could get her voice. He was offering her the chance she had wanted. Incredible! "Th — there's another girl?"

Strange how his amused laugh reminded her of Daniel Spencer. "Hardly. I will be busy with law. It will take some time to get established the way I choose to do. I don't intend to rely on my family name and reputation. I intend to do it on my own."

Something more like respect than she had ever had for him flooded Betty's mind. "I think you should, Prescott." She dropped her lashes. "I also think you're right about breaking our engagement. After all, you'll be busy, and I'm not the type to sit at home without escorts while you're playing lawyer —" She swept a look upward that had always brought fire to his eyes. Not this time.

"Don't play games, Elizabeth."

The command in his voice, as unexpected as a bite from a pet dog, startled her. "Games? I?"

"Yes, you." He was smiling much as her father would smile. In the few minutes since she had entered the little room Prescott seemed to have added inches to his stature, years to his age. For one moment she felt he had grown beyond her and almost frantically clutched at the familiar. "But Prescott, you just said —"

"I said don't play games. You aren't in love with me. You never have been. It's all been arranged, convenient."

Betty's mouth flew open. "Why, Prescott dear, how can you even think such a thing? I've always been fond of you." Her protests died. "Or is it that you don't love me?"

To her amazement Prescott did not answer immediately. Instead he stared at her as if seeing her for the first time. Again she was uncomfortably aware of the similarity between him and Daniel. The thought flared her into action. "Is it because of Daniel Spencer? That's it, isn't it? He has turned you against me." Two tears of fury sparkled on her lashes.

Prescott threw back his head and laughed. It shocked Betty more than anything else could have done. Prescott was laughing at her! She rose defiantly, haughtily. "I believe I do not care to speak with you any more, Mr. Wetherell."

Prescott caught her hand, forcing her back into her chair. The laughter still tugged at his lips. "Elizabeth, I wouldn't have believed it. Yes, Dan Spencer has had something to do with this. In fact, he has had everything to do with it. You're in love with him."

Changing from rosy red to snowy white, Betty's face was a study in emotion. "How dare you say such a thing!"

"Because it is true." The finality in Prescott's voice silenced Betty. "Can you look me in the eye and swear you are not in love with him?"

She turned her head away indignantly. "Why should I? How could anyone care for a country lout like him? Are you insane?"

"No, Betty. Just glad I know the truth." He paused. "You asked if I still love you. I am not sure. I have cared a long time, always knowing deep inside it was not returned. Now — I just don't know." He rose to tower over her, a stranger from the Prescott she had played with since childhood. "I believe you could find a great deal of happiness if you would change and be the woman Daniel Spencer needs."

Betty desperately grasped for the reins of control. "Why should I change? I could never fit in his world even if I did care, and why you should think I do is a mystery to me!"

"He would never fit into your world. You would have to go to him."

Betty escaped from her chair, feeling as if she had to get out of the room before she went into hysterics. "Of all the improbable situations! My fiance of a few weeks comes to tell me he wants me to break our engagement —

and follows it up by recommending I change my whole life in order to qualify as a fit bride for his best friend! Prescott, have you been reading too much fiction?"

Prescott gathered up his hat and coat from a nearby rack. "I will expect to see a formal withdrawal of our engagement in tomorrow's papers. Good night, Elizabeth." He stopped just inside the door. "If ever you need help of any kind, come to me. I'll be there." The door opened and closed. He was gone.

"Prescott!" Betty threw wide the door and hurried after him. "Did you — does Daniel know — is he —?"

"He knows I came here tonight and why. Good night."

Betty pressed cold hands against her flushed face. Could the scene she had played in the little sitting room be real? It was real. Prescott stood watching her, waiting for her to speak. As in a trance Betty saw herself strip off the ring with the heavy stone and lay it in his hand. "You might as well take this."

"Thank you, Elizabeth." This time she did not run after him. Instead she stood slowly watching a part of her childhood walk away, head up, chin high. The fingers of her right hand involuntarily felt for her third finger, left hand. How bare it seemed — but how light. Suddenly she was glad. It was over — the sham engagement she had hated. She was free.

No, she was not free.

Prescott's words haunted her. "You're in love with him."

He had not said Daniel cared for her. Hot and cold by turns, Betty forced a smile and entered the dining room. It would be time for dinner soon. She must prepare herself to tell her parents the engagement was broken. Yet why did it not seem a staggering task? All she could think of was Daniel Spencer. In love with him? Absurd. Was it possible the trap that she had laid had sprung, catching herself instead of her prey?

She pushed back all thoughts of Daniel when her parents entered. Once they were served and the maid gone, she tossed out her news. "I broke my engagement to Prescott tonight." Her voice started out small but gained assurance. "He is going into law, and I don't intend to sit around and wait until he gets around for a wedding."

The effect was shattering. Her father's wine glass came down with a little crash. Her mother's lips compressed in a thin line. "And just what do you intend to do?"

Betty looked up, surprised. "Just as I've always done. Have a good time." Catching the flabbergasted look on her mother's face, she added airily, "There are more fish in the sea and better than have ever been caught. I won't have any trouble replacing Prescott."

"You had better watch your step, miss." Betty was alarmed at the purple color tinging her father's face. "I'm getting tired of your flirting and carrying on. Pretty soon no decent man will have anything to do with you!"

"Then I'll find someone who will." Stubbornness matched stubbornness in father and daughter as they glared at each other.

"Hush. Here comes Sally with dessert," Mrs. Courtland warned. A strained silence fell until the maid left the room.

"I won't have it, I tell you!" Mr. Courtland thundered. "I thought you were finally going to settle down and do what any self-respecting young woman would do — marry and have children. There will be no more of this dilly-dallying, Elizabeth. You will marry Prescott Wetherell as planned and on the day planned, or I'll know the reason why. I won't have you single any longer, driving men to distraction. When you were younger it was amusing. Now it isn't. You will marry Prescott!"

Betty sprang to her feet, knocking over her water goblet. "And I say I shan't! You may be my father, but you can't marry me off the way you'd sell a prize horse. I am a person. I have rights."

"Rights? You have nothing except what I give you!" Mr. Courtland's rage increased. "Do you have some other good-for-nothing on the string?"

Death itself could not have kept the rich blood from coursing into Betty's face. Her father saw it and jumped to conclusions. "Who is it? Who is he, the dishonorable man who would make love to you even while you are engaged to another man?"

"He has never made love to me. He despises me!"

Her father did not even hear. He brought down his fist to the heavy table with such force the silver jumped. "I demand to know his name, the man you fancy, or you will be locked in your room until you regain your senses!"

"I refuse to be treated as a child!" Betty stormed. "I told you there is no one who has tried to come between Prescott and me. Can't you understand? Prescott himself sees we could never be happy." It was her trump card. If it did not work, nothing would. She had seen her father in spells of rage before but never directed at her. She clutched the table edge with fingers white at the knuckles. "Will you listen? *Prescott asked me to break the engagement!*"

If her father had been enraged before, now his fury knew no bounds. His roar could have been heard throughout the Courtland mansion. "Then if that is true, and I will make it my business to find out, it must be because he knows you are unworthy to be called a Wetherell." He shoved back his chair with an oath, overturning it in his haste to get out of the room.

"Go to your room and stay there. I mean to have a talk with Prescott, and when I come back —" he shook his fist at her "— God help you if you have done anything that will reflect on the name of Courtland!"

White-faced, degraded by his accusations, Betty could not defend herself. Her own father, charging her with sins she could only guess at! She turned, walked up the stairs, entered her room, and locked the door. Let him rage and question. Her heart was as dead as if it had been pierced by a bullet. How could he believe some terrible thing of her? Sobs rose, shaking her entire body, but not one tear came. Her grief was too deep for tears.

What would Prescott say? Fear greater than shame flooded her body. What if some chance word caused her father to believe that Daniel Spencer — she could not finish the thought. Her father would never accept the innocence of their friendship, not now. He would seek Daniel out and either horsewhip or kill him. If there were a God, how could He permit such a horrible thing to happen? In her confusion Betty vaguely sensed it might not be God's fault, but her own. There was no time to think of it now.

She snatched up her bell, ringing it furiously, and admitted Abbie into her room moments later. "Get out my driving things and have the small carriage brought around." She forstalled Abbie's protest. *"Don't argue. It's a matter of life and death!"* Her fumbling fingers were already busy with fastenings.

For once Abbie did as she was told. The look in her mistress's face had been awful. But she was adamant when Betty was ready. "I am going with you." Nothing could change her — neither threats nor pleading. "Come on, Miss Betty. If it's life or death you can't stand there arguin' with me."

The next instant they were racing down the servants' stairs, out into the night. Without waiting for Sam's assistance, Betty climbed into the carriage and snatched the reins, giving Beauty an unaccustomed touch. Beauty snorted and leaped ahead, taking the corner at incredible speed. Abbie held on and braced herself, wisely asking no questions.

A tiny voice resounded in Betty's brain. *What if you are too late? What if he is dead? It will be your fault.* Deep inside a cry too faint to reach her lips formed, winging its way to the pitiless stars above. *Please, if You're there, don't let me be too late.*

5

Betty reined Beauty sharply to the right and groaned. "Oh, no. Father's already there." Her stricken face stood out sharply in the gloaming. "Abbie, I'll hop out. You drive Beauty around where she can't be seen when my father comes out." Leaving no time for protest, she slowed Beauty, threw the reins at Abbie, and disappeared around the side of the Wetherell mansion.

She could not go in the front door. In all likelihood, the men would be in the library. If only she could have reached there first. Her mind raced faster than her feet as she crept close to the library window. She had to get inside, just in case anything were to happen. Wait! Prescott had showed her a tiny alcove off the library, barely room for one person to study. It was hidden from view by heavy curtains and had a door to the main hall. On feather feet she slipped further around the house to a side door where she could sidle through. Luck was with her. Moments later she had entered the alcove and hidden behind the curtains, holding both hands over her mouth to still the heavy breathing. From her vantage point she could see Prescott and Daniel slumped in chairs before the fire. Her father was nowhere in sight. Dare she call out and warn them?

She hesitated, and in that split second lost her opportunity.

"Mr. Courtland, Mr. Prescott." The wide library door swung open. The impassive butler ushered in her father and went out, closing the door behind him.

"Why, Mr. Courtland!" Surprise was evident in Prescott's face. "My father is not at home this evening."

"I came to see you." Courtland wagged his head toward Daniel. "Who's he?"

"Didn't you meet my friend Daniel Spencer the other night? Sorry. Daniel will be filling the pulpit this Sunday."

Eyes like steel drills bored into the young minister. Behind her sheltering curtain Betty rejoiced to see that Daniel did not flinch. "So *you're* the fellow who's turning down our offer to build some ramshackle church in the far West."

"That's me." Daniel's smile was disarming.

"Humph!" Courtland turned back to Prescott. "I'd like to speak to you, alone." His voice was ominous, and Betty shuddered.

"Certainly." Prescott raised his eyebrows and motioned to Daniel. "You can go out through the alcove if you like."

Betty froze to the spot as footsteps, quick and light on the heavy carpet, neared her hiding place. A strong hand swept back the curtains. Her eyes pleaded with the man who stood there looking down at her, terror evident in her clasped hands. Hesitating only a moment, Daniel stepped into the alcove and drew the curtains behind him. He could not step forward. Betty was in the way. Neither could he stay in his ridiculous position, half in, half out of the alcove. He motioned toward the exit door, and Betty shook her head violently. She could see the contempt in his face for one more "Madcap Betty" trick. Hot color filled her face, but she grasped his arm, pulling him to the bench beside her.

Daniel's lips opened to speak. She put her hand over his mouth and shook her head again. She could feel his heart beating as she crouched beside him on the tiny bench, gently pulling her heavy skirts back, thankful they were not rustling.

"My daughter tells me you are not getting married." Her father's accusation stilled the two eavesdroppers.

"That is correct." Betty shifted and moved the curtains an inch so she could see into the library. The same strong hand that had opened the curtains gripped her shoulders hard, pulling her back from sight. Her father was facing the alcove. He evidently had not seen the movement. "May I inquire as to the reasons? Elizabeth has said that you asked that she break the engagement. That tells me that you have found out something to her discredit. If it is so," he pounded his heavy cane against the floor, "if it is true, I will cut her off without a cent!"

In that moment Prescott Wetherell was magnificent. Rising to his feet he glared icily into the eyes of Mr. Courtland. "How dare you doubt your daughter's honor?" Contempt shone in every pore of his skin. "Elizabeth Courtland may be high-spirited and full of mischief and fun, but she is the soul of honor! She would rather die than demean herself in any way!"

The granite face did not change. "Then why have you asked her to release you from your betrothal plans?"

"Because neither Elizabeth nor I would ever be happy together. I am going on to become a lawyer. I have always known that she loved me as a brother, not as a husband."

"Rubbish! It is not for women to say whom they shall love. Love comes to them after marriage, at least to nice women!"

The fire died from Prescott's face and he dropped heavily into a chair. "I regret to say I disagree entirely. Elizabeth and I have drifted with the tide of yours and Mrs. Courtland's and my parents' plans. Now we must choose our own lives.''

"My daughter will do as I say! And I say she must have some other reason, or she wouldn't have agreed to break the engagement. I demand the name of the man!''

Betty turned pale as death, and the arm cradling her tightened, sending a surge through her like nothing she had ever known. Prescott's infrequent kisses had been almost brotherly and had meant nothing. Now the touch of this man threatened to undo every shred of pride she knew. It was all she could do from flinging her arms around him, begging him to hold her so forever.

Prescott's voice roused her from the daze she was in. "Do you dare to insult your own daughter?'' His indignation knew no bounds. Tall, strong, he snatched Courtland by the lapels of his coat. "I will not allow you to stand in my home and speak such vile things of Elizabeth! You should be thanking God she is pure and clean instead of what you are thinking! Then you should go home and get down on your knees to her and apologize.''

"Apologize? I? I never apologize. It's a sign of weakness.'' Courtland's face was purple again, veins standing out. He jerked free and stepped back. "I'll have the name of the man, and when I get it, I'll kill him like I would a snake that threatened my home!''

Prescott's face was nearly as dark as Courtland's. "What if Betty were guilty of unspeakable things? Whose fault would it be? What have you ever given her except her own way? Have you taught her to believe in God and respect Him? Have you given her any reason not to do what she chooses? Have you commanded respect by your own life or demanded it because you are a Courtland?'' The words hurled themselves like bricks, each striking harder at the hypocrite facing him.

"I suppose your parents have done better?''

"No!'' Prescott, who never swore, uttered a rough oath. "But I am learning that life is more than prestige and money and what 'they' think. I pray to God that I will one day become the man I'd like to be.''

"Like the preacher who was in here?'' The sneer on Courtland's face darkened. "A white-livered coward who will spend his life preying on weak-minded women?''

Betty's gasp was lost in Prescott's reply. She had never seen him look so, face flaming with passion. "If I can ever become half the man Daniel Spencer is, I will be thankful.''

"Bah! I will continue this no longer.'' Courtland whirled toward the door, then back as a new thought struck him. "Is this minister interested in my daughter?''

"If he were, it would be the greatest compliment any woman could be paid. But why should he be? Outside of a pleasing personality and a pretty face, what could Elizabeth offer a man like Daniel Spencer? He needs someone who can stand up to life, not a pampered doll like your daughter. She would have fit into my plans, but never his."

"That will be all, sir!" Courtland advanced, cane raised.

"Yes, it will be all." Prescott reached for a pull rope and waited for the butler. "Show Mr. Courtland out. It is quite past time for him to go."

Courtland muttered incoherently and stomped after the butler, but paused to say, "You will regret this little conversation for the rest of your life. I will see to that!"

A curious tranquillity filled Prescott's eyes, lifting the corners of his mouth in a half smile. "Such is the reward for believing in your daughter, sir — the thing you should have been doing. If I had agreed with you, would you have killed me for insulting her?" Only the closing of the door answered him, its slam muted by its well-oiled hinges.

"Quick, you must go!" Daniel was on his feet, pulling Betty up.

He was a fraction of a second too late.

"Dan? You there? I thought I heard movement —" The curtains were thrown back, revealing the shrinking Betty and white-faced Daniel Spencer huddled in the tiny space.

"Elizabeth!" Was it the realization that she had overheard the whole thing that sent the deathlike look over Prescott's face?

Elizabeth finally found her voice. "I came — he said terrible things to me at home — I was afraid —"

"There really was no way out without her father discovering her," Daniel added as he helped her into the library itself. "I regret to say that any other alternative was out of the question."

"You heard it all? His accusations?" Prescott's eyes were filled with shame for her father.

"For the second time. He hinted at things I don't even know about at the dinner table." She looked up at Prescott. "If I knew how to thank you, I would."

"Don't!" The fierceness of his exclamation cut her off. "To think that you had to listen to that! It is despicable."

"But why did you come here?" Daniel interjected.

"I had to. I didn't know what he might do, if he found out I — we — that you had been seeing me."

Color swept to Daniel's hairline. "He thought what he wanted to think without any cause whatsoever?"

"Yes." Betty's head drooped like a flower, too tired to look up. "If he had known that Prescott had sent you to take me places, I don't know what he would have done. So I came here."

"Family pride like that," Prescott said, his voice cold. "Inexcusable!"

Daniel looked deeply into his friend's eyes. "Did you mean what you said about wanting to find your place in life — with God?"

"I never meant anything more." Prescott's gaze was steady, unshakable, leaving Betty feeling as if a charmed circle had been drawn around the two men, shutting her out. It hurt unbearably.

"Daniel, take Elizabeth home. She can slip in without her father knowing." Prescott was in command, but Betty shook her head. "Abbie's waiting outside." Before they could stop her she slipped back through the alcove, out the door, and back to where the carriage stood with a trembling Abbie holding the reins. A minute later the two men in the library heard Beauty's hoofbeats as she slowly turned toward home.

"Hard lesson for her." Daniel poked up the already blazing fire, his face in half-shadow.

"Maybe it was what she needed. She's been known for some of her madcap ways. It's time she learned that there is responsibility in life."

"To what *they* think?" Daniel's lip curled.

"No, to herself." Prescott dropped back in a chair. "Daniel, I believe that Betty is capable of being another Mrs. Minister if she had direction and guidance such as you could give her."

"Never! I don't even want to discuss it!"

But long after Prescott had said good night, his guest remained in the library, remembering his decision earlier in the garden. As he watched a final spurt of fire before it died into ashes, he recalled how his heart had lurched at the softness of Elizabeth Courtland in his arms.

"I don't feel like going to church this morning."

"You're going." Mrs. Courtland was grim. "That friend of Prescott's has been filling Prescott full of wild stories. Your father says we're going to find out what it is about him that has hypnotized a person like Prescott into becoming an absolute boor!"

Despite Betty's misery at the thought of facing that same minister, especially in a preaching capacity, her lips twitched. *So Father thinks Prescott a boor, simply because he defended me. Perhaps the day will not be so bad after all.*

First Church was in for a shock — a series of shocks. The first came when Daniel Spencer entered the pulpit wearing an ordinary business suit instead of a clerical collar. "The idea," Mrs. Courtland hissed in Betty's ear. "If he thinks he can come in and start wearing that kind of clothing he might as well get it out of his head. We want no minister who can't respect God enough to dress properly!"

"Sh!" Betty could feel disapproving glances. There was no use reminding her mother that Daniel Spencer had no intentions of being their minister, even though they did not attend frequently. She was glad she could see him without being seen. A large woman in front of her screened her, but Betty could lean slightly and see around.

"*All* have sinned and come short of the glory of God." His Scripture reading was electrifying. "*All* we like sheep have gone astray." Several of the members who were prone to doze through the service for the sake of putting in an appearance shook themselves and sat up straight. This young upstart dared come in *their* church and read Scripture in that manner, emphasizing *sin?* It took the well-prepared anthem by the highly trained choir to soothe ruffled feathers. Perhaps he just had that way of speaking. Betty was reveling in the indignation around her, paying little heed to what was being said. Daniel certainly was speaking to those hypocrites in the church. Not once did it occur that ALL meant her as well.

The anthem was over. Now Daniel Spencer would step forward, congratulate the singers, and read a discourse. Betty settled back along with the others only to be shocked into uprightness.

"I will not be using the sermon I prepared." Each word fell clear-cut, like a stone plopping into the pool of silence. "I find that there is a message the Lord wishes me to being in place of the one I had written out."

Never in the history of First Church had such a thing happened. Flags of color flew in Betty's eyes as she met Prescott's amused glance. Purple lights highlighted the deep blue. What was Daniel Spencer up to?

Folding his hands before him on the pulpit he leaned forward, then laughed lightly and stepped from behind the massive piece of furniture. "This is a beautiful pulpit, but it puts me too far away from you. It sets me apart as someone special, on a little higher plane." He deliberately stepped down from the platform to the floor in front and smiled again. "That's better. You know, this is what the Lord wants — for all of us to be closer together — and to Him."

First the Lord had a message; now he presumed to say what the Lord wanted. The congregation was paralyzed. It had been a long time since a minister had dared tell them the Lord wanted anything more of them than to attend on Sunday and drop a sum into the offering box. Yet there was not one person who did not lean slightly forward to meet whatever new thing would come next.

"You have asked me to fill your pulpit. You have asked me to accept a call to be your pastor, shepherd of your flock." He looked around, straight into the eyes of the disapproving board members who felt it out of place for him to discuss such things in church.

"I appreciate your invitation. Yesterday I spent a long time in prayer. I asked God what I should do about taking this church." Somehow his eyes seemed to have discovered Betty and were speaking to her. "When I came to Grand Rapids I knew I would not take this church. Yet, certain things happened that made me wonder; perhaps God had a work here for me to do."

In the little pause Betty's heart beat rapidly. Was she part of the reason he reconsidered? Joy flooded through her, only to be drowned by his next statements.

"I asked God what to do." The ripple was barely discernible, yet he caught it. "I always ask God what to do, and I hope you do too. It pleases our Father to give us direction." Again his eyes sought out Betty's corner.

"I asked Him if I should give up the plans I had to build a church in a little town named Pioneer, in the far West. It had been pointed out that perhaps someone else could best serve there and leave me free to serve you."

Betty's blood raced.

"Yes, I asked God. He said no."

Dumbfounded, Betty made no pretense at hiding behind the large woman. Along with the rest of the congregation she gaped at the man in the plain business suit who dared turn down their honored call so casually.

Something in his dark eyes called to her as he said quietly. "It was not an easy decision. It took struggle. The place I will go is far different from here. It will be small. I will often be discouraged by lack of numbers." Again he took a step toward the congregation. "As I prayed, the garden where I knelt faded. In its place was a small building that had once been a store. I never saw the building. I only heard of it.

"Years before I was born, a young man starting out his ministry felt called to start preaching the gospel in a little village on the Great Plains. He had been assured there would be those who would listen. What he had not been told was of the man who ruled the little village. The leader employed most of the people there or purchased their produce or in some other way controlled their living. He hated ministers. So when he found the former owner of the empty building had rented it to the young minister for a week, he was furious. He demanded the owner cancel the agreement.

"The building owner would not do so. He didn't care what the man thought; he was leaving for another town. The leader took another way. He visited people, and spread the word. No one was to attend the church service. If they did, there would no longer be a market or a job.

"The people were appalled, but what could they do? They had no money to move on. So regretfully, families who had looked forward to the series of meetings stayed home. The building owner fell ill and was unable to attend.

"The young minister came in eagerly. He swept the building and built a fire. He even managed to find a few sprigs of green to decorate a bit. The stove smoked, and the fire went out; but he only laughed. It had taken the chill of non-use from the room, and the evening was pleasant. He opened every window wide, letting the good fresh air finish the task of ridding the room of its odors.

"When seven o'clock came he was surprised to find no one there. Had the notice been changed to seven-thirty? No, the notice on the door said seven. He waited. Five after, ten after, fifteen after. By seven-thirty, he realized the truth. No one was coming.

"Outside the window huddled the town leader, peering in, enjoying the young man's discomfiture. To his amazement the dejection suddenly turned to action. The minister found a hymn book among his possessions.

" 'Abide with me, fast falls the evening tide,' in a strong voice came rolling out the open windows, down the streets, into homes of poor people. Doors opened. People poured out. The order had been given for no one to attend church. Who could be singing like that?

" 'Touched,' the town leader pointed to his head and whispered as others crowded beneath the window just out of sight. But others came closer.

" 'What's he doin' now?' A glance inside confirmed the truth — the minister was offering an opening prayer.

" 'Lord, I thank You for this opportunity to meet with You. I pray that You will bless the reading and speaking of Your Word this night. Amen.'

"Another hymn, then the young minister picked up his Bible and read a Scripture. People peered in to make sure someone had not slipped inside. The room was empty except for the minister who had gone on and was preaching — *to an entirely empty room!*

" 'Who's he a-talkin' to?' someone wanted to know.

"The town leader could only shake his head, eyes popping. Not one of those men or women left his spot by the window. They were spellbound by the simple words about Jesus Christ that the minister spoke to an empty room.

"When he finished, the young minister sang another hymn, gave a closing prayer, and stepped from the pulpit and into the yard. He gave no sign his 'congregation' had all been in the yard.

" 'Service tomorrow night at seven,' he called cheerily. 'Good night.' Then he walked down to his boarding place."

The magnetic voice stopped. There was not a sound in the entire First Church.

Daniel Spencer again took up the story. "The next night the little building was packed. In the very front row was the man who had passed the word to stay away. When the service was over he was first to shake hands with the young minister.

" 'Tell me, why did you go ahead with your service last night when no one else was here?'

"The young minister gripped the man's hand and looked him straight in the eye. 'Sir, God was here. My appointment was with Him. If others did not choose to come, it did not release me from my appointment.' "

Again Daniel paused, his eyes sweeping the silent congregation. "Friends, that little building is gone now. In its place stands a church where over a hundred people worship every week. If it had not been for that young minister who kept his appointment with God, it would never have come to pass. Why should I care about a young minister who preached to an empty room long ago in a dusty town? Let me tell you why."

Betty drew in a shaken breath, gaze fixed on his face. It was illuminated, reminding her of the face of an angel in a treasured childhood picture she once owned.

"The man who ran the town, the man who tried to run the preacher out of town, and the man who was first to recognize truth when he finally heard it through the lips of a young man called of God, was my own grandfather." His eyes seemed to bore into the hearts of his listeners, searching, probing to depths hidden from all save God. "If I can reach even one person the way my grandfather was reached, I will have fulfilled my calling — and it must be in Pioneer that it starts."

Betty collapsed against the back of the pew, drained. But Daniel Spencer was not through.

"I could stop now and let you all leave thinking this is my calling, without applying it to your own lives. I tell you this day, each one of you is being called of God to exemplify His qualities in whatever part of life you occupy." He relentlessly turned toward the board. "You, sirs, are required by God to find the minister for this great church that *He* would have you have." He turned back to the rest of the gawking congregation. "There is not one man, woman, or child within the sound of my voice who is not being called just the same way to be the best. Whether businessman, lawyer, doctor, wife, mother, or student, God has a call for you. Find it. When you do, you will be of all people most happy and blessed."

Slowly Daniel Spencer walked to his place. The last song was sung. The benediction was given. The congregation spilled out on the sidewalk, some laughing self-consciously, denying by their mirth the validity of what was said.

"Theatrical claptrap!" Betty's father muttered.

"Too bad. He has such nice eyes. But that cheap emotional story about his grandfather —" Mrs. Courtland's eyebrows lifted, completing her opinion.

Betty stood in a sea of comment, most of it adverse. They were coming out of the spell cast by what had happened inside, ready to complacently go on living the way they always had. Was she?

"What do you think of him now?" Prescott managed to whisper before meeting Courtland's frown and melting into the crowd.

His words fell on empty air.

Hands over her traitorous heart, torn apart with feelings new and untried, Betty had fled.

"You aren't going without telling Elizabeth good-bye!"

Daniel Spencer's lips involuntarily twisted with pain, and he looked away from Prescott. "I have to." Moodily he stared through the window at the heavy curtain of rain. "In spite of everything within me crying out that it is wrong, I have learned to care a great deal for her. Seeing her again would solve nothing." He impatiently stepped to his trunk and tightened a fastening. "You can tell her I said good-bye."

"I'm not sure if you are taking the coward's way out or doing the honorable thing!" Prescott admitted. "Since you feel nothing could come of it, perhaps you're right, but I don't know what Elizabeth is going to do when she hears you've gone."

"She'll find someone else. She always has, hasn't she?"

"Until now. This time I'm not sure she will."

"Better to wound her vanity than have her build false ideas about being the wife of someone she could persuade to accept First Church and fit right into society." He laughed shortly. "Except I don't believe First Church is quite so eager to have me take the pastorate since I spoke there!" He turned moody again. "I really am not sure why I ever came to Grand Rapids — to break your engagement, upset the Courtlands, or turn the congregation upside down?"

"Don't forget, Dan, if you hadn't come I would still have been on the society treadmill. Now I have hard work to look forward to — and getting to know your God better."

A rush of feeling swept away Daniel's dark reflection as he clasped Prescott's hand. "That's true. It's worth everything to hear you say that." He cleared his throat of the husky note. "I know you don't want me to refer to it, but I have to, this once. I don't know when I'll be back, if ever. Prescott, you are the finest friend I have ever known, and the most understanding."

"Don't make me out a saint. I'll admit when I first saw how Betty watched you I felt some pangs. Yet as I honestly searched myself and her, I knew it wasn't you who had come between us. It was Betty — and me." That time he was the one to laugh, slapping Daniel on the shoulder. "Come on, or you'll miss your train. I wish you would, you know!"

45

Long after the train left the station, speeding west into a new and strange land that would swallow his friend, Prescott Wetherell stood on the platform watching. The next thing was to tell Elizabeth Daniel had gone. It was not going to be easy. He could not go to the Courtland home with things the way they were. He would have to send a note.

It was the hardest note he ever had to write. Short. He made no effort to soften the fact that Daniel had left without trying to see her.

> Dear Elizabeth,
>   Daniel Spencer left this afternoon for his assignment in Pioneer. He asked me to tell you good-bye for him.
>   Faithfully,
>   Prescott

Calling a servant, he ordered, "Deliver this to Miss Elizabeth Courtland and see that it goes directly to her, not into the hands of anyone else."

"Yes, sir." If there was curiosity behind the impassive face it was well hidden. Yet Prescott sighed when the man was gone. How would she take it?

He did not have to wait long to find out. Almost before his man could return, he heard flying hooves. Beauty! Through the library window he could see Elizabeth tumble from the carriage practically before it stopped, race up the path, and pound on the front door.

He was there to meet her. "Why, Elizabeth!"

She lifted her tearstained face to his. "Is he really gone? Without a word for me?"

It almost melted Prescott's reserve. "Come in, child." He led her to the library. "He said to be sure and tell you good-bye."

"Good-bye!" Betty choked over the word. "Was that all? Didn't he leave any other message for me?"

"What message could he leave?"

Betty lifted her head proudly. "He could have said — he should have — I don't know, but Prescott, he's gone!" Never had he seen her so distraught. Her dark hair was disheveled, her eyes hurt. "I'll never see him again."

"No, you probably won't." Prescott stepped closer, lifted her chin, forced her to look into his eyes. "Elizabeth, do you care that much?"

For the space of a heartbeat Betty thought of denying. What good would it do to tell Prescott of the feelings that filled her? She could not lie. "I care."

His grip tightened, almost to the point of cruelty. "Why? Because he's the only man who never fell at your feet at first glance? Because he was a challenge?"

"No!" She wrenched free, eyes nearly black with emotion. "Don't ask me why I care! He's nothing — rude, boorish, a hick preacher with not enough sense to snatch First Church when it was offered to him on a silver platter! He thinks I'm a cheap flirt, without anything a man needs to have in a wife. But, oh, Prescott, why did he go without me?"

"You don't mean you would have gone with him! You, Elizabeth Courtland? I can't quite see you milking cows and keeping house and cooking for him." His sarcasm increased. "What could you offer such a man as Daniel Spencer?"

"My love."

It stopped him short. "You can't really mean you love him. You've only known him a few weeks. You're entirely unsuited to each other. Why, even Dan said he would never tell you how he felt because you could never be happy —"

"He said *that*?" Glory trailed in Betty's face like streams of water seeking the ocean.

"Forget it!" His command was sharp. "I never meant to let you know."

"Know what, Prescott?" Color stained her white face. "That — that he cares?"

"It doesn't mean a thing that he cares or that he was attracted to you. He'll go into Pioneer and someday laugh at the idea of ever having given you a thought. He'll find someone who will stand beside him in that wild land and be the helpmate he needs."

"No!" She flinched as if he had struck her.

Again he held her arms, pinioning her so she had to look at him. "Even if you could learn how to be a wife, the kind he needs, could you ever learn to know the God he serves?"

Betty stared into the demanding face, a Prescott different from the gay companion she had always known. At last her answer came. "No, Prescott, I could not." Seeing the disappointment that came into his face she cried, "How could I? I don't even know if there is a God!"

"You really think you could fill Daniel's life as he deserves?" He dropped her arms, eyes chilled.

"What difference does it make about his God? If he wants to believe it, so what? It doesn't change how he feels about me." She warmed to her subject. "If two people care about each other, none of what they believe needs to matter. I've money, plenty of it. My grandfather left it in trust for me. You think Daniel Spencer would stay in Pioneer if he knew he could have me by going elsewhere?"

"Didn't he know that before he left?"

"How could he?" Her angry flush should have warned him of the tantrum to follow. "I certainly did not tell him, and I hope you didn't!" Her scornful accusations were in sharp contrast to her earlier woebegone state.

"You honestly think you could ever win him away from what he thinks God wants of him?"

Betty's eyes blazed with anger. "God! I will fight God with everything in me for Daniel Spencer! He's the only man I ever wanted, and I intend to have him, regardless of the cost!"

"Elizabeth!"

She was adamant. "I mean what I say. If I had known sooner he was attracted to me, instead of disapproving the way he acted all the time, do you think he would ever have left without asking — no, without begging me to go with him?"

"So you will fight God for Daniel Spencer and turn him into a tame cat, the way you have done with men all your life." Arms folded, Prescott stated the case quietly.

"You needn't act like judge and jury. If there really is a God, He wants Daniel to be happy."

"I can't believe you think you could ever make him happy!"

Betty drew on her gloves as she stepped toward the door. "I cannot imagine not being able to make any man happy, if I choose. Even you, Prescott."

She was unprepared for his stern reply. "I wonder."

"I really must go. Abbie will be wondering where I wandered off to. Thank you for the information. I will use it — to the best of my ability."

"You should be turned over my knee and spanked. You are nothing but a spoiled, greedy child, snatching what you are told you can't have!"

"And you, Prescott Wetherell, are insufferable!" Anger turned her eyes to purple. "If you think I'm so terrible, maybe you'd better be thankful to that God of Daniel Spencer's you escaped me!" She flounced out, but not before hearing Prescott's quiet response.

"Perhaps I should."

Betty drove home slowly, heart pounding. So Daniel cared! The instinct that had driven her, had taunted her to cling to him in the little study that day had been true. He cared! His lean, handsome face formed before her. His lips did not smile with mockery; they smiled with welcome. Closer,

closer — "Beauty!" A near miss with a great branching tree when Beauty swung a corner too wide brought Betty back to reality. Somehow she managed to get home and to her room. It was no punishment being alone as her father had ordered. It was time to think and to plan.

He would write. When Daniel got to that forsaken place he would write, maybe even within a few days. Betty's heart leaped. What would it be like to get a love letter from Daniel telling her he had found out he could not live without her? All the censure he had given was forgotten in the knowledge he cared.

It was the beginning of a new era for Betty Courtland. Each day she eagerly awaited the mail, only to turn away heartsick. Invitations poured in by the score as well as notes, flowers, and candy from the string of admirers who had suddenly focused their attention on her. There were many showers, teas, and luncheons. But not one word from Daniel Spencer.

If only she had not quarreled with Prescott she could get news of Daniel from him. But she was too proud to do that, too proud to admit that she had not heard from the man who had gone away without a word.

One night she overheard her father and mother talking. At the top of the stairs she stood unseen but frozen to the spot when she heard her name.

"What's got into Elizabeth?"

"I'm sure I don't know!" Had her mother's voice always been so querulous? "I found her in the kitchen the other day actually watching the cook bake a cake! When I asked her what on earth she was doing, she just said, 'Maybe someday I'll have to bake a cake. I was just watching how it was done.'"

"Elizabeth bake a cake? What foolishness is she up to now? You don't suppose she's grieving over Prescott, do you?"

"Of course not! She never loved him. She's just moody."

"Maybe we should send her to my sister and brother-in-law in New York for the winter. I'm getting tired of her doldrums."

"I hardly think that is necessary, Mr. Courtland." Her mother's voice was icy. "I don't approve of letting a young girl travel alone, and I certainly can't be spared from my committee work to take her."

Courtland sighed. "She'll be twenty-one in a few months. I never thought my daughter would be an old maid!"

"Well!" Even without seeing her, Betty could imagine her mother bridling. "If she is, it is from her own choice. But I admit, something's going to have to be done about her. She's even been driving out to see Emma practically every week! It's one thing to give to charity, but to deliberately seek out the company of one's former cook —"

Betty missed the rest. Biting her lip in vexation she slipped back into her room and deliberately banged the door coming out. The conversation below ceased as she ran down the stairs. Yet she did not miss the scrutiny of her father at dinner.

"Elizabeth." His colorless lips seemed ill at ease forming words of kindness. "Are you ill — or anything?"

For one ghastly moment she stared, then her face chilled. "No, I am not ill — or anything. I have not been ill — or anything. I will not be ill — or anything."

"Silence!" The head of the house thundered. "I won't have you answering me back!"

Betty sprang to her feet. "Then don't ask questions that are little more than veiled insults. Ever since I broke off with Prescott you have acted as if I were some wanton creature. Either I am your daughter and trusted as such, or I will no longer remain in your house!"

"Elizabeth!" Mrs. Courtland threw up her hands in horror.

"You will do as I say!" His heavy fist balled, and he glared at her with eyes gone suddenly red. "That broken engagement has never been explained satisfactorily. Until it is, you are suspect. Prescott Wetherell would not have asked for release if you had not brought it on by some action of your own!"

"I meant what I said, Father." Very pale, very calm, Betty stood up and walked toward the staircase. "I will not listen to such talk."

"Come back here." He pounded the table for emphasis.

"I will *not* come back." Under her breath she added, "Ever." Running to her own room she locked the door, ignoring the pounding and the sound of her father's voice demanding an apology a few moments later.

With fumbling fingers she threw open her wardrobe door, heedlessly snatching a few garments. How long it was until another knock came at the door she never knew or cared.

"Please, miss, it's Abbie." The whisper came through the keyhole. "I've brought you some dinner. Let me in quick before I'm seen."

Betty unlocked the door and Abbie slipped inside, carrying a tray. Her face was splotchy. "If I'm caught, I'll lose my place."

Betty stared at her — the maid who had been with her so long. "Abbie, I have to get away. My father has accused me of unspeakable things. Will you help me?"

Abbie gasped. "How can I help?"

"Carry out this carpetbag with my things under some towels, as if you had washing. Then get Beauty hitched to the light carriage. Sam will do it if you tell him, and do it quickly!"

"How will you get out? Your parents are still in the dining room!"

"I'm going out the window." Betty had been making rapid plans while she worked. Now she slipped from her long skirts and dropped them out the window. Slim, clad only in slips and shirtwaist, she whirled toward Abbie. "I'll climb down the big tree. Now hurry!"

It was easier than she had thought. The branches grew close, and she stepped from one to another, down, down. Once she almost fell as a limb broke but clung to the tree trunk and felt for safer footing. When she reached the bottom she put her skirt back on and headed around the house to Beauty and the carriage.

"Where will you go, Miss Betty?"

"It's better that you don't know. All you know is that you saw me drive away with Beauty. I'll get in touch with you when I can."

"Will you be all right?" Betty could see tears running down Abbie's freckled face, her hands clasped earnestly.

"I'll be fine. Remember, all you know is that I drove away." She gathered the reins and lightly touched Beauty with them. "Good-bye, Abbie — for now." Quietly the faithful horse stepped forward. Betty did not look back. The mansion she had lived in was already part of her past. Where could she go at this hour of night? A vision of an open hearth and bubbling stew rose before her. Emma! The little cottage would give her shelter until she could plan ahead. Money was no problem. Betty's legacy from her grandfather had come to her when she was eighteen. There would be more when she was twenty-one. She could stay with Emma until then and — no, it would be the first place they would look for her once they discovered she was gone.

The miles paced off under Beauty's hooves as she planned. A daring idea formed, was rejected, and came again, more insistent than before. What if she were to board the train and go to Daniel Spencer? When he learned her own father continued to think ill of her he would have to marry her!

"I'll go to Pioneer. He will feel sorry for me, know I have compromised my good name by running away. Once we're married I'll show him what the difference between his precious Pioneer and having me can be." She was almost surprised when she reached the darkened house she sought. Wild plans filled her head.

"Emma?" She pounded on the door and was rewarded by a sleepy voice. "Emma, it's Elizabeth Courtland. May I come in?"

"Miss Betty!" The old woman's face was a mass of wrinkles in the hastily lit candle. "You here, this time of night?"

"My father has cast me out. May I stay here with you until I know what to do?"

"Of course, lassie. But what's the trouble at the big house?"

"Because Prescott and I decided to break our engagement Father thinks I have done something dishonorable." It was out in words, and Betty cringed at the shock in old Emma's face. "I haven't, Emma, I haven't!" All the emotion she had held back during that awful scene rushed over her. "Is it my fault that I don't love Prescott?"

"Or that you do love the other young man, Mr. Spencer?"

Betty dropped to a worn chair, head in hands. "Yes, I love him."

A hand, work-hardened, stroked her hair. "Don't cry. Does he love you?"

"He loves me but thinks I couldn't be a good minister's wife."

"Aye, I can see how he would feel that way."

"I can, Emma, I know I can. I can learn to cook and sew and everything else I need to know, can't I?"

"If you want to badly enough." She straightened from her crooning position over the young woman she had cared for since she had been a child. "Now, off to bed with you. Things always look worse at night."

Betty knew she could not sleep a wink. She was shocked to open her eyes and find morning had arrived. There was a great sore place inside when she thought of her parents, yet as all her plans rushed over her, joy overrode the sadness. The heavy porridge with cream heartened her for what lay ahead. Somehow she must get word to Abbie to pack her trunk. But why not take Abbie with her? If ever she chose to return it would be so much more respectable if her maid had gone along.

Just as dusk fell Betty quietly pulled Beauty up a short distance from her former home. Now if only she could attract Abbie's or Sam's attention. They adored her and would not tell. Luck was with her. In a brief time her father and mother walked down the steps. She could hear the rustle of her mother's skirts and her complaining voice.

"Really! I don't see why you didn't force Betty to open her door. The idea of letting her sulk inside for an entire day isn't my idea of how to tame her. You should have made her answer when you called!"

Betty's heart leaped. They thought she had been in her room all day!

"Let her sulk. She'll come out when she gets hungry enough. Now let's go. The Fosters hate to be kept waiting!" Her father passed close enough for her to have reached from the shrubbery and touched him. A pang shot through Betty, not for the cold man he was, but for the kind of father he might have been. What if he had been like Daniel's father?

Her reverie was interrupted by the carriage leaving. Now was her chance. They would be gone for hours. The Fosters held late parties.

"Abbie, Sam!" She sped inside, closing the door behind her. "Help me." Staring into their stunned faces she stamped her foot. "I said, help me! Sam, get my big trunk. Abbie, pack your clothes."

"My clothes!" Every freckle stood out on Abbie's face.

"Yes. I'm going to Pioneer, and you're going with me!"

Abbie fell back from Betty's advance as if she were a spirit. "Pioneer? Out West?"

"Must I do everything myself? Do as I say! Get everything you own that can be packed easily. We have to be out of here before my parents come back."

"But — but —"

"Don't you want to come with me?" Betty paused in mid-flight up the stairs. "I need you, Abbie." Her face suddenly looked old. "Mother and Father have made it impossible for me to stay. I'm going to Daniel Spencer." Her voice trembled, and it was not all acting. "If only you go, I will at least have one friend."

Abbie responded to the forlornness of her voice rather than the orders. "Then if you need me, I'll come. Hurry, Miss Betty, or we won't be away before the master comes back."

Incredibly they finished what was needed long before the Courtlands were due home. Betty even took time to hastily scrawl a note.

> Daniel Spencer cares for me and I for him. I am going to
> him. Abbie is with me, so all is respectable.

She hesitated. Could she honestly sign it "With love?" Her lips tightened. She would not be a hypocrite. Scribbling the word *Betty* at the bottom she placed it in Sam's hands and disappeared into the night.

When Daniel Spencer waved good-bye to his friend Prescott it was with little hope that he would ever see him again. Grand Rapids was rapidly disappearing in the lurch and sway of the train that carried Daniel away. Where was the excited flush he had anticipated, the knowledge of carrying the gospel to those who needed it so much? For one moment he almost hated Elizabeth Courtland for ruining the special moment he had waited for for so long. If only he had never met her.

Fixing his lips in a grim line Daniel turned his eyes to the passing countryside. Rolling hills, farms, trees such as the one that had sheltered him when he and Betty had their long talk the first time they had driven together.

"God, have I been untrue?" He did not realize he had spoken aloud until the curious look from a man across the aisle brought him back to the present. Daniel leaned back against his seat. Why must he be tormented? He had fought his fight, set his course. Must he be haunted by shadowy eyes that changed from deep blue to purple, hair so dusky as to be part of the wraiths around him? Yet what a follower Betty Courtland would make, if her loyalty could ever be fixed on God. He dwelled on that for only a moment, then firmly pushed it aside. She was foreign to his faith, his belief, his work. He would not allow himself to moon like a stupid schoolboy.

The decision carried him miles toward his destination. After changing trains in Chicago he closed his eyes, little caring for the tall buildings. They would be part of his past.

Somewhere in the Dakotas Daniel roused to a voice. The conductor was entering his car calling. "Is there a doctor here or a minister?"

"I'm a minister." He sprang to his feet.

"Come with me, please. There's a lady dying and calling for a minister."

Daniel followed the conductor down the narrow aisle, clutching chair backs when the train swayed around a corner. It was not far — just two cars ahead. In the first car the conductor had found a doctor, a man not much older than Daniel but with lines in his face showing that he had seen much of life that was not pleasant.

"There, sister, what seems to be the matter?" The doctor's cheery greeting brought faint color to the white face of the patient.

"My heart. My physician warned me not to take this trip, but I wanted to see my daughter out West." The little old lady clutched her chest as another spasm of pain shook her.

Instantly the doctor was on his knees beside her. "Well, let's just have a listen." His stethoscope was already in his hand when he reached her. "Hm."

"It isn't good, is it?"

"No. I'm afraid your physician was right." The doctor's words were gentle in spite of their frankness.

"A minister?" Her faded eyes searched the area.

"This man's a minister, ma'am." The conductor respectfully stepped back for Daniel to approach her.

"I want to talk with him — alone." Her breathing was labored. Daniel glanced at the doctor and caught his look. The next moment he and the conductor were gone.

"I'm not afraid to die," the little lady told Daniel. "I just thought it would be nice — if someone said a prayer. I know God. He and my husband are waiting for me."

Daniel felt his throat tighten in response. He put one of his big hands over her frail one. "I'm sure they are. Why, they're probably getting ready for you right now."

"Could you —" she was growing perceptibly weaker. "Would you —" Her fingers clasped Daniel's strong ones.

"Dear Lord, welcome this child to Thy care. Help her to go with joy to meet You. Bless us all, for Jesus' sake, Amen."

"I'm glad you were here." She opened her eyes and smiled. "Tell my daughter I'll be waiting —" Her grip loosened.

It was a long moment before Daniel could get up from his knees and step into the aisle where the conductor and doctor waited. "She's gone." The doctor disappeared inside and returned shortly, nodding.

"She left instructions," the conductor told them. "Before she called for you she told me what to do."

Strangely silent, Daniel turned back toward his own car to be halted by the hearty grip of the stranger doctor. "Brother, would you like to talk a bit?"

Daniel measured him with his eyes, taking in the carelessly worn suit, the steady face. "Of course."

"I'm Gordon Stewart." He held out a well cared-for hand.

"Daniel Spencer." They dropped into Gordon's seat and the empty one next to it.

"Glad you were aboard. When there's nothing left for me to do, you people come in handy."

In spite of the little smile Daniel could feel his hackles rise. "Not just when there's nothing you can do."

"Sorry if I trod on your toes." The doctor's face looked weary. "I guess I just never could understand why men became ministers."

"Perhaps for the same reason you became a doctor." Daniel still smarted under the other's casual comments. "Why did you, by the way?"

"It's what I always wanted — to help people."

"My very reason for becoming a minister." Somehow Daniel found himself telling the stranger who was rapidly becoming a friend all the things that led to his accepting the call to Pioneer. Only once did Gordon Stewart interrupt. "You say you're going to a little dump in the Northwest to build a church? Why didn't you stay and work in some city church?"

"Why didn't you stay in some city hospital?" Daniel shot back. "You just told me you broke free because of rules and regulations — because you couldn't be free to practice medicine as you saw fit. Why should I be any different?"

Gordon's hearty laugh restored peace. "I guess you shouldn't. Tell me about this town of Pioneer."

The churning wheels ate up miles while they talked. Far into the night, their low voices vibrating with dedication to their chosen fields, they shared. Two who had come together by chance — or was it?

"Do you believe things just happen, or are they planned?" Gordon demanded at one point. "For instance, were you on this particular train because it led where you wanted to go? If so, why not a train a day earlier or a day later? If you were on for a reason, was that reason to be with the woman when she died, to comfort her? I overheard her telling you she was glad you were there."

Daniel's mind was racing. Did he dare say what he felt? Breathing a quick prayer for just the right words he leaned forward, intent on the thoughts coming with lightning rapidity. "Gordon." They had long since dispensed with formality. "What if I told you I believe I am on this train not because of her, although I was able to minister, but because of you?"

"To convert me?" Disappointment shaded the question.

"Not at all." Daniel flashed a smile. "That might be a side effect, but that isn't what I meant."

Gordon's suspicious glance did nothing to help the conversation. "Just what do you have in mind?"

"Why don't you go to Pioneer with me? There's no doctor there, but plenty of work."

"Are you out of your head, man? Why would I go to a place like that?"

"To help people."

The challenge lay between them, given, not yet taken up.

"I can help people wherever I go."

"But will they need it as much as the people in Pioneer?" Again Daniel leaned forward, deadly serious. The more he thought of it the more right it seemed. If only such a man as Gordon Stewart could be convinced to practice in Pioneer.

"I have the chance for a job in Seattle."

"Will it really be any different from the one in Chicago?" Daniel ignored Gordon's black look. "There are many doctors in Seattle. There are none in Pioneer." A thought crossed his mind. "Of course, if you are in it for the money —"

"Money? Never! I am a doctor because I have to be one."

Daniel took heart. "Then why not be a doctor where you are needed desperately? There are loggers in Pioneer who are brought into town injured, needing medical help. The nearest doctor is thirty miles away over rough roads that are barely passable. The nearest hospital is another twenty miles past that, again on roads that can become little more than ruts in winter. Sometimes trees are down. Women in childbirth have had babies while waiting for someone to clear a tree from the road. Some have lost their babies, simply because there was no doctor. The man who encouraged me to go to Pioneer told me all that. He also said that in at least seventy-five percent of the deaths, if there had been a doctor, the patients would have survived."

"A layman's opinion."

"Yes. But a qualified layman. He served as doctor's helper during the Civil War. He's too old now to be of much help, but does what he can." Daniel could feel defeat creeping through him. Why had he thought he could interest this man in Pioneer?

"Why do people live in such an isolated spot?"

Was there more than curiosity in the question? Daniel countered with another. "Why do people live in any particular spot? Because it's all they know — or where they make a living — or where they are sent by a Higher Power than themselves."

"And you believe I am being *sent* to Pioneer, as well as yourself?"

Daniel stood and stretched. The cynical smile on his new friend's face did not escape him. "I believe no man on earth can decide that for another. Good night." He turned on his heel and made his way to his berth.

It was not their last conversation about Pioneer. In spite of his unwillingness to even consider practicing there Gordon had an insatiable interest in the little town. He pumped every detail Daniel knew from him.

"Maybe I'm presuming," Daniel told him. "Perhaps you have a wife or family who would hate it there."

"No wife or family. The girl I loved died a few years back. I couldn't help — a congenital heart defect." Daniel saw the lines deepen into furrows and understood the look in Gordon's face. "So many others who seemed to have less to live for, and yet Susan was taken. Why?"

"I won't even attempt to answer that question."

"Good. I've heard all the platitudes about there being a reason." Gordon stared out the window. "I wonder if Susan would want me to go to Pioneer?"

"We'd make a good team," Daniel contented himself with saying, not allowing his exultation to leap into his face and be seen. It was too tremulous, too cobwebby a beginning. "Besides, the little railroad that goes in and out of Pioneer daily runs both ways. If you looked it over and decided against it, you'd still have time to take the Seattle opening."

"Maybe I will."

From then on the conversation was not of the past but of the future. Somehow, once Gordon made his decision to look Pioneer over, there did not seem to be any doubt in Daniel's mind as to the outcome. How could anyone, especially a doctor, see the need in a place like Pioneer and turn his back on that need?

With a start Daniel realized he had not thought of Grand Rapids or Elizabeth Courtland as he had thought he would do. In the face of what lay ahead, they receded into a dreamlike trance. Was it another lifetime that he had held her for the one brief moment in the little study, feeling her softness almost to the point of yielding? Now it seemed long ago, something that had nothing to do with Pioneer and Gordon Stewart. The country had changed from plains to mountains to desert and back to mountains. When they reached the small village where they would board the train for the last of their journey, Daniel was too full for words. There was a wooden platform with trunks piled high, a black monster, breathing fire and belching smoke, a high, clear whistle calling them on, and blue skies like he never before had seen.

Yet with every inch of those last miles Daniel could feel his nerves tighten. He refrained from looking at Gordon, who had grown silent.

What would they find? In spite of all the preconceived ideas, even the country they traveled through was unfamiliar. Great stretches of untouched timberland passed before them. The train slowed as a buck, his doe, and two spotted fawns crossed the shining tracks that cut through their territory. Daniel and Gordon caught glimpses of mighty rivers and glistening streams.

"I'll bet there are fish in those streams." Gordon suddenly grinned at Daniel. "Of course if what you say is true, a man won't have much time for fishing — at least not my kind of fishing. Now, you are a fisher of men, I've heard tell. Wonder who might catch the most?"

Pioneer dawned on them before they were quite prepared. They rounded the last curve, the whistle triumphantly announced their arrival, and it lay before them — a huddle of crude houses in a raw land. Carved from the forests that towered to the edge of what they called a town, Pioneer could by no stretch of the imagination be called inviting. Dust lay thick in what must be Main Street. It clung to a series of buildings that were the seven saloons Dan had told Gordon made up most of the "business." A little apart stood a ramshackle building marked General Store. Long benches on the porch gave evidence of visitors, as did the worn boards of the flooring.

"Whew! Not the most elegant place in the world!"

Daniel had expected crudeness. Still his heart sank. For himself it did not matter. Seen through Gordon's eyes, it was pathetic — this hamlet in the wilderness that *dared* call itself a town.

"What's that?" Gordon lifted his head as they stepped down.

A passerby called back over his shoulder, "Speeder whistle! Someone's hurt and comin' out from the logging camp!"

Forgotten was the sparsity of Pioneer. Before the speeder with the injured man stopped Gordon was there, black bag in hand. "I'm a doctor. Let me in here!" Daniel saw the bloodstained bandage around the man's leg and the agony of his face even as one of the loggers on the speeder said, "Widowmaker got him."

"Widowmaker?"

The logger looked at him scornfully. "Dead snag."

"Is there a place he can be taken?" Gordon addressed the same logger. "I've got to get this leg sewn up right away, or he'll bleed to death!"

"Bring him to the hotel." The big logger was already elbowing his way through the anxious crowd that had gathered. "Easy, there, men." Daniel was amazed at the gentle way the patient's comrades lifted the hastily improvised stretcher.

"You'll have to help me," Gordon told Daniel. "Had any experience?"

"A little." Daniel was already stripping off his coat and rolling up his shirt sleeves.

"Good." They beat the patient to the hotel. "You have hot water?"

"Sure, Doc." Someone must have run ahead. The hotelkeeper was lifting steaming kettles from his huge wood stove.

"Good." Gordon motioned to Daniel. "Bring my instruments as soon as they've been sterilized." He was already on his way to the little room where the logger was biting his lips until the blood came to keep from screaming.

Daniel would never forget their introduction to Pioneer — the tense faces of the loggers. the only partially relaxed logger. What pain killers Gordon had could not work rapidly enough to spare him all the agony of the cleansing of the deep wound, followed by countless stitches.

"There. As neat a piece of stitching as I've done in some time." Dr. Stewart washed his hands and rolled his shirt sleeves down. "I'll just keep an eye on him and in a few weeks he'll be good as new."

"Thanks, Doc." The head logger had stood by for orders during the entire operation. "And thanks —" he looked at Daniel inquiringly.

"Daniel Spencer. I'm your new minister."

Blankness greeted his statement. "A preacher?" It was followed by a loud "ha, ha." "Well, you're shore a good one. Never knew a preacher before who'd jump in and help like you did today. Andy'll be pretty glad." His statement gave Daniel a lot of insight into just what kind of preachers those loggers had evidently known.

"Are there rooms we can rent here?" he turned to the hotelkeeper.

"Shore. Don't s'pose you'll be stayin' long. They usually don't." It was further enlightenment on the status of religion in Pioneer. Daniel's jaw was set.

"I'll be staying."

"So will I." Gordon looked directly into the crowd of men. "Why isn't there a better place for injuries than here?"

The head logger's face turned a dull red. "No need for one. Didn't have a doctor. Why have a horspital?"

"You have a doctor now." Grim, steady, Gordon gathered up his instruments.

"Then we'll have to see about gettin' a horspital."

Was the man joking? Daniel shot him a glance and found something in the rough man's face that reassured him. It was no joke. It was as simple as that. If a hospital was needed, it would be provided. The beginning of warmth for the loggers in front of him stared out through Daniel's dark eyes. "Dr. Stewart needs a place while the hospital is being built. Is anything available?"

The leader scratched his head. "Well, there's the Smith shack. They up and moved off — said they weren't comin' back. It ain't much, but it has three rooms."

"Fine." Gordon held out his hand to be crushed in the other's grip. "Will you show us where it is?" He turned back to Daniel. "You're going to live with me, aren't you?"

Daniel hesitated. With patients coming in all hours of day and night, could he accomplish what he had come to do? Yet the Master he followed had taken care of the sick and helpless even before showing concern about their souls. "I will if you want me."

"Better stay here a few nights," the hotelkeeper advised. "That Smith place needs a good cleanin'. We can get some of the women to help, if you like."

"That won't be necessary." Daniel caught a glance of approval from Gordon. "I'll clean it while Dr. Stewart gets a room set up for his work."

"You shore ain't like the other preachers," one of the loggers commented, moving toward the door. "Well, my woman'll be glad to help, anyway."

"Ours, too."

But the logger leader stopped just inside the door, heavy calk boots scratching the already scarred floor. "Better take the help, preacher. Pioneer takes care of its own — and it 'pears like you 'n' the Doc are goin' to be part of us."

"Well!" Gordon turned back to Daniel when the others had gone, eyes sparkling with higher interest than Daniel had seen before. "In the words of our new friend, it 'pears we're goin' to find plenty to do in Pioneer."

"It also appears we'd better take a look at that Smith cabin. Might as well see what needs doing."

"Yeah, but let's go ahead and keep our room here until it's cleaned. I don't hanker to move into a place that's been left for the birds and squirrels. Wonder why the Smiths 'up and moved off?' Seems like quite a place to me."

"Then you have no regrets?"

Gordon's fine eyes darkened. "After seeing the need here? Who's going to have time for regrets?" He stepped through the door in the direction of the cabin that had been pointed out. "I have a feeling we're going to be two busy people for the next few months."

"I hope so." Daniel did not see the quick glance Gordon gave him. For one second only, he thought of the contrast between Grand Rapids, First Church, Prescott, and Elizabeth, and all they stood for rose to protest against the appalling primitiveness of Pioneer. The next moment he was following Gordon down the overgrown trail toward the Smith shack where they would create a semblance of a home.

"All it needs is a good cleaning," Gordon exulted. "I can take the biggest room for my office and the alcove to sleep. You can have the middle size room. There's even an extra door. You won't have to be bothered when patients come." He looked like a boy on a camping trip. "There's a fireplace, but I reckon we'd better eat at the hotel. I'm not much of a cook. Are you?"

"Not me! I can if I have to, but I hate it. Besides, since we don't have to rent rooms, the money can pay for meals." Daniel was catching some of his comrade's enthusiasm. "We can —" he broke off. "What's that?" A buzz like a swarm of bees was followed by a knock on the door.

"Why, hello!" Daniel looked over the small army of women. How had word gotten around so fast? Each was armed with broom, cleaning cloth, and pail of hot water.

"Shoo! Out of here." The foremost woman waved her mop threateningly. "When we heard there was a doc and a preacher in town we just grabbed our stuff and came. You git out of here so we can clean!"

"It really isn't necessary, Mrs. —"

"Sloane. My husband's head logger. Now git out of here, will you? You'll have plenty to do once you move in." A murmur of assent went through the crowd. "Oh, there'll be a potluck after church on Sunday, so you'll want to plan for it."

"Potluck? Church Sunday?" Gordon sounded as confused as Daniel felt.

"Shore. We got a preacher and a new doc, and we can use the schoolhouse. I hear tell as how there's goin' to be a new church, but no sense waitin' 'til the Lord sees fit for it to git done. We'll have preachin' Sunday."

Gordon and Daniel fled from the swarm, laughing all the way up the trail. "Well, so there will be church Sunday! I've had my introduction to Pioneer." Gordon's eyes danced. "Now it's your turn!" He turned back toward the station for their baggage. "I have to admit — I'm curious to see just what you choose to talk about in your first sermon in Pioneer!"

Daniel grinned a bit sheepishly. "Oh? You're not half so curious about that subject as I am. I get the feeling it's going to be quite an affair."

Daniel Spencer straightened up and rubbed his back. No sign of an ache. The hard days of work had toughened him. It did not seem possible that so much had been achieved in the short weeks since he had come to Pioneer.

Before him lay a low building, raw logs shining in the sun. Tom Sloane had been as good as his word. Every spare moment the loggers had pitched into work on their "horspital." Crude, compared with hospitals he had seen, it boasted four separate rooms, one of which Gordon Stewart would occupy.

"It's not that I haven't enjoyed bunking with you," he told Daniel. "This way I can be closer to my patients. You can have a little more peace and quiet for your work too."

Daniel smiled. The bond of friendship that had grown between the two was like the one he had shared with Prescott Wetherell. For a moment a pang stirred him. Prescott! In the busy days, working long after dark by the light of kerosene lanterns, he had managed to hold back thoughts of Prescott — and of Elizabeth. He smiled again, grimly this time. What would she think of Pioneer? His mouth twisted. The very rawness of the place answered his question. She would hate it.

"Sorry I haven't been more help building," Gordon regretted. "Seems like every sick person in Pioneer just waited until I came. I even pulled a tooth the other day. The littlest Sloane boy had a swollen jaw, and Mrs. Sloane said she 'reckoned I'd better git it out' since they couldn't go to a dentist — takes too long." He grimaced. "Can't say I enjoyed that. What we need in Pioneer is a dentist."

"And a laundry. And a bakery. And a —"

"Hold it!" Gordon threw back his head and laughed. "Our town will get them all in time."

"Our town?" Daniel's eyes were dancing. "I thought you were 'jest stoppin' over fer a spell.' " He dodged the sweet-smelling wood chip Gordon hurled at him.

"Say, aren't they a grand bunch of people? I wish some of the earthborn snobs in cities could see how happily these people live — for the most part." He frowned. "Saturday nights are something else. The drunken sprees some of these men go on give me a lot of heads to patch."

63

"Isn't it strange." Daniel dropped to a stump, clasping both hands around one knee. "They fight Saturday night, yet most of them have been coming to the Sunday preaching. The other day Andy sidled up to me and slipped me a bill. He said, 'It ain't much, but reckon it'll help.' I've never known a freer-handed, more open-hearted bunch of people."

"I know." Gordon shaded his eyes. "Tom Sloane told me that just because the boys let off steam didn't mean they didn't want better things for their 'womenfolk.' He thinks your coming is one of the best things that's happened to Pioneer."

"Not to say anything about your own part," Daniel jeered. "I suppose Pioneer doesn't think a thing of your being here!"

"Don't fool yourself." Gordon struck an exaggerated pose. "I've never been so praised and appreciated in all my days of doctoring. Catch me ever going somewhere else!"

"Put 'er there." Two hard hands met in perfect understanding. "I wouldn't trade all of Pioneer's inconveniences for New York City itself."

"Or for Grand Rapids?"

The pressure of Gordon's hand increased until a weaker man would have cried out with pain. Daniel had long since told Gordon of Elizabeth Courtland and his opportunity to stay in Grand Rapids at First Church. "Especially not for Grand Rapids."

The next day Elizabeth Courtland and Abbie Tucker arrived in Pioneer.

It had been a long trip. Once they were successfully away from Grand Rapids some of Betty's glee diminished, but none of her determination. "We'll just enjoy the trip, Abbie," she confided. "I've got plenty of money. In the spring I'll be twenty-one, and then we'll have more than we'll ever need. I'm going to show Daniel Spencer that he's a fool to stay in a dump like that Pioneer must be." She fell to brooding, leaving Abbie wide-eyed, staring out the dirty train window.

Madcap Betty's plans were interrupted in Chicago. She and Abbie changed trains successfully after getting instructions from the porter. But when they were seated Betty gasped, "Abbie! My bag — it's gone!"

"Miss Betty! How could it be?"

"I remembered when we started up the steps that someone jostled against me." She frantically looked on the floor beside her. "It must have been stolen!" She turned a despairing face toward the freckle-faced girl who had begun to be more friend than maid on their trip. "What shall we do?"

"I have our tickets," Abbie reminded. "You told me to carry them. I also have a few dollars you gave me."

A little color returned to Betty's pale face. "Thank heavens! At least we won't be put off the train."

"You could wire back for money, couldn't you?"

Betty shook her head violently. "No. I secured all the money I could before we left. There will be no more until I'm twenty-one, and we have all this winter to get through." Her frown lifted. "Oh, I'm being ridiculous! Daniel will marry me as soon as we get to Pioneer. I won't have to worry about money at all." She went on, planning happily. "Of course, you'll stay with me as my maid, Abbie. Daniel wouldn't want us to be separated." There was real warmth in her look toward the little serving maid.

"Besides, I could always get a job," Abbie volunteered. "I'm used to hard work."

"That won't be necessary." Betty relented and smiled. "You can cook until I learn how!" An instant later a frown replaced the smile. "Abbie, Mr. Spencer mustn't know we don't have any money."

"No, ma'am." Abbie started to add something but refrained, and Betty leaned her head back against the plush seat, eyes narrowed, mind scheming.

While the train carried them west, Abbie relaxed and enjoyed the changing countryside, leaving Betty to do the planning. Betty was not interested in the changing countryside. She only wished it would change faster. When Abbie roused her to look at something of particular interest her only reply was, "Yes, Abbie, it's nice," before she drifted back into anticipation of Daniel Spencer's face when she stepped from the train. Never once did she take into consideration that he might not be there. She was so caught up in her own dreams that she had no thought but that Daniel would be there with arms outstretched to welcome her.

Daniel was not there when they pulled in.

Haughtily, Betty descended. She had primped as well as the limited means on the train permitted, even changing into her best silk dress. She surveyed the other passengers on the last lap into Pioneer with satisfaction, ignoring their gasps at the daring garb she wore and rejoicing that not one of them could equal her magnificence. Now she stepped from the train — and sank into icy slush over her boot tops!

Her eyes darkened with rage. "Why hasn't this been cleared away?" Only Abbie paid any attention to her, quickly stepping forward to help her onto the platform. She might as well not have existed for all the notice the residents of Pioneer paid her.

"Sir!" Her imperious command to the tall, good-looking man near the depot door brought him around to face her.

"You were speaking to me?" The almost amused tone set flags flying in her already overheated face.

"Will you be so kind as to tell me how to find Daniel Spencer?"

Was the stupid lout so void of understanding that he could only stare? "Daniel Spencer?" He sounded like a parrot she had once seen.

"Yes. Daniel Spencer." She stamped an increasingly cold foot. "I am Elizabeth Courtland, his fiancee."

From somewhere behind her Abbie gasped, but Betty stood her ground. She *was* Daniel's fiancee; he just did not know it yet.

"I — see." The stranger surveyed her coldly, then turned to Abbie, his face warming a bit toward the shivering girl. "And this is —?"

"My maid, Abbie Tucker." Betty stamped her foot again. "Really, Mr. Whoever-you-are, it is inexcusable keeping us standing here in this cold. Where is Daniel Spencer?"

In answer, he swung wide the door to the depot, letting out a blast of warm air from the pot-bellied stove. "Step inside, please, Miss Courtland, Miss Tucker."

Betty marched in, closely followed by a frightened Abbie. The quick glance the depot agent shot her was not lost. Betty drew herself up even taller and turned to the stranger closing the door. "Will you be so kind as to inform me where Daniel Spencer might be found? Or would you take a message and let him know I am here?" She fumbled in her pocket and removed some coins, holding them out.

"Your money isn't needed, Miss Courtland." The stranger's manner matched her own for haughtiness as he stepped back, face sternly set against her. "I am Dr. Stewart, Daniel Spencer's best friend. Dan isn't here."

"Not here!" Betty's stare equaled the depot agent's.

"No." Dr. Stewart warmed his hands by the stove. "He is about fifteen miles up the river on a call to an Indian family."

Betty sank weakly to the hard wooden bench nearby. Up the river! "Then Abbie and I will just have to get back on the train and go where he is." She rose, some of her assurance returning.

"Ha, ha!" She whirled, furious with the braying of the station agent, getting even angrier at the impossible situation. Was that hick *daring* to laugh at her?

A glimmer of pure devilry shone in Dr. Stewart's eyes. "Sorry, Miss Courtland. The train doesn't run up the river."

"Then how did Daniel get there?"

"By canoe."

Betty shuddered. "Canoe! You mean one of those dreadful dugout boats?"

"Not dreadful if you're used to them."

"Where can we find one?"

Every trace of laughter vanished. "You can't go to the Indian village, Miss Courtland." Dr. Stewart's glance was even. "I'll take you and Miss Tucker to Dan's cabin. You can stay there until he gets back. He shouldn't be gone more than a day or two."

Betty was silenced. She watched the husky doctor shoulder her suitcase and Abbie's. "Maybe you can get Andy to haul the trunk over," he told the agent. His eyes swept the array of bags and boxes. "And the rest of the stuff." Contemptuously he opened the door for them.

If Betty lived to be a hundred she would never forget that first walk in Pioneer. She stumbled after the long and easy stride of Gordon Stewart, biting her lips to keep from calling out for him to come back and help her. Her feet were frozen. Her long skirts dragged in the slush no matter how she tried to hold them up. By the time they left the town behind and entered the clearing in the trees she was almost numb. She could hear Abbie panting behind her and was thankful when the doctor set down the suitcases and opened the rough door.

"Come in." A match flared, there was the pungent smell of kerosene, and Betty took her first look around Daniel Spencer's home.

All the pride Daniel had put into his little cabin, all the work the good ladies of Pioneer had done went unnoticed. Betty's sophisticated gaze dismissed the cheap curtains, scrubbed hard wood floor, and handmade spread on the big bed. Her gaze riveted on the open fireplace, ashes long dead in it. Nothing mattered now except to warm herself.

"Build a fire, Abbie," she directed, but the doctor forestalled her.

"I'll do it. Miss Tucker can get out dry garments for you both."

Betty opened her mouth to protest, but he was already kneeling by the fireplace, shaving kindling into long curls, setting them ablaze, then feeding chips and sticks, finally banking it all with a great log.

"Get into dry clothes," he ordered. "I'll be back soon."

They needed no urging. The blazing fire had taken the chill from the cabin. By the time the doctor knocked at the door again, both girls were bundled up in the warmest clothing they had brought and were toasting in front of the fire.

Betty was amazed when Dr. Stewart entered with a basket. From it he took rough bowls, heavy iron spoons, and crude knives. He lifted the cloth and set bread on the small table by the fire with a pat of butter. Finally he took out a heavy black kettle and set it in the fireplace, carefully hanging it on the big hook over the flames.

"Hot stew. Cooled off some while I brought it from the hotel."

Betty started to thank him, but he had already turned to Abbie. "Miss Tucker, do you think you can cook over an open fire?"

"I think so." Some of her freckles were covered by the blush from the dancing flames.

"Good. It's too cold for you to want to go to the hotel tonight." He casually inspected the cupboard. "Plenty of cereal for tomorrow. There's a bottle of milk just outside the door in the snow. It's fresh. You can get along all right for breakfast." He glanced at his watch. "I have office hours in a few moments. I'll see you tomorrow."

"Mr. — Dr. Stewart?" Betty hesitated.

"Yes?"

"Where are — where is — how do we —?"

Dawning comprehension filled his eyes with laughter. "Plenty of water to wash in. Pump's right outside the door. You'll see it's well-wrapped against the cold, so it won't freeze up." He motioned toward a bucket. "Hang the bucket on the crane in the fireplace to heat." From behind the curtain into the alcove he drew out a huge washtub. "Portable bathtub."

"What about the — *facilities*?"

"Outhouse is about a hundred yards down the trail." Ignoring Betty's shocked look he opened the door. "Good luck." They could hear his merry whistle as he walked away.

"Well!" Betty stared at Abbie. "Did you ever see the like? 'Outhouse is about a hundred yards down the trail,' " she mimmicked. "Ridiculous. Didn't these people ever hear of indoor plumbing?"

Abbie's eyes were round, but she skillfully grabbed a heavy towel and removed the now-bubbling stew pot from the stove. "Maybe that's why they call it Pioneer."

It was the final touch needed to set Betty off. She laughed until she thought she would have hysterics, rocking back and forth, clutching Abbie to keep her balance. When she finally subsided, she sank back in her chair. "At least we can eat."

"It smells good too." Abbie dished out the steaming stew. "I'm sorry Mr. Daniel isn't here, but at least we have a place to stay. What if we hadn't met Dr. Stewart? We don't have any money for the hotel."

Abbie's practical assessment of their situation dampened Betty's mirth. "I know. But as soon as Daniel comes back we'll be married, and everything will be all right." Betty began eating the rich stew. "Abbie, at least I have you! What would have happened if you hadn't come with me?'' She finished her supper and sat back while Abbie removed the dishes, then jumped up with flushed face.

"Starting right now I'm going to learn everything. You can show me how to do the dishes, cook, and pump water. I have to learn.''

"But, Miss Betty,'' Abbie exclaimed in horror, "you'll ruin your pretty hands.''

Betty's mind was set. "Pretty hands aren't the most important thing in the world, Abbie. Now teach me!''

By the time the dishes were washed and the girls had brought in enough water for both to bathe, they were exhausted. Neither had slept enough on the long train trip. Now Betty curled under the despised homemade coverlet gratefully. Every bone in her body ached. Was that what it meant to be a minister's wife? She could hear the soft, even breathing where Abbie lay asleep in the alcove. Gradually her own eyes closed.

"What was that?"

Through the night air came a horrible screeching sound, bringing Betty bolt upright in bed, Abbie flying to her mistress' side. *S-c-r-e-e-e-c-h!*

"Oh, Miss Betty!'' Abbie landed on the big bed and was hauled under the covers by Betty. "What is it?''

"I d-d-don't know,'' Betty said through chattering teeth. "D-did we bolt the door?''

"Yes.'' Abbie burrowed deeper. "There's a big wooden latch that drops down. Nothing can get in.'' She crept closer to Betty who put her arms around her while waves of fear threatened to swamp her.

For a long time they lay tense, maid and mistress, clutched in a mutually encouraging grip. At last some of the tension began to leave. Betty's voice was muffled by the covers, against Abbie's shoulder. "Abbie — maybe we shouldn't have come.'' Her heart raced in the long silence.

"There isn't anything we can do about it now. We're here.'' The practical Abbie curled into a ball and dropped off to sleep. But long after her grip loosened, Betty lay wide-eyed in the darkness. Yes, they were there, and there wasn't anything they could do about it now. If only Daniel Spencer would hurry home from up the river with the Indians.

Elizabeth Courtland woke to a new world. Strangely enough, she felt rested; it must be late. Her faithful watch said nine o'clock, but how dark it was — and how cold. Grateful for the warmth of the still-sleeping Abbie, Betty closed her eyes again. She would wait until Abbie woke up and built a fire before she got up.

The next moment she reversed her decision and carefully slipped from bed without disturbing Abbie. If she planned to be a minister's wife in this horrible place, even until she could persuade Daniel to leave, she had to show him she could make it. Her feet cringed from the icy floor, and her fingers were nearly numb before she could pull on heavy stockings and walk to the blackened fireplace. Perhaps there would be a few coals left to get her started.

There were no coals. The ashes lay gray and dead. Betty swallowed hard and caught up the big knife Dr. Stewart had left by the pile of kindling. Even her warm wrapper did not hold off the chill of the room. With unaccustomed fingers she hacked away at the soft cedar, managing to make a few shavings. Gently she put them in the fireplace and struck a match. They flared. Overjoyed by her success Betty watched them burn, then frantically realized she should have added chips. By the time she gathered the chips her small flame had gone out.

Her second try was more successful. Forcing her freezing hands to carefully add chips a few at a time, then a stick of wood, she felt a thrill. She had actually built a fire! She waited only to see that the stick was catching, then put on more wood as she had seen the doctor do. When it blazed up, she crept back across the cabin and into bed, cuddling against Abbie, her thoughts busy.

Daniel would be home today, or at the latest, tomorrow. The icy apprehension of the night before melted in that thought and in the gradually warming room. He would come, she would tell him about her father, and they would be married. She closed her eyes. Married to Daniel! A flush touched her pale cheeks. With a man like that, even the primitive conditions could be endured until she could change them.

Abbie stirred, opened sleep-filled eyes. "Why, Miss Betty!"

Betty laughed, seeing the puzzled look as Abbie glanced around, then realized where she was. "No more Miss Betty, Abbie, just Betty Courtland, then Mrs. Daniel Spencer."

"Why," Abbie's wondering gaze fell on the crackling fire, "there's a fire. Did Dr. Stewart come?"

"No, Abbie. I built it myself."

Abbie sat bolt upright in bed. "You!"

Betty flushed under the innocent criticism, and her chin lifted. "Yes, I. From now on I learn to do everything there is to do."

Abbie flopped weakly back on her pillow. "But, Miss Betty, I mean, Betty, I meant to —"

"I know you did, Abbie." Betty sobered. "But you must let me learn; you must teach me. I have to show Daniel Spencer I can fit into his world before I can take him back to ours."

Abbie was speechless, but Betty hopped from bed. "Let's get up. I'm starving. Didn't he say something about cereal in the cupboard? Besides," she made a face, "I'm going to have to take that hundred-yard walk."

Abbie could not have moved if her life had depended on it. She watched as Betty determinedly slid into layers of petticoats, struggled into her dress, and backed up to the bed to be buttoned, then slipped through the door. She was not gone long.

"Of all the inconvenient —!" Her hands were red from the cold. "Honestly, Abbie, that outhouse is the coldest place I've ever been." She sighed. "Well, there isn't any other choice, but just wait until you've been out there!"

Abbie finally came alive and hopped out of bed. It only took moments for her to slip into her warm undergarments and the dark gray dress she usually wore to work. She glanced anxiously at Betty's silk. "Miss — Betty, don't you want to wear something else? I don't know how things get washed out here, but if you get that dress dirty we might have a terrible time getting it cleaned."

Betty looked down at the fancy dress and back at Abbie. "I suppose you're right. I just wanted to look nice when Daniel came, but —" Her eyes roamed the cabin and lit on a large towel. "I can put that around me. Besides, until the other baggage comes, I don't have any other choice."

Somehow between them they managed a creditable breakfast. Abbie found the cereal and cooked it in the hanging black kettle. Betty discovered a long handled fork Abbie told her was for toasting bread, and after dropping the first two pieces in the ashes and flames, she managed to turn out two more that were only burned slightly.

"It isn't quite like breakfast at home, is it?"

"No." Abbie turned her head to hide her pity, thinking of Betty propped up at home against lacy pillows with a breakfast of hot rolls, freshly squeezed orange juice, a puffy omelet, and perhaps sausage on a tray before her.

"But that's all right." Betty was determined not to think back. "I knew it wouldn't all be easy."

Before they quite finished breakfast a knock was heard. Dr. Stewart stepped inside, a slight smile thawing the frozen look Betty associated with him. "Well! I see you're all set up. Miss Tucker, you evidently know how to adapt to circumstances. That's a good looking fire, and I see you made breakfast."

Betty was suddenly, hotly angry. "I'll have you know *I* made that fire, Dr. Stewart, *and* toasted the bread!"

The smile she hated flashed. "Amazing. Congratulations, Miss Courtland. I wouldn't have suspected it."

Leaving her tongue-tied with rage, he turned to Abbie. "Miss Tucker, I wonder if you would like a job?"

"A — a job?" Abbie faltered, glancing across at Betty.

"Yes. You look like a sensible girl, and I need someone to help me in the hospital. Ever done any nursing?"

"Just taking care of Miss — of Betty when she was sick."

"You're strong and can learn. I'll teach you what you need to know. It will involve staying with patients when they are in the hospital and needing care I don't have time to give. What do you say?"

Abbie glanced back at Betty helplessly, an appeal in her eyes. Betty thought rapidly, seeing recognition in Abbie's eyes of their dwindling funds. There might not be too many chances for work here. Everyone probably took care of their own work.

"If you want to, Abbie, go ahead." To stress her complete indifference she added, "I can take care of everything here while you're gone, especially until Daniel gets back."

Dr. Stewart's bland innocence did not deceive her. Betty ground her teeth as he said, "Oh, of course. Anyone who can toast and build a fire should have no trouble with other household chores."

Abbie's voice was small. "If you think I can do it, Dr. Stewart, I'll try."

"Good girl!" His look was warm and approving. "If you don't mind, I could use you right now." He bowed elaborately to Betty. "That is, if Miss Courtland doesn't mind."

"Not at all." She managed to rise with some of her natural haughtiness, even to smile. "It is the neighborly thing to do. Isn't that the word they use out here, Mr. — sorry — *Dr.* Stewart?"

For just an instant she was rewarded by admiration in his eyes, but he merely turned to Abbie. "We'll go then. Good morning, Miss Courtland." With another bow he opened the door for a half-frightened Abbie to scuttle through and then added. "Have a pleasant day."

Betty stared at the door closing behind him, torn by an impulse to call Abbie back. How could she spend the entire day in this isolated cabin? Yet after she was married to Daniel wouldn't she be spending many such days, especially if Abbie continued her work with Dr. Stewart? Soberly she collected the dishes they had used for breakfast and stacked them. Abbie had thoughtfully filled the big bucket with fresh water and hung it on the crane. She tested it for hotness in the small tin dishpan she found, valiantly struggled with the pump until she had a pan of cold water to temper it, and washed the dishes, drying them carefully and putting them away.

The fire was dying, and she dared not let the room chill. Hastily she rebuilt it, this time carrying a huge log to roll in behind the flames. Sparks flew, and she beat them out.

"Oh, no!" There were holes in the white towel she still wore for an apron. What if she had not put it on? Her best dress would have been ruined. Her hands were sooty and her hair coming undone by the time she got the fire well banked.

"Elizabeth Courtland, Daniel Spencer was right. You really aren't good for much," she told herself as she passed a small square of looking glass. Her image grimaced. "Well, I can learn. I'll show that man — *and* Dr. Stewart, if it's the last thing I do!"

A quick partial bath restored some of her spirit. Emma had said she could learn, if she wanted to learn badly enough. She surveyed the cabin. What should she do next?

"The bed. It needs to be made." Some of the quilts were on the floor from where she and Abbie had huddled against the night noises. "Get up there, you," she threw the quilts in a heap, then tried to smooth them, ending up by taking the whole thing apart. Finally, red-faced and gasping, she managed to get everything in fairly neat order. Even the top coverlet quilt was smooth. Again she felt that little thrill that had come when she built the fire. She had never given any thought to satisfaction that comes from work well done.

"I guess there are just a lot of things I've never thought about!" She dropped to a rude chair by the fire and stared into it. "Everything's just always been done. I never noticed how much there was to do." Now her eyes spied crumbs under the table and litter on the hearth. A worn broom stood in the corner, and Betty attacked the floor with vigor. Moments later she was coughing at the dust she had stirred up. Gradually she slowed her strokes until they caught up the offending dirt but did not raise dust. She swept it directly into the fireplace.

"Well, Abbie should be home soon. It must be late," she peered outside into the gloom. A few snowflakes had begun lazily drifting down. She glanced at her watch. Twelve o'clock. Had it stopped? It must be later than noon! She shook it. No, it was ticking steadily. Disheartened she dropped back into her chair. What did people *do* in this country when all the work was done?

"I do believe I'm hungry again." She foraged the cupboards, but everything was packaged or needed to be cooked except one slice of leftover bread and a little milk in the jar. She toasted the bread and drank the milk. It would have to do. But what about dinner? Dr. Stewart would bring Abbie home and wonder why she had not started any dinner preparations.

For a moment she toyed with the idea of going to the hotel for a hot meal but decided against it. There was so little money left it might not cover their meal, and if Daniel were delayed — she firmly shoved the thought aside. She had boasted that she could handle things in the cabin; now she had to make good.

In the cupboard she found a package of rice. Good! She loved it. If she cooked rice, they could have something hot. There were glass jars of fruit. Had someone given them to Daniel? She peered at the neat rows, wondering why there was so little. Did Daniel eat at the hotel instead of cooking? He must or there would be more provisions. Well, once she learned to cook that could stop.

There were no instructions with the rice, but she knew it must take water to cook, so she confidently put a small amount in the hanging black kettle over the fire and added some rice. It did not look like very much. Maybe she should add more. They could reheat it for the next day. She put in the rest of the package and stirred it. Funny, it did not look like enough water now. She added a dipperful, reluctant to have to struggle with the pump out in the cold for more.

"It still doesn't look like much. Maybe I'd better fill up the kettle." By the time she got back in with skirts wet again and dumped in water to the top of the kettle she was out of sorts. "Why would anyone in his right mind choose to live in this place? Daniel did not have to come. He chose to come." She grimly rotated in front of the fire, drying her bedraggled skirts.

"Miss Courtland," a hail from outside brought her to the door. Could Daniel be home? It was only the station agent with a strange kind of sled affair. Face beaming, he pulled the sled to the tiny porch of the cabin. "Brought your duds."

Betty rather resented his familiarity but forced a smile. "Thank you. Bring them in here," then. "Please." She must remember she was not at home where one ordered servants about.

The agent was panting and puffing by the time he took in all the bags, boxes, and the huge trunk. Betty had directed him to put them all in the little alcove. The spare room seemed to be a study of sorts. For now, they could stay in Abbie's cubicle.

"Right cozy little place here, ain't it?" the beaming man eyed the cabin, making Betty glad she had cleaned it. "Nothing like what it was before the preacher came. All the womenfolk jumped in and made curtains and gave him the bedding and stuff."

Betty looked around with new eyes. Then the furnishings had been gifts. They took on a little more importance. "That was kind."

"I hear tell you're going to be his woman."

For one awful moment Betty thought she would have hysterics. That red-faced man calling her Daniel's "woman" seemed the height of impertinence. Elizabeth Courtland — to be Daniel Spencer's "woman!"

Her silence did not daunt the friendly agent. "Pioneer's a whole lot better place since he came, him and the doc. Soon's the town gits wind you're here, they'll be coming to call." He held out his hand, and she reluctantly shook it.

"Welcome to Pioneer, Mrs. Minister."

Betty's hand still felt the warmth of the hearty shake as he closed the door behind him. Some of the warmth stole into her troubled heart. Mrs. Minister! The ignorant man could have no way of knowing what the words meant to her. They had succeeded more in reconciling her to her surroundings than anything else could have done.

Betty forced herself to survey the cabin, seeing it again through newly awakened eyes. It was not more than crude logs, yet they were chinked against the cold. The panes in the little window were shining clean. Those cheap curtains, evidently made from friendship for "the preacher," were crisp and clean. She moved to the bed, fingering the quilt, noticing for the first time the tiny, tiny stitches. Someone had made that quilt, setting those stitches one at a time — and giving it to Daniel, in love.

I don't belong here. The shattering truth rocked Betty until she felt physically ill.

"I don't belong here!" she cried out to the open rafters, the fireplace with its now bubbling burden, the cupboard with curtain in front of it. "I can never fit in. I don't know anything!"

Depression grayer than the outdoor gloom swept through her and in desperation she threw herself on the newly made bed, fighting tears until from sheer nervous exhaustion she slept.

Daniel Spencer was tired. The trip to the Indian village had been one of sadness. The chief's son was sick. Gordon Stewart had confided, "There's no cure. Too far gone before I came — consumption."

So Daniel had made the long trip to give what comfort he could. The impassive brown faces did not hide the chief's sorrow or that of his family. The dark eyes steadily watched Daniel as he talked with the child, tried to make him understand that the "happy hunting ground" was even more beautiful than the world he would shortly leave. In the time Daniel had been in Pioneer he had learned to blend the language of his own faith with the vocabulary of the Indians rather than impose strange new terms. Now he spoke to the child about Jesus, the "Great Spirit's Son," who had come to earth to die that children such as Bright Arrow might go to be with Him.

The canoe trip back down the river was silent until they beached just outside of Pioneer.

"Daniel Spencer, when Bright Arrow dies, you will say the words?"

Daniel gripped the chief's hand. "When Bright Arrow dies, you bring him here. I will say the words."

He stood for a long while watching the chief turn the canoe and paddle back up against the current, going with him in spirit, entering the rude abode, waiting for the end.

If only they had come sooner! If he and Gordon Stewart had been in Pioneer even months earlier, Bright Arrow could have been saved.

Dog tired, discouraged, he started for his cabin. At the edge of the trail toward the little hospital he hesitated. Should he go see Gordon for a time? No, it was office hours. He would go home, rest from the sleepless night of the trip, and see his friend later.

The snowflakes that had lazily descended earlier had grown in intensity, turning hard, stinging his eyes. He walked rapidly, glad to be back. There was nothing worse than feeling totally helpless to do anything. At low ebb, now all he wanted was to get home, and the little log cabin had become a real home.

He increased his stride, visualizing the warm fire he would build and the sleep he would get before going to the hotel for dinner. No, maybe he would eat whatever was on hand instead of going out again.

Just a few more yards now. His cabin loomed up. The sense of smell heightened by his months in pure air stopped him in his tracks. Something was cooking. His mouth stretched in a grin. Gordon must have suspected he would be back tonight and come over to fix dinner. Funny, there was no light in the cabin.

He dropped his pack on the tiny porch floor with a thud and pushed open the door, sniffing again. Something was burning and badly. From the light of the open fire he could see his kettle with lid raised off by something white boiling over and over into the coals below. He snatched an old towel and seized the steaming mess. Rice? Why would Gordon —?

From behind him, in the shadowy corner of the room where his bed was came a gasp. Dropping the sticky kettle to the hearth Daniel whirled toward the sound.

"Who are you and what are you doing in my cabin?"

He struck a match — and gazed directly into the frightened face of Elizabeth Courtland.

10

"Daniel!" It came out as little more than a whisper. Relief flooded away her fear. Daniel had come home; everything would be all right. She could see his fingers tremble as he lit the kerosene lamp, then held it high, still disbelieving what he saw. "Madcap Betty? What is this, another of your stunts?"

She was cut to the quick. For him she had given up everything, only to have him speak in that harsh voice. Where was the loving welcome she had dreamed of ever since leaving Grand Rapids? Disappointment choked off any self-defense she might have made. Even in the pale yellow lamp-light she could see how Daniel had changed. He was no well-dressed city visitor. Before her stood a man whose shadow loomed behind him on the rough walls, perfectly at home in those awful surroundings. Gone were city clothes, replaced by a dark blue shirt open at the neck and dark blue pants. Yet even as she tried to adjust to his strangeness, something within her cried out to be in his arms.

Daniel's words fell like hard little stones, bruising her already shattered composure. "I've seen a lot of bold stunts but never anything to match this. Just what do you think you're doing?" He marched to the alcove, contemptuously looked at the trunk, bags, and boxes. "What made you think you could come out here and move into my cabin while I was gone?"

Betty bit her lip, stripped of pretense. "I — I — Prescott told me —"

"Prescott told you what?" His voice was granite overlaid with lead. There was not a trace of weakening.

Betty licked her lips, finding words hard to get out. "He said you cared —"

She was not prepared for his harsh laugh. "With what right did he tell you such a thing? I left no message for you but good-bye."

It was too much for Betty. She hurled herself against the wall between them. "How can you, a professed man of God, speak to me like this?"

"It is because I am a man of God that I must."

Hope died. He would never believe that it was more than one of her stunts. For one moment Betty passionately regretted the name she had built for herself. Madcap Betty! Well, if he thought it of her she might as well live up to it.

"You don't think you can stay here, do you?"

It was her turn to laugh, although her lips had gone white. "I could if I were your wife." She saw the effects of her taunt, the involuntary step he took toward her before thrusting his hands into his pockets. She laughed again, noting the brittleness of the sound in the otherwise quiet room. "I built a fire this morning. I toasted bread, swept your floor, and made your bed. I put rice on for dinner —" Her eyes fell to the ghastly mess on the hearth. She was silenced. A drift of white disaster mutely bore evidence of her failure.

Daniel's face was no longer pale. Dark color and a beating pulse in his throat shone in the dim light. With one stride he caught her by the shoulders and swung her off the bed and to her feet. "And you think that is what it means to be a wife? Don't push me, Elizabeth Courtland! Why did you really come out here?"

For a moment Betty thought she would sink through the floor. A great leap of hope spurted. "Because of what Prescott said." She faced him steadily, conscious of the gripping fingers that would leave bruises as their mark. "And because — I —" she threw her head back defiantly, "I care."

"I don't believe you."

She wrenched free, rage tumbling out almost faster than she could speak. "I don't care if you believe me or not. I couldn't stay in Grand Rapids. My father has never stopped believing the worst of me. I brought Abbie, and we came here thinking you would take care of us." Was there an imperceptible lessening of the strain in his face? Betty dropped her eyelashes and played her last card, swaying toward him. "I found out life wasn't worth anything without you, Daniel." Every wile of her coquettish youth shone in her confession.

"Even if it was true, which I doubt, it wouldn't matter."

Betty stared. How could he stand there, arms folded? Why had he not taken her into his arms?

"You don't think I'm sincere, or don't you think I'm good enough for your royal palace?" She gestured around the sparsely furnished cabin.

"No, Betty Courtland, you aren't. My God is head of this household. He always will be. I don't think you'd find it comfortable living here with me — or with Him."

The infinite sadness touched her more than all his anger had done. Betty reeled backward and would have fallen if the bed had not caught her. "I — see."

A poignant light came into Daniel's face. "Betty, can you honestly say you could marry me and live here under those conditions?"

Betty's mind raced, her heart rejoicing. He cared! He must care to look like that! And yet — live with the shadow of his God over them? She shuddered.

Daniel's lips tightened; the light in his eyes went out. His voice was colorless as he turned away. "I'll arrange for your baggage to be moved to the hotel, Miss Courtland. You mentioned Abbie was with you?"

"Yes." A stranger had taken over her voice. It could not be she answering in that calm way. "Dr. Stewart gave her a job." Mustering the shreds of her dignity Betty stood. "Thank you for sending my baggage." She stumbled blindly toward the door. She was arrested halfway.

"Betty." Was there pleading in his voice? Another moment and she would fling herself into his arms, beg him to marry her regardless of that God of his. One more step to freedom — she took it, stepped outside into the snow, and ran. The mark of his tracks showed the way. Pounding steps behind her increased her speed. Soon he was up with her, turning her around, laying her cloak across her shoulders. In the last dimness with snow falling around them his eyes looked like black coals in a white blanket. "You can run away from me, Betty, but you can never outrun God."

She clutched the cloak and ran again, only pausing when she came to the rude board hotel. It would not do to appear breathless before those inside. What would they think if they knew their precious minister had practically thrown her out? Her lips curled. Why think of him? She would stay overnight at the hotel and go back to Grand Rapids in the morning.

No! A little moan escaped her lips. She could not go back to Grand Rapids. There was barely enough money to pay for her dinner. She would have to ask Daniel for money.

"Never!" She set her white teeth into her lower lip until she could taste the sickish taste of blood. "I'll starve first!" Yet as she paced the cold porch of the unfriendly hotel hopelessness overcame her. What could she do except ask him? She could write Prescott for money, but it would take time to get it. Her father was out as a possibility. Would Gordon Stewart lend her train fare? She could not ask. He was Daniel's friend and would report straight to Daniel.

She had to get the money, at least enough to get by until she could write Prescott. Through the windows she could see tables of men seated before steaming platters of food. Memory of her sketchy meals made her mouth water as the tantalizing dinner odors crept through the cracks. Her eyes narrowed. There had to be a way.

"I'll do it!" Suiting action to thought she entered the hotel door, taking a deep breath.

Instant silence fell as every eye turned toward her, the same silence that used to greet her entrance back home at a social event. It did wonders for her bruised ego. She lifted her chin, put on her most charming smile, and crossed the room to the man in the white apron who appeared to be the proprietor.

"Something I can do for you, miss?" He took another keen look at her. "Say, ain't you the preacher's gal?"

She fought down an impulse to walk out and only smiled again. "I am Elizabeth Courtland. I would like a room, please, and dinner."

"Of course." He beamed at her. "Will Mr. Spencer be joining you?"

"Not tonight." She dropped her eyes demurely. "He just got in from up the river and all."

"That's fine." The proprietor elaborately led her to a small table a little way from the others, giving her a feeling of privacy. "We call it supper out here instead of dinner, miss. I'll send one of the gals."

"Thank you, Mr. —"

"Just Buck. We ain't much for misterin' out here." He was warming under her smiles just the way she had hoped.

Betty decided it was the strategic moment to strike. "Buck, I'm wondering if you would give me a job waiting tables."

"You?" If the horrified look on his face were an indication, she was in for a battle.

Betty lowered her voice and leaned forward mysteriously. "I hope you can keep a confidence."

He perked up immediately. "I shore can."

"You see," Betty began, "I've always wanted to write a book about a place like Pioneer."

"A book? You mean about folks like us?"

"Yes." Her eyes glowed. "Back East people really don't know anything about the kind of men who open up the wilderness and make it safe for women and children. They think it's all rough and wild." Good heavens, could he possibly swallow that?

Betty stifled a nervous giggle and lowered her voice even more. "It's a surprise, even for Mr. Spencer. My friend Abbie is working for Dr. Stewart now." She had had to substitute 'friend' for 'maid.' "I thought if I could wait tables it would give me the chance to get to know a lot of Pioneer residents." She flashed her famous smile again. "But I have to confess, Buck, I don't know much about waiting tables."

"Why, that's all right, Miss Courtland," he gave her a conspiratorial wink and a fatherly pat on the arm. "You can learn."

Betty had one more trick. It *had* to work! She risked everything. "Of course, since I'm new and all, I wouldn't expect to be paid. It's to give me experience and get me acquainted."

He fell for it even better than she hoped. "That wouldn't be right at all!" His genial face took on an unaccustomed scowl. "If you work, you'll be paid the same as the other girls. Board and room and —" The paltry sum he mentioned almost brought a gasp of indignation. Just in time Betty remembered her part and smiled brilliantly.

"I insist, Miss Courtland." He swept over her with a glance, and the worried look returned. "Just one thing —"

"What's that?" *If hearts can stop, mine will,* Betty thought. *Everything has gone so well. What can hold it up now? I have to have the job!*

"The other gals are all called by their first names." Buck looked doubtful. "And your clothes — ain't you got anything not quite so fancy?"

Betty's heart bounded. "I'll expect to be called Elizabeth, of course." She hid an inward shudder at the thought of those crude loggers calling her that. At least she would not have the humiliation of them calling her Betty. "And when my trunk is unpacked I have other clothes. I don't have any aprons, though."

"We have aprons." The beam came back to his face. "Does Mr. Spencer know what yore aimin' to do?"

"Sh!" Betty twinkled her eyes and placed her fingers over her lips. "I'll take care of him."

"Ha, ha!" Buck's laugh drew every eye in the room. "Well, I'll send supper, and you can start tomorrow. Four-thirty."

"You mean I don't work until afternoon?"

"I can see you have a sense of humor, Miss — Elizabeth. We start servin' breakfast at four-thirty so the loggers can get out in the woods."

Once more Betty stifled a gasp and shudder. "It's going to be quite an experience." But when he had gone it was all she could do to get down the tasty supper. In order to be ready for work at four-thirty in the morning, what ungodly time would she have to rise?

Somehow she managed to finish a meal and stumble up the stairs behind Buck.

"You said you had a friend, Abbie? You want two rooms?"

"Of course —" But Betty hesitated. Two rooms would cost twice as much. She was getting hers free, but if Abbie took one it would have to be paid for. The quicker they got the money for passage together the faster they could get out of this terrible place. She went on smoothly, as if she had not thought rapidly. "— No, we can share."

"Right in here." He held the lamp high. The room was small, barely big enough for two iron beds, a chest of drawers, and hooks on the wall covered by a curtain serving as a closet door. At least it was clean.

"It's very — clean." Betty could not do better than that.

"You bet. Our maids keep this place clean. I'll get you a pitcher and bowl." He set down the lamp. "Want I should bring your friend Abbie up when she comes?"

"How will you know her?"

His tobacco-stained lips split in a grin. "When you live in Pioneer, you know outsiders. 'Sides, Doc'll probably bring her over." He looked around the room again. "If you need anything else, just holler."

The door closed behind him, leaving Betty alone in the strange room that would now be home. Compared to the cozy cabin she had left earlier, it was nothing. So bare. Yet what did it matter? She and Abbie would be gone soon. How many weeks would it take with their two salaries combined to pay fare home?

Homesickness overwhelmed her. Even her father's sternness melted a little in the face of the terrible longing for home. If only she could be free, waiting for Prescott to come to take her to a dance or a luncheon. Why hadn't she been satisfied with what she had instead of chasing after a man who did not want her? Outsiders, Buck had said. He was right. She and Abbie *were* outsiders. She fought a rising hysteria. Should she "holler" the way he told her to if she wanted anything? What she wanted was to be safe back in Grand Rapids where she could forget anyone named Daniel Spencer existed.

"Miss — Betty!" Abbie's eyes were round with shock as she interrupted Betty's misery.

Betty noticed Buck in the background and hurriedly drew Abbie in, talking to cover what she might blurt out. "This is our new room, Abbie. You can have the bed by the window. I've already unpacked what we'll need for tonight." She forced a smile to the waiting proprietor. "Thanks, Buck. See you in the morning."

"G'night." He was gone, mercifully leaving Betty and Abbie alone.

"But what are you doing here?" Abbie demanded, eyes still popping. "Dr. Stewart took me back to Mr. Spencer's cabin, and he was there, but you weren't!" She looked straight at Betty. "You didn't quarrel, did you!"

"Quarrel!" Betty almost shrieked the word. "It was more like a fight to end all fights."

"Then you aren't getting married?"

"Never! At least not to him."

"Then what're we going to do?" Abbie dropped weakly to her neatly made bed.

"I've got a job waiting tables here. You can keep on with Dr. Stewart. When we get enough money we're going home."

"But, Miss — Betty! Don't you love Mr. Spencer?"

The storm broke. "Yes, I love him! I even thinks he loves me. But we'll never be married. He told me God lived in his house, and I wouldn't be happy there." Betty's face flamed through the tears. "He's right. I don't even know this God he talks about all the time. Even if I did, I'd never be second to some unseen something. I'm going to work and go back to Grand Rapids, and someday Daniel Spencer will come crawling, begging me to marry him. When he does I'll laugh in his face and tell him to go find that God he thinks so much of."

Abbie gasped, her face reflecting her horror. "That's blasphemy!"

"Is it?" Betty's eyes were great purple orbs. "He told me I couldn't outrun his God. I'll show him. Just wait and see."

Abbie held her tongue, unable to speak in the face of such fury. Finally she suggested, "We'd better go to bed. I have to be up early tomorrow. Dr. Stewart has a man coming in before work and wants me to see how he does dressings."

In spite of her anger and woe Betty caught something in Abbie's voice. "You like what you did today, didn't you, Abbie?"

"Yes." The little maid's eyes glowed. "Dr. Stewart says I have natural ability. Miss — Betty, when we get back to Grand Rapids, if you don't need me, that is, do you think I could learn more about being a nurse? Then when you do get married and have babies I could take care of them when they were sick."

Betty stared. She had never seen Abbie so excited. Her answer came slowly. "Why, I don't see why not." She sighed. "But first we have to get there. At first I thought I'd write Prescott for train fare. Now I think I'll just wait until we can earn it. Then when we leave I can throw in Daniel Spencer's face the fact that we had to go to work in his precious town even to get money to leave!"

"How long do you think it will take?"

Their eyes met. "I'm afraid most of the winter, Abbie. Can you stand it?"

Abbie's eyes were sober. "It won't be me that has trouble standing it, Miss Betty. I'm afraid it's going to be you."

Abbie's words proved true. By the end of the first day on her job in Pioneer, Betty Courtland thought she would die. Unaccustomed to any work at all, standing on her feet, carrying heavy platters of food in white hands that had never held anything heavier than Beauty's reins was sheer agony. By the time breakfast was over she was too tired to eat. Buck sent her upstairs for an hour's rest warning, "We get a big dinner crowd."

Dinner? Betty remembered. To her it was lunch. She threw her weary body on the hard bed thankfully and did not rouse until Buck tapped on her door. He sounded apologetic. "Sorry to wake you, Miss Elizabeth, but it's time to set up for the crowd."

Betty hurriedly splashed water from the basin on her face and pasted on the stiff smile she had worn that morning. She managed to get through the meal and help clean up, then stumbled toward her room that had become a haven. It was Abbie's entrance that woke her.

Abbie was full of chatter, perched on her own narrow bed while Betty freshened up. "I'm learning so much! Dr. Stewart says he couldn't ask for a better helper." Her eyes glowed, then the lamps in them went out. "Oh, he and Mr. Spencer will be in for din — supper tonight."

Betty unconsciously squared her shoulders. The moment she had feared was upon her. Neither Daniel nor Dr. Stewart had appeared at breakfast or the noon meal, although she had started every time the heavy door opened.

"I wonder what he's going to say when he sees you here?" Abbie looked worried.

Betty moistened her lips with the tip of her tongue. "I don't know. It really isn't any of his business, anyway." She finished smoothing her hair and tossed her head with some of the old haughtiness. "The sooner I get it over with, the better."

Abbie followed her down the stairs, scooting into a far corner and watching her former mistress with concerned eyes.

"Hello, Miss Tucker. Ready for a good, hot meal?"

Dr. Stewart's bright greeting spun Abbie back to attention. She smiled back at him. "Oh, yes, Dr. Stewart!"

"Where's your friend? Not down yet?"

Abbie gasped as Dr. Stewart and Daniel Spencer dropped to chairs at her table. "Why, she's —" The words choked in her throat as Betty crossed the crowded room to their table.

The sound of her voice brought both men to their feet. "May I help you, gentlemen? You wish the full din — supper menu, of course?"

"*Betty!*" Daniel Spencer's face had gone brick red, then deathly white.

"I am known as Elizabeth during my working hours, Mr. Spencer." She deliberately turned her back on him and smiled at Dr. Stewart. "Will you have coffee now or with your supper?"

"Now, please."

"And you?" She turned back to Daniel, in perfect control of herself, at least outwardly. Inwardly she quivered like the small dish of strawberry jelly she had placed on the table earlier.

Daniel did not answer; he merely stared until Dr. Stewart sat down, pulling Daniel with him. "Bring coffee for all three of us, Elizabeth. That is, if Miss Tucker doesn't mind our having supper with her?"

Abbie was shocked into speech. "No, I don't mind, not at all."

"Very well." Betty sensed a wave of bitterness threatening to engulf her. How things had changed! Out here she was "Elizabeth," her former serving maid was "Miss Tucker." She shrugged impatiently, careful not to let her face show any of her hatred of the situation. Even her hands were steady as she poured the coffee.

"Is this another one of your jokes? Or are you going home tomorrow?" Daniel finally found his voice and demanded in a low tone.

"Home? Oh, you mean to Grand Rapids?" Suddenly her laugh was clear to every corner of the listening room with staring men. "Buck has promised to be patient. I'm going to learn to cook and clean and whatever needs doing. Abbie and I will be staying here in the hotel all winter, at least." There was nothing in her words to give the wide-open ears of the hearers anything to talk about.

"Impossible!"

Again, Dr. Stewart's warning hand kept back further comment. Daniel lapsed into silence as Betty Courtland moved gracefully around the crowded room carrying food, laughing at the sly sallies of some of the loggers. Andy, in particular, seemed charmed by the Eastern girl. Daniel overheard him say, "Ma'am, you don't know how much good the doc 'n' the preacher have done. Glad yore here."

Betty just smiled, conscious of Daniel's eyes following her. She had always been a good actress, taking parts in home plays for friends and the like. Now she used every bit of her amateur skill and grew almost radiant. "Why, thanks. Andy, isn't it?" Her magnificent eyes deepened. "Daniel and I are both thankful you feel that way."

Abbie gaped, and Dr. Stewart stifled a chuckle; but Daniel Spencer rose and stalked through the door, letting it bang behind him. Andy's grin got wider. "Say, he shore was in a hurry. Don't s'pose he's a mite bit jealous, do you?"

Betty stared at Andy, the seed of an idea sprouting. "Why, no." Twin dimples flashed as she confided, "Besides, we aren't married — yet." For one moment the response in the man's eyes frightened her, and she drew back; but he laughed, and she moved on to serve the next man.

"Miss Tucker." Dr. Stewart's stern voice drew Abbie's eyes like a magnet. His face was serious. "Better tell your friend she can't use her Eastern charm out here. It's dangerous to flirt with these Pioneer men. You've probably noticed that we're short of women, especially young, attractive women. These men are simple. If a woman asks to be insulted by her actions, she also lowers herself in their esteem. They don't understand all the modern goings on that Betty Courtland was used to back East."

"Well!" Betty herself stood at their table, coffee pot poised.

Dr. Stewart rose and reached for his hat. "I meant what I said, Miss Courtland." Even in her rage she rejoiced that he had not called her by her first name. "You're lighting a fuse to dynamite if you flirt with these loggers."

Venom sprayed through her until her voice was hoarse, almost undiscernible. "I will act in any way I see fit, Dr. Stewart."

"Not in Pioneer you won't. You're supposed to be the minister's fiancee. As such, you've been given a pedestal. See that you don't fall off." He tipped his hat, more to Abbie than to Betty. "Good night. I'll see you in the morning, Miss Tucker."

"Elizabeth." Buck's call sent Betty scuttling for the kitchen. "Take this extra platter of chicken to the big table, will you?"

It was only the beginning. By the time Saturday night came Betty was too tired to care if she lived or died. How many weeks of it could she stand before she just curled up and expired? The work was hard. The men were courteous but also curious. Every meal at least one asked, "When are you and the preacher gittin' hitched?" She always managed some light answer but inwardly boiled. What right did these oafs have to ask her such personal questions?

Abbie fared better. She was totally absorbed in her new work. She came home nightly with tales of Dr. Stewart's kindness. "He's so gentle, Betty!" The "Miss" had long since been dropped in sharing the same plight and room. "He delivered a baby today, and I've never seen such a look in a man's eyes for a squallin', little red baby."

Betty shuddered. The last thing she needed was to think of squalling babies. She had troubles enough of her own. "Too bad it didn't die. Who'd want to grow up in such a place?"

"Betty!"

"You needn't glare at me, Abbie. I didn't really mean it." She crossed to their bit of a window and looked out. "Did you ever see such desolation?"

"Dr. Stewart says when spring comes it will be beautiful."

"I don't think spring will ever come."

"Tomorrow's Sunday. Are you going to the church service?" Abbie held her breath. Betty was so unpredictable lately that she never knew what to expect.

"I suppose so. Buck said they have meals at different times 'so's those who want to, kin go to the meetin.' I almost laughed in his face."

"I really kind of like it here. When you get to know some of the wives and children, it's not so bad —" But Abbie saw Betty was not listening.

The next morning Betty did not admit it, even to herself, but it was good to lay aside the plain garments that she had chosen for work and put on something prettier. She chose a blue dress that matched her eyes at their bluest, with tiny bands of red braid down the front and a row of red buttons to match. She even dug into the bottom of the mostly unpacked trunk for a matching hat with red plumes.

"Oh, Miss." Abbie's shock brought back her former servitude. "Miss Betty, you aren't goin' to wear that to church?"

"And why not?"

Abbie's face turned crimson with embarrassment, but she bravely held up her chin. "I heard one of the women talking about red hats or anything red. Out here it's considered — bad." She brought the last word out reluctantly.

"Bad!" Betty's lip curled. "Of all the backwoods —"

"It's what they think. And you're the minister's fiancee — or at least everyone thinks so."

Without a word Betty ripped the red plumes from the hat, leaving only the blue with a tiny line of red trim. She had already confided to Abbie what she meant to do. "I'll live according to all their traditions, show them what a perfect minister's wife I'll be. Then when I'm gone, he can explain just why I left — if he dares!"

If she meant to shake Daniel by her presence, she failed utterly. He preached as she had heard him preach before, sincerely, from the depths of his heart. Betty pressed her handkerchief to trembling lips to deny the stirrings of her own heart. What if she did believe in his God? What if everything he said was true? Marriage with Daniel Spencer could be a glimpse of the heaven he spoke of, right here on earth.

"Miss Tucker, may I have the honor of walking you to your hotel?" Dr. Stewart stepped forward when church was over.

Abbie shot a frightened glance at Betty, then nodded and took his arm. Betty was left standing alone.

"Waitin' for the minister, huh, Elizabeth?"

She hated the familiarity and almost turned an icy stare at the innocent Andy, who had surprisingly been in church in the little one-room school. Framing for the church was up, but the weather had kept it from being finished.

"Why —" She made up her mind and swept Andy a glorious smile. "Why, yes."

"Here she is, Preacher." Andy turned to Daniel as he stepped out of the building.

"Thanks, Andy." Daniel stepped down and took her arm, leading her gently away from the worst muddy spots in the road. Once away from the loggers' curious eyes he asked, "How long are you going to continue this farce?"

"Farce?"

His jaw was set in the way she had learned to know. "Yes, farce. If there is anything more ridiculous than you working in that hotel I don't know what it could be."

"I consider that my business."

"It's my business because you chased out here after me."

In that moment she hated him. Every indignity she had faced, every humiliation heaped up in a pile to accuse him. "It's all your fault! Why did you ever come to Grand Rapids, anyway?" Regardless of any watching eyes she jerked free and faced him, stamping her foot on the muddy road. "Do you think I like being here? Do you think I'd stay if there were any other way —" She broke off, appalled at how close she had come to giving her penniless state away.

"Any other way to get what you selfishly wanted." He had misunderstood her completely. "You are still the same spoiled child I knew in Grand Rapids. I hoped, once you were here, you might see the value of these hard-working people who are trying to carve out homes."

Betty's unruly heart leaped. He could not speak so to her if he did not still care.

"I fail to see why anything I do should interest you at all. Good day, Mr. Spencer." She turned, caught the hem of her skirt on a partially hidden boulder and would have gone down if he had not snatched her.

"I will walk you to the hotel. No use advertising to the whole town just how things stand between us."

"I am no more eager to advertise than you." She spoke no more until he opened the hotel door for her. "Thank you for walking me home, Daniel." The added sweetness was for the benefit of anyone who might be listening.

"My pleasure, I am sure." Daniel's farewell left Betty seething. It was the last time she would go to church. Let Pioneer make of that what it would.

But when the next Sunday came Betty could not face the four walls of her own room in her hours off duty. Even sitting through the torture of Daniel's sermon, aching to be at peace, was better than brooding in the little room that was not even all hers. There was not even privacy to cry if she wanted to do so. Abbie worked long, hard hours and needed her sleep. Betty did not realize her consideration of Abbie was something that had grown since coming West. She only knew Abbie needed rest. She herself was usually so tired from working she fell asleep the moment her head touched the uncomfortable pillow.

And then the snows came — not little flakes, but great, soft winter whirlings that left the ground blanketed with beauty. Even Betty's spirits rose. The world was clean. The defects of Pioneer were covered with that mantle of freshness. That night sleigh bells rang outside the hotel. Dr. Stewart bounded in. "Miss Tucker, Miss Courtland, we're having a sledding party. Will you come?"

Refusal trembled on Betty's lips. She was tired. She had had to help cook that evening and burned one hand painfully in the process of lifting bread from the oven.

"Could we, Betty?" The longing in Abbie's face decided her.

"Go ahead, Abbie."

"Not without you," faithful Abbie pleaded. "You need to be out."

"Yes, Miss Courtland." Dr. Stewart's keen eyes seemed to see right through her. "The fresh air will be good for you."

"Is Mr. Spencer — Daniel going?"

"No. He's tied up."

Betty's heart bounced again. Why not? She dropped her eyelashes as she used to do when she was belle of the ball back home. "That's too bad. Well, maybe I'll go anyway."

"Good! Put on your oldest, warmest things."

Fifteen minutes later the girls were bundled into the big sleigh along with about a dozen more laughing young people. Betty looked around her astonished. "Why, where did you all come from?"

The shout of laughter warmed her heart. "Most of us are home from school," a girl near told her. "Sue and Abigail and Tom and James and I all go to Normal School, and we're home for the holidays." She counted off on her fingers. "The others are either friends or relatives who have come to spend Christmas with us."

"Christmas!" Betty's shocked repetition was lost in the general uproar. She had lost track of time. What would it be like to spend Christmas in Pioneer? For one moment she felt nauseated, remembering the beautiful home she had left, the gigantic Christmas tree with dozens of tiny tapers. Sam and Abbie had always been near with buckets of water in case the flames touched the branches. She drew in a quick breath of the clear, cold air. Would she ever spend Christmas in her own home again?

The evening went by in a blur. All Betty could remember afterward was the beauty of the night and the feeling of security being tucked in between others of her own age. Problems seemed suspended as the group shouted songs, laughed, and finally ended up at a farmhouse for steaming oyster stew. It was the best thing she had eaten since she arrived in Pioneer. When she was working the food odors took the edge off her appetite, and she had lost a tremendous amount of weight. Now she ate as if she were starving, never noticing the relief in Dr. Stewart's eyes.

"Your friend seems happier tonight," he whispered to Abbie later.

"I'm glad." The little maid turned her trusting, freckled face toward him. "It hasn't been easy for her."

"And you?"

"I love my work. It makes all the difference, you know."

Dr. Spencer's eyes widened as he looked into Abbie's upturned face. "Yes, it does." His gloved hand felt for her little mittened one under the blanket that covered them both. "Abbie." It was the first time he had called her that. "You'll never know how much it means to me for you to be working here."

"Thank you, Dr. Stewart." But the shy glance from blue, blue eyes held more than appreciation.

Betty had missed the whispers but looked up in time to see Abbie's face. Stupefied, she could only stare. Abbie, looking like that? And Dr. Stewart — he actually looked human. But before she could digest what she had seen they were at the old farm. Light streamed through the welcoming door.

"Why, I thought we were going home!"

"Not us," Dr. Stewart told her, eyes shining. "This is another family who have kindly provided dessert for us." He helped both girls down. "Can't you smell that peach cobbler?"

Again Betty ate until she could hold no more. The peach cobbler had been topped with heaps of thick whipped cream, billowing over the edges like the snow drifts they had seen on the way out.

"Too bad Daniel couldn't be with us," Dr. Stewart remarked casually, his eyes intent on Betty's face.

"Yes, isn't it?" Betty's eyes challenged his in the moonlight now highlighting every white, burdened branch. "But then, if I'm to be a country minister's wife, I suppose I have to get used to it."

Dr. Stewart was still for a long moment, then said, "Yes, if you are to be a country minister's wife, you will have to do just that."

Was there the slightest emphasis on the word *if*? Betty turned to the girl closely packed on her other side with a bright remark about what fun this was, but inside her heart thumped with fear. Just how much did Dr. Stewart know about her?

Suddenly the joy of the unexpected evening fled, leaving Betty more alone than ever before, especially when she saw Gordon Stewart turn to Abbie with the same warm look of approval she had intercepted earlier.

It was Christmas Eve. Work at the hotel was over. Most of the men were home with their families or anxious to get through and ready for the "big doin's" at the schoolhouse.

Betty did not know when she had ever been so tired. Her lips trembled as she hung up the last dish towel. One of the other girls had been sick, and Betty helped clean up. Dejectedly she made her way upstairs.

"Oh, Betty," Abbie's eyes were like two stars in her highly freckled face, "Hurry! We don't want to be late for the program."

"I don't see how you can get so excited about a hick town Christmas program." Betty bit off the rest of her complaint. The faraway look in Abbie's face told her Abbie was not even listening.

"Abbie, you've grown positively pretty since we came here."

"Do you really think so?" Abbie took a step nearer, peering into Betty's face.

"Yes, I do. You look happy." Betty could not keep the unconscious envy from her voice. "Funny. I was the one who was going to find everything I ever wanted in Pioneer, but it's you who is happy."

Abbie fell to her knees by Betty's bed, both hands taking Betty's sadly disfigured ones in her own. "Miss Betty, I am happy. I wasn't going to tell you, but —" Her face suffused with color. "Dr. Stewart — Gordon — has asked me to marry him." She faltered before Betty's shocked expression.

"And you —"

Abbie's eyes were wells of happiness. "Do you remember so long ago when you asked if I'd ever been in love?"

"Only too well." Betty took in a deep breath, trying to smother her pain.

"I told you no. I can't say that any longer." Her face grew serious. "From the first time I saw him I knew I loved Gordon Stewart."

"Are you sure, Abbie? It's not just because you work with him and he's a kind man?"

"No. When he told me about the girl he loved who died I knew he'd never love anyone else. I was wrong. He has learned to love me."

"But if you marry him you may have to spend the rest of your life in this hole!"

"It isn't a hole to me. Not when Gordon is here." Abbie rose and crossed to the window, looking into the black night with courage in her eyes, a slight smile on her lips.

"You'd really stay here forever, just because of Dr. Stewart?" Betty was horrified. "Or will you try and get him to go back to civilization once you're married?"

Abbie whirled from the window. "Oh, no! This is our home."

Betty fought the urge to throw herself on the bed and cry her heart out. Even Abbie had betrayed her.

"I've been thinking, Betty." Abbie was back at her side. "With the money we've both saved, you'll have enough to go home right after the New Year. I won't need mine. You can have it."

Betty's lips quivered at the generosity of the other girl. "You'll need it, Abbie. You'll want sheets and pillowcases and everything to set up house-keeping."

"No, Dr. Stewart already has enough. I want you to take the money. Your papa and mama will forgive you if you tell them you're sorry. You can marry Mr. Prescott. He will give you everything you ever wanted."

"Except the man I still love."

Two strong arms crept around her. "Oh, Betty! You mean you still love Daniel Spencer — after all this time?"

Betty flinched from the pity in Abbie's voice but bravely lifted her chin. "I can't help it, Abbie. It won't do any good. I've worked and tried to hate him, but I can't. If only I could be his wife!"

"Would you be content to stay here in Pioneer?"

One lone tear escaped the tightly shut lashes. "I don't know. I only know that when I go back to Grand Rapids it will be slamming the door on something that could have been very precious. If it hadn't been for his God, things would have been different."

"I wonder."

Betty's eyes popped open, anger rising. "Just what is that supposed to mean?"

Abbie's gaze was steady, unafraid. "I mean if he had been just like everyone else, all the other young men in Grand Rapids, you wouldn't have cared any more for him than you did for them. The reason you fell in love was not in spite of Daniel Spencer's God but because of Him!"

"That's not true." Betty flounced to the mirror, watching Abbie's dim reflection instead of her own. Abbie did not budge an inch, even when Betty stubbornly repeated, "It's just not true."

"Isn't it?" Abbie gathered her cloak, tied her bonnet strings. "What do you think makes him different? It's his belief, his partnership with God." Her face softened at the misery in Betty's image. "Come on. Go with me to the program. You'll like it. I understand there's something on the tree for everyone in town."

Betty sniffed. "I suppose that was Daniel's ridiculous idea."

"It isn't ridiculous. It's a time when the whole town can join together for a little while and enjoy each other." Abbie hesitated in the open door. "Aren't you coming at all?"

"No."

"Then, good night, Betty. Merry Christmas." The little figure that had suddenly acquired a new dignity disappeared from sight. Betty could hear her light steps running down the stairs to meet Dr. Stewart. In spite of herself she crossed the room and looked down through her little window. Dr. Stewart had tucked Abbie's arm through his own. The flaring light from his old lantern shone for a moment on their laughing faces, sending another pang through Betty. What if Daniel should look at her like that?

Hot tears stored up through all the long, hard working hours threatened to flood Betty's eyes. She held them back and frantically fumbled in her trunk for a dress. She would go to the program after all. It could not be worse than sitting alone in this prisonlike room, envying Abbie with all her heart.

Betty slipped into the last available chair in the back corner when she got to the church. It had begun snowing again, and she gladly relinquished her cloak with its heavy hood to a smiling man she recognized as the depot agent. Curiously she surveyed the packed building. Abbie had been right — everyone in town must be there! What if she really were the minister's wife, part of the watching crowd? For the first time she saw them as individuals, not just loggers and wives, store owner, doctor, or teacher. She caught the kindly approval in glances sent her way, and her heart beat wildly. What if they knew it was all a hoax and she would be leaving as soon as she got the fare? Would that kindly regard change to stern disapproval?

Something stirred, born of Abbie's news and the fact that it was Christmas Eve. Maybe it would not be so bad living in Pioneer with Daniel after all.

She turned back toward the little platform built from a few hastily thrown together planks. A large Christmas tree stood near. The children were intent on presenting the Christmas pageant. Betty craned her neck to see around the burly shoulders of the man in front of her.

"I'm sorry. There is no room in the inn." The youthful innkeeper looked down his nose at the miniature Mary and Joseph.

Betty winked back tears, furious at herself. What was wrong with her? So she had never been to a Christmas Eve program before. She had danced Christmas Eve away at balls and parties. Must she make a fool of herself? Still she found herself listening intently.

"I have a stable. You can go there." The innkeeper gestured, and Mary and Joseph turned away.

In wonder Betty watched the rest of the pageant, unable to withdraw her gaze. What a lot of work! Every child knew his or her part perfectly. The background scenes had been painstakingly formed. Had Daniel done it all? She could have helped. She often painted for her own pleasure when she was growing up.

Then it was over. The little group around the manger with the shepherds who had come to worship and the look of love Mary gave to the real baby in her arms lent reality to the scene. Daniel Spencer stepped to the side of the group. He looked thin and tired in the glow of the candles on the tree, but exalted. Betty's heart gave one leap, then settled back in dullness.

"I'm not going to preach tonight. In a few moments we will distribute the Christmas gifts — something for everyone. I just want to ask one question. You have seen our children portray the search by Mary and Joseph to find room for the Christ Child. My challenge to you this Christmas season is: Will you find room in your heart for the Christ Child? He is still looking for a place to abide. Or, like the innkeeper, will you turn Him away? If you do, you can know He goes sadly. Once more, is there room in your heart for God's Son?"

Betty could not stand any more. A wild impulse to rise and cry out, "I will make room" was stopped only by action. Stumbling over knees in the semidarkness she got to the door, snatching her cloak from the agent who held it out to her. She had to get away. Was that then the secret of Daniel Spencer's success — a personal magnetism that hypnotized people into accepting his God? Almost hysterical, Betty ran through the snow-covered town back toward the hotel. At least she would have privacy. It would be a long time until the Christmas tree was dismantled of its gifts and Abbie returned.

There was no peace in her room. The light showed her distraught face. The darkness held Daniel Spencer's accusing eyes. Had they looked directly at her? Or was that God looking at her from the corners of her room?

"God, if You really are, what have You to do with me?"

For what seemed hours she paced the floor, finally sinking to her bed in sheer exhaustion, only to be roused by Abbie.

"Betty?" A wave of cold air from Abbie's garments brought her back to reality. "I thought I saw you at the program."

It took all of her control to answer carelessly, "Oh, I dropped in for part of it."

Abbie's concern showed with the hastily struck match and the yellow glow of their little lamp. "You didn't stay to receive your present. Mr. Spencer asked me to bring it." She stooped to pick up something from the floor by the doorway and crossed to Betty's bed. "These are for you."

Betty was speechless. Red roses, a whole dozen of them. She hadn't seen roses since she left Grand Rapids. "But how — who —"

"There's a card."

Betty held the card in her hand and silently read it in the dim light.

MERRY CHRISTMAS, ELIZABETH.
Daniel

The tears would no longer be denied. Betty cradled the roses to her breast, tears softly falling to the heart of the beautiful flowers.

"He must have had them sent in on the train," Abbie told her, eyes still wide. "Betty, he must love you a great deal to do this."

Long after Abbie slept, Betty stared into the darkness. One of the red roses caressed her cheek, its soft petal and gentle fragrance reminding her of the sender. Some of the storm of the early part of the evening had passed. But just before sleep finally claimed her, Elizabeth Courtland, proud and haughty Eastern beauty, whispered, "What shall I do? Oh, what shall I do?"

It was several days before Betty saw Daniel again. Through Abbie she learned that he had gone to the Indian village to spend time with the people he had learned to love. That time she did not shudder. It all fit what she had learned of him since she came to Pioneer.

Then one night he was at the table with Abbie and Dr. Stewart.

"Good evening, Miss Courtland."

Betty's heart sank beneath the long white apron protecting her dress from her work. She had hoped the roses would soften the hostility between them. She had no way of knowing the fight Daniel experienced within during his trip to the Indian village, or that he had seen and correctly interpreted her turmoil the night of the program.

Now she merely answered, "Good evening, Mr. Spencer. I'll bring coffee right away," and turned from him without meeting his eyes. When she returned it was to hear him say, "Gordon, I wish you'd go to the Indian village with me tomorrow. Some of the children seem to have a red rash. Looks like it could be measles." His brow wrinkled. "You know how hard these diseases are among the Indian people. They don't have any immunity to it. Strange thing, though, it's only on their stomachs."

Gordon's keen eyes flashed. "Is it small red spots? Are you sure they don't appear on arms and legs?"

"I'm sure." Daniel leaned toward his friend who had turned pale. "What is it? Something other than measles?"

Gordon glanced at Abbie and Betty, openly staring at him, and clamped his lips shut. "I can't say. We'll leave early in the morning." He finished his meal in silence.

"What do you think he suspects?" Betty whispered to Abbie after the two men were gone.

"I don't know." Abbie's face was solemn. "But it doesn't sound very good, does it?"

The next night Abbie rushed in, wild-eyed. Seizing Betty's hand she managed to draw her aside from her work. "Don't tell anyone, but there's typhoid fever in the Indian village." Betty gasped, but Abbie rushed on. "Dr. Stewart came back as soon as he discovered what it was. Half the village is sick and many of the others have symptoms. Dr. Stewart and Mr. Spencer will stay with the Indian people and take care of them." Her hands were like ice. "I wanted to go with them, but they wouldn't let me."

"Well, I should hope not." Betty was indignant.

"You don't understand! They could get it and die."

Only Abbie's quick clutch saved Betty from falling. "You mean —"

Abbie could not hold back the truth. "After Dr. Stewart was gone I read everything I could find in his medical books about typhoid fever. It comes from drinking impure water and is passed on by flies. Betty, Mr. Spencer was bound to have drunk the same water the Indian people drank while he was up there."

"What can we do?" Sheer terror lay in Betty's face.

"Wait — and pray."

Abbie had predicted well. All Pioneer waited and prayed. The only ones who visited the Indian Village were the doctor and the Indians who brought him down by canoe for supplies and waited at the river. Abbie carried on at the hospital, valiantly doing her best, assisted by those loggers with rudimentary knowledge of first aid. Betty continued her work, no longer aware of the long hours. In her state of numbness she could only wait. She tried to pray but did not know how, except to sometimes whisper, "Help him."

News from the Indian village was not encouraging. Many of those who contracted the disease died. Others were weak, still needing care. January slipped into February without notice. Every time the doctor came for supplies he looked grimmer. Then one day Abbie came home with different news.

Betty was sitting in their little room, staring blankly at the wall when Abbie came in. "What is it?"

Abbie's thin face, worn with work and worry, looked sick. "You know they found the source of the impure water some time ago." She paused, and Betty's nerves screamed.

"Well, Dr. Stewart thinks the village is over the fever." She turned away, her voice muffled. "He came home today — with Mr. Spencer."

"Is he —?"

Abbie flung herself into Betty's arms. "He's sicker than any of the others. Dr. Stewart said he had to get him back here for there to be any chance at all." Tears were running freely. "He was so run down taking care of others —"

Something snapped inside Betty. "He's not going to die?"

"I don't know." Abbie's reply was a wail. "Dr. Stewart said it would take a miracle to save him."

"Then that's what he's going to have." Betty snatched her cloak and started for the door.

"Where are you going?"

"I'm going to take care of him. Tell Buck, will you? He will understand."

"But Betty, you can't!" Abbie jumped up in horror. "Gordon won't let you into that cabin. He said no one in Pioneer except himself can go in. I'm to leave supplies at the edge of the clearing, the way I did while he was at the Indian village. He won't take any chance of sickness spreading through Pioneer."

Betty's pale, determined face did not waver. "I won't spread it. I'm going to that cabin, and once I'm inside, nothing on earth will get me out of it." She swallowed fiercely. "I may not know anything about Daniel Spencer's God, but I know this — if there really is a God like Daniel believes, He's not going to let Daniel die. I'm going to be right there to see to it!"

She yanked open the door and turned back to Abbie. "If you ever prayed, Abbie Tucker, you'd better pray now. I'm not good in that department, but let me tell you — Daniel Spencer is going to get well, and when he does, I'm going to marry him no matter what it costs. If I have to live in Pioneer the rest of my life and learn to serve the God he worships, I'll do it. There's nothing or no one, including Daniel himself, who can change that.''

The door slammed behind her. But the white-faced little maid huddled on her knees by the side of a hard bed scarcely heard. She had been ordered to pray; it was all she could do. Daniel Spencer's God would have to do the rest. As Dr. Stewart had said, nothing could save their minister except a miracle.

13

"What are you doing in this cabin?" Dr. Stewart's iron grip and fierce whispered demand nearly undid all her determination.

Betty raised her pale face and jerked away, panting from the run through the snow from the hotel to the little log cabin in the small cleared area. Disheveled, breathless, she managed to get out, "I'm here and I'm staying. If you try and put me out I'll scream until every person in Pioneer comes running to see what's happening!"

The doctor's red-rimmed eyes from lack of sleep burned into her very soul. "Another act, Miss High and Mighty?"

She caught the lapels of his rough coat and peered into the now bearded face. "This is not an act. I have to be here with Daniel."

Something in her pleading face snapped the bonds of Dr. Stewart's better judgment. "Can you take orders?"

"I can."

"Then get out of that wet cloak. There's work to be done."

Daniel Spencer's gaunt face was etched forever on Betty's heart as she entered the sick room where he lay. Burning with fever, unconscious of her presence, he tossed and turned constantly, arms reaching out. Mumbled and incoherent sentences escaped his parched lips.

For one moment she hesitated. Dr. Stewart spoke in a low tone. "Are you sure you want to be here?"

"I *have* to be here."

He was convinced. "Then do as I say." He rolled up his sleeves and motioned for her to do the same. "He didn't let me know how far advanced his symptoms were, and I was so busy I didn't notice. It wasn't until the last case in the Indian village was on the mend that he said, 'Gordon, old man, we'd better get home. I think we're in for some rough weather.' "

"You love him, don't you?"

"Like a brother." He shot her a keen glance under bushy brows. "And you?"

"With all my heart."

"Then why —" he cut himself short. "I have no right to ask that."

"It's all right." Betty was glad to be able to talk it out with this man whose skill would give Daniel the finest earthly attention possible. In whispered voices, hands busily bathing and sponging the feverish, tossing

101

man they both loved, she told Dr. Stewart, "I was intrigued at first, then furious at how useless he thought I was. Later I knew he was the only man for me. I broke my engagement to Prescott, Daniel's friend. My father thought I was — was unworthy of the Courtland name. Perhaps I was. Not through anything I had done wrong, but by my demand for admiration. Then I came to Pioneer."

Dr. Stewart's hands slowed, then stilled. He wiped them on a towel and motioned her into the other room. His eyes never left her face as she spoke.

"I hated it, all of it." Apology shone in her dark blue eyes, along with honesty. "I think I hated you too. You were his friend. I was — nothing." She took in a deep breath, staring into the fireplace where she had once built a fire and cooked rice until it ran over the edge of the pot to the coals below.

"Why didn't you leave and go back to Grand Rapids?"

Betty forced herself to meet his eyes. "I almost did. My parents wouldn't have helped me, but I know Prescott would have sent money for train fare." A faint smile hovered on her pale lips. "I imagine you're glad I didn't go and take Abbie."

She did not wait for a reply. "Daniel doesn't know it, but I am penniless until spring and my inheritance comes. Abbie and I had most of our money stolen on the way here."

Dawning realization touched Dr. Stewart's face. "You mean — then working at the hotel wasn't to humiliate Dan? You really needed the money?"

"Yes. At first I was just going to work until I got money from Prescott. But I never wrote Prescott for money. I decided to earn it myself. I had to prove I could."

"To Dan?" His voice was gentle.

"I think more to myself." Again her eyes met his squarely. "You know, he was right. Before I came here I couldn't do anything except paint or embroider or play the piano." She looked at the work-roughened hands. "I'm proud of the way they look now. These hands know how to cook and wait tables and do dishes and sweep. They show it. If my friends in Grand Rapids could see them they would shudder with horror — just as I would have done last fall."

"Why didn't you tell Dan the truth?" Dr. Stewart's piercing gaze saw through her, demanding an answer.

"I couldn't. He told me the night he first came home from the Indian village how things stood. I even told him I loved him, wanted to marry him."

"And?" The word cracked like a rifle.

Betty met his question head on. "He said God lived in this cabin, and I would never be happy here in His presence."

Dr. Stewart grunted. "What did you say?"

If it had been possible for Betty's face to turn even whiter, it would have done so. Yet she had determined to bare her soul. "I told Daniel nothing. I shuddered — and ran away."

In one stride he was at her side. "You did that, to a man like Daniel Spencer, a proud man who has fought his own feelings for you all these months, trying to follow the God he serves?"

"Yes." All the condemnation of that same God fell on Betty's defenseless shoulders. Then with some of her old fire she cried, "What else could I do? I don't know his God."

"Have you ever tried?" A tiny pulse beat in Dr. Stewart's forehead. "I didn't know God either, until I came here with Dan. In the months we've worked together I've learned that God is just what Dan says — loving." He turned away from the fire, hiding his face for a moment. "When the girl I loved died, I hated God — if there was a God. I, a doctor, couldn't save the one I loved! Then I met Dan. I still don't know why God let her die. I do know that I've found peace and contentment — and Abbie. I know Dan's God allowed everything to happen as it did. He didn't make Susan die. But neither does He want me to spend my whole life mourning.

"As I've walked this clean land, breathed in air free from the grime of cities, seen snow cover the harshness, I look forward to spring and rebirth. I know *I've* been reborn, Elizabeth. I am not the same man who came to Pioneer only a few short months ago. Abbie is not the same woman; neither are you." He cleared his throat, then finished gruffly, this time facing her, "Only Dan is the same. The reason why is that he brought faith in Christ with him. The rest of us had to find it here."

Something akin to hopelessness touched Betty, sending a cold breath across her body. "But I haven't found Him."

"You will." For the first time since trying to throw Betty out of the cabin Dr. Stewart smiled.

"I — I tried, a little. I tried to pray when I knew you had gone to the Indian village. Then on Christmas Eve — the manger scene, I felt —" Betty helplessly threw her hands wide. "Does Daniel Spencer hypnotize people into believing in something that doesn't exist? Or if God does exist, why does Daniel feel He's interested in individuals?"

"I asked myself that question a hundred times, Elizabeth. Now I feel like Dan; I can only believe God is and cares. Why things happen as they do is not for me to know, at least not at this time." Infinite sadness touched his face. "I don't know why God would allow Dan, of all people, to be stricken with typhoid fever. I can only do my best and let that same God take care of the rest."

A low moan from the other room snapped them back to their duties. Daniel's fever had risen again, in spite of the cooling sponge bath.

All night long, the next day, and the next night Dr. Stewart and Betty took turns watching and bathing Daniel. There was no improvement. If anything, the fever rose higher, his cries became more incoherent. His emaciated form seemed scarcely alive. His cracked lips uttered meaningless sounds and the once strong hands now picked at the coverlet.

Betty grew thinner, whiter, unable to eat even when Dr. Stewart forced food on her. Daniel worsened. If he died, everything on earth would stop for her. Was this God's punishment for her making war against Him? She voiced the question to Gordon but she was only partially satisfied when he shook his head and said, "God is not vindictive or small, Betty. He loves us so much He sent His only Son, that whoever believes on Him might not perish, but have everlasting life. Surely you have heard Dan preach that."

"It didn't mean anything," she confessed, eyes gigantic in her peaked face. "I was too busy hating God for taking Daniel."

"And now?"

"God could never forgive me." There was hopelessness in her voice.

"When you know you are a sinner and ask Jesus to forgive you and live in your heart, you have that forgiveness." He looked at her sternly. "But you can't just make a sham and think it will save Daniel's life. The transaction has to be between you and God, and it has to be real."

Betty's head drooped as Dr. Stewart slipped into the other room. She was so tired of fighting. Her idea of making God the object of her selfishness had been insane. Was it true what Gordon had told her? Could forgiveness really be that simple? There was no problem in admitting she was a sinner. Neither was there a problem in knowing Jesus must have been waiting a long time for her to acknowledge Him.

"Is there room in your heart for God's Son?" Daniel's challenge at the Christmas Eve service struck her with the force of a blow.

What had she done? Even while she had fought tears at the thought of Mary and Joseph's being turned from the inn of old, she had steadfastly refused to admit that same Jesus was seeking room in her life.

With shock Betty realized that neither her position nor her wealth could make her acceptable to the God she had chosen to battle. A conviction began to grow. Daniel was right. So was Gordon Stewart. Her head reeled.

Before she could think it all out or even more than recognize something wild and sweet that came with the knowledge, Gordon returned. His face was haggard. "I don't know why he isn't dead." Unashamed tears stood in his eyes. "I can do no more. I've prayed and given the best care of which I am capable. Still he's dying."

Betty gave a terrible cry of protest, automatically snatched up her cloak, and flung wide the door, answering Dr. Stewart's curt, "Where are you going?" with, "I am going to find God — and His Son."

"Betty, come back —" The closing door cut off his cry.

Betty struggled for footing in the fresh snow, her brain on fire. Where should she look for God? She had to find Him, tell Him there was room in her heart for His Son. She had to tell Him she was a sinner and ask for forgiveness. She had to let Him know that no matter what happened with Daniel, she could fight no more. She was His — for keeps.

Would even God's great love cover the deliberate way she had acted? Were her sins too great for forgiveness? No, Dr. Stewart had said God's love was so great He allowed His only Son to be crucified to save the world from even such sins as hers.

Now her only question was — where could she find God to tell Him, to confess what she had done, and to claim the promise of forgiveness and salvation through Jesus. How strange that those phrases came to mind! Or was it? She had heard them many times, especially since coming to Pioneer. Even while she had ignored any application to her own life they must have been working into her heart and soul.

The church! She had felt God there on Christmas Eve. Her faltering footsteps started down the way she thought was back to town. Then she remembered. She could not go there. She was a possible carrier of the dread typhoid.

The hotel, where she had felt the same on Christmas Eve? No. Abbie and the others must not be exposed.

"Where are you, God?"

The mocking wind caught her words, whirled them away, ate them alive before they had gone a foot from her lips.

A great fear entered her. Now that she knew the truth, what if she could not find God to tell Him? Yet God was a God of love. He would not hide Himself from her cries.

Like a wraith from the past words from months before flickered in Betty's mind. Dan's voice, urging her on, giving strength. Reverent and deep and sincere. "My God is head of this household. He always will be."

With a cry of joy Betty struggled to her feet from where she had fallen heavily a few moments before. Why, of course! Why had she run into the storm in search of God? He was there all the time! Why hadn't she known it sooner?

If God was in the cabin, He was also in the storm. He was there right now beside her. He was everywhere. All she had to do was tell Him.

Elizabeth Courtland, proud society belle, dropped to her knees. The icy wind was unheeded as she bowed her head. "I'm sorry, God. I wanted my own way. I wanted it so much I would have done anything to get it. Forgive me. I am sorry for everything. Most of all for not making room in my heart for your Son, Jesus."

She hesitated and one tear escaped the tightly closed lashes to tremble on her face then drop to the ground and freeze. "I'm not even sure I can understand how much love You had to send Your only Son to die — for me. I thought I loved Daniel more than the greatest love on earth, but it's nothing compared to Your love. I accept that love and the gift of Jesus. I know now Jesus is the only One Who can save me, and I thank You for sending Him."

Something deep inside Betty melted, something she hadn't known was frozen. The single tear gave way to others, but they were not tears of sadness now.

With a start, Betty came back to the present. Her cloak had fallen back and while she still felt warm inside, her hands and face were freezing. She peered through the ever-deepening gloom. Which was was the cabin?

She hastened to the left and plunged into untrodden snow. She turned back to find herself caught in hanging underbrush, fighting snow-laden branches that had suddenly become a trap. Abbie had told her never to be out in a storm. People who had become lost were later found frozen to death within a few hundred yards of Pioneer.

"I will not die out here!" Determination gave her strength. "I have so much more to live for now." She tore at the brush, worked through — only to find herself facing a large unfamiliar tree. She fought back through the thicket and the branches that gleefully held her as her own.

Finally Betty could go no farther. "I'll stop and rest for just a moment." She sank onto a big log. The storm lulled her into closing her eyes. If only she could sleep for a few minutes! With tremendous effort she opened her eyes. "No, I mustn't. If I go to sleep I'll die."

She struggled back to her feet, still talking to herself. "It doesn't seem so bad now. If I die, I'm forgiven. I'll see Daniel again."

A spark flared. "Coward!" She came back to full consciousness. "God expects you to do your best. Now that you know Him, you must tell others, just as Daniel did." Faces from Grand Rapids formed in the little thicket ahead: Prescott, her parents, others. "God, if Daniel lives, we can work together. I need him. If he doesn't make it —" she set her teeth in her lip, hard "— I'll go on and do what I can."

She paused. "But, oh, if I could just tell him I've truly accepted Jesus before he dies!" Her foot hit a hidden root and it threw her. Snow surrounded Betty, was in her mouth, up her sleeves, under her long skirts.

Was that God's eye looking at her? She focused on the bobbing movement. "I'm here, God."

Strong arms picked her up. It was Dr. Stewart.

"Where's God?" she asked stupidly. "I saw His eye looking at me."

Dr. Stewart sounded funny. "You saw the lantern." He picked it up with difficulty and helped her back to the cabin, taking great steps through the snow.

"God was there. He's everywhere. So is Jesus. I did what you said. I told Him how wicked I had been. I told Him I didn't see how He could still love me but that I knew He did. I told Him I wanted His Son, Jesus, as my Savior and asked Him into my heart."

Even in the dim light of the lantern she could see Dr. Stewart's face light up. His arms tightened about her. "Thank God!" Another few strides and they were inside the cabin. Betty stripped off her wet cloak and ran to the fire.

"Betty." Dr. Stewart's voice stopped her. "It wasn't a bargain for Daniel's life?"

She spun around. "No, Gordon. Once I left this cabin I didn't think of Daniel except as someone from my past. The only important thing was to be forgiven."

There was humility in his face as well as gladness. "Forgive me. I had no right to ask."

"You had every right." She looked toward the bedroom. There were no moans now. "No matter what happens, I found out tonight that Jesus Christ is the most important thing in life. Nothing else matters." She quietly slipped into the little room.

Dan lay as she had last seen him, eyes closed, pale as death. This time instead of reaching for a soft cloth, Betty clasped his hands between her own. She must reach the man who had traveled so far toward the fine line between life and death it seemed impossible for him to be snatched back.

"It's Elizabeth, Dan. I'm here." Her voice was clear, but there was absolutely no response.

"I just want you to know I accepted the Lord Jesus Christ into my heart and life tonight. I've been forgiven for everything, even fighting against God. I also want you to know that if He takes you, I think I'll stay in Pioneer, at least for a time. Did you know Abbie and Gordon are getting married? I don't have any money until spring, but when I do we can have the church you wanted. If you can't be here, we'll try and find another minister." Her lips quivered as Dr. Stewart quietly came in.

"Is it all right to keep talking?"

"Go ahead." The slump of his body told her it didn't really matter.

"You said God is head of your household. I know now He isn't a far-off something, but Jesus Christ, alive and living in His followers."

On and on she talked, often rambling. At last Dr. Stewart motioned her away. Before she went she bent low. "Good-bye, my darling." She drew away, repelled by the chill of his lips, to stand before the fire once more.

Betty looked around the rude cabin. She belonged — now. If Daniel died, perhaps she could buy it and spend her life here where she had met her Lord.

Dr. Stewart's hand fell on Betty's shoulder. The timbre of his voice sent a surge of feeling through her. "There is a slight change. The crisis is past. He is sleeping naturally."

Color filled her face. "You mean there's a chance?"

"A slim one. One in a thousand. Sometimes there is a final rallying before death. Other times the patient recovers after much care. He is in God's hands."

The words that would have struck Betty dumb with terror a few days before now sent a burst of hope through her. "We will pray."

The long way back was an uphill fight. There were times when the death shadow hovered close, but as the last storm of winter ended, Daniel Spencer crept slowly back to life. He was strangely apathetic, even when blue sky could be seen outside the window and an apologetic sun sent feeble rays to earth.

Dan did not yet know Betty cared for him, or even that she had been there. He did not ask about her, and Dr. Stewart let her stay with him only while he slept.

"I'm afraid of his reaction." He turned away from the hurt in her eyes. "He doesn't know how you've changed."

Days later Dan stopped his friend as he prepared to leave the bedroom. "Say, old man, isn't anyone else sick in Pioneer? Seems you're here taking care of me. What about the others?"

"Oh, I've had some help." Gordon tried to sound disinterested.

A flicker of interest crossed Dan's face. "Abbie still here? I thought she and Miss Courtland would be gone by now."

"Not yet."

Dan looked puzzled.

In the other room Betty crept nearer the doorway, trying to hear above the thudding of her heart. "I thought they were going when spring came?"

"Abbie isn't going at all. We're getting married as soon as you're able to do the job." Gordon grinned at his patient.

"Well! Good for you. She's a fine girl. Miss Courtland is staying for the wedding, I suppose. That's nice of her."

To the eavesdropper just outside the doorway his apparent lack of interest cut deep. From her vantage point she could see Dr. Stewart's eyes narrow as he dropped back into a chair. "You don't know just how good Miss Courtland has been, Dan. She's been here helping me the whole time you've been sick."

Dan raised himself on an elbow. "Here? Madcap Betty's been playing nursemaid to me?"

Gordon's sober face helped restore that same nurse's composure. "I thank God she was and is Madcap Betty! She came here the night I brought you from the Indian village, as soon as she heard you were sick."

"And you let her stay?" Dan sounded incredulous.

"I had no choice. She forced her way in and threatened to scream her head off if I threw her out."

It sounded to Betty as if the doctor was enjoying himself.

"She cooked and cared for you. She followed orders like a soldier. She lost weight and couldn't eat. Still she stuck."

Dan was staring. "Betty Courtland did all that for me?"

"It isn't all she did." Gordon went into a brief description of the hours of desperation they had shared and then added in a quiet voice, "I finally had to tell her you were dying. I could do no more."

The ticking of the old clock sounded like a cannon in Betty's ears.

"What did she say?"

If Betty had doubted interest, his question told her those doubts were unworthy. His eyes blazed darker than she had ever before seen them.

"She looked at me and gave a cry that was almost inhuman. She ran for the door. It was the worst storm of the winter. I asked where she was going —" Dr. Stewart stopped for breath.

"What did she say?"

"She said" — Gordon's voice was almost reverent — "she said, 'I am going to find God — and His Son.' " He seemed to anticipate the next question hovering on Dan's lips. "I had told her earlier how God loved her so much He sent His Son to die in her place. I also told her she couldn't pretend in order to save your life.

"I called for her to come back. She ignored me. I had to check on you again, but when she had been gone a long time, too long, I knew I must go to her. She was not far away. She was turned around." Gordon drew a ragged breath. "When she saw my lantern she thought it was God. She wasn't scared. She had confessed herself a sinner and accepted the Lord Jesus Christ out in that storm, just as Abbie and I did not long ago.

"I listened at the doorway when she told you about it, wanting somehow for her words to pierce your unconsciousness. She also told me other things, Dan. Betty stayed in Pioneer because she had no money to do anything else and was too proud to ask for help. She also stayed to prove she could be worth something. Daniel Spencer, if I didn't already love Abbie Tucker, I would follow Madcap Betty Courtland to the ends of the world!"

"Gordon!" Dan's face contorted. "It wasn't delirium? She *was* actually here? She held me in her arms, told me —" He sank back as if too weak to go on. "That moment I knew I was crossing from life here to life eternal, did she kiss me?"

"That is only for her to say." Gordon stood. "A doctor sees many things that are sacred. He keeps them to himself. I only told you what I did to be fair to Betty." Gordon clasped Dan's hand. "Once you told me of your mother. 'Mrs. Minister,' I believe she was called. I think there's going to be another 'Mrs. Minister' right here in Pioneer as soon as you are able to attend a wedding." He cleared his throat and walked through the door, nearly falling over Betty, who was huddled behind the curtain. "Miss Courtland, I believe your patient wants to see you."

Betty hesitated. The moment she both hoped for and dreaded was here.

"Come here, Betty." The command in his dark eyes reached across the room and across the awkward moment that should have been between them.

"Oh, Daniel," she choked. She stumbled to his bed, dropped to her knees beside him, and buried her face in the coverlet.

"Look at me, Betty."

She forced herself to meet his compelling gaze.

"Why? Just to prove you could?"

She could not bear the sadness mingled with hope. "Because I love you." She cast pride aside as once she threw off discarded garments. "I have always loved you. If you died, my world would be ashes."

His hands cradled the tearstained face turned toward him. "You really mean it? You will actually live here in Pioneer with me, stand the hardships and do the work God has given me to do?"

"It's my work too."

Her fervent response sent flames leaping into the watching dark eyes. "You know God is still first." His steady gaze never left her own. "There can be no more choosing between you."

Betty's answer was firm. "I also know I am second only to the Lord Jesus, as you are to me. I have been called to serve even as you are called, but in a different way. Even if you had not lived, the Lord would still have been head of this household." She broke off, lips trembling. "But, oh, Daniel, I am so glad He didn't take you away when I had just learned what it was to really care!"

"Betty." Two arms that would grow strong again and protect her from whatever life had to offer encircled her, drew her close. His lips claimed hers. Betty sighed, responding with all her heart. His love was everything she had dreamed of and more.

When he finally released her, her face was flushed, her eyes shone. In that moment Betty saw into his very soul and thanked God for the man he was. His whisper carried only to her listening ears.

"Mrs. Minister — welcome home."

Flip over for another great novel!
HONOR BOUND

HONOR BOUND

by

Colleen Reece

Flip over for another great novel!
THE CALLING OF
ELIZABETH COURTLAND

Barbour Books
164 Mill Street
P.O. Box 1219
Westwood, New Jersey 07675

Typesetting By
Typetronix, Inc., Cape Coral, FL

89 90 91 92 93 5 4 3 2 1

HONOR BOUND

The door to the playroom swung inward. Honor Brooks looked up from the table where she and five-year-old Heather had been making letters.

"Miss Brooks, Heather" — Ben Stone beamed as he looked down at his daughter and her governess — "how would you like to go to the Grand Canyon?"

Honor was speechless. Heather was not. "Daddy, Daddy!" She flung herself into her father's arms. "Are we really going?"

"We certainly are." Laurene Stone indolently posed in the doorway. "Since President Wilson signed it into a National Park it's really quite the place to go." Her usually petulant face showed a spark of interest. "I understand El Tovar Hotel is sumptuous. Several of my friends are going for the summer, and Ben needs time away from his law practice." Her cool eyes were almost fond as they swept over gray-clad Honor. "It will be good for you, too. You can take Heather out in the fresh air and sunshine."

"That's very kind of you." Honor blushed.

"It will take about a month to get ready. I'll have all new clothing, of course. You're good with a needle, Honor. Would you like to remodel some of my present gowns for yourself?" A look of dismay crossed the carefully made-up face. "You weren't planning to go into mourning, were you?"

"Laurene!" Honor had never heard Ben Stone thunder before. Was this how he talked to lying witnesses in the court room?

Now Laurene had the grace to blush. "I didn't mean to be rude, or anything. It's just that at the Canyon and all — your brother wouldn't want you to wear black, would he? And being with Heather every day —"

Honor lost the rest of the explanation as a small hand slipped into hers. Heather stood with one finger in her mouth, her earlier joy of the news about their trip gone, showing clearly how the scene was affecting her.

"You're right, Mrs. Stone. Keith would never want me to wear black." She even managed a wan smile. "Your gowns are lovely, and I believe I can make suitable garments from them."

"There!" Laurene turned triumphantly to her husband. She pulled a bell rope and waited as a maid responded. "Sally, have Jimson bring down the trunk of clothes by my closet."

1

Heather crossed to her mother but looked back at Honor, eyes still anxious. "They're really pretty. You'll look nice in them."

Honor forced herself to smile at Heather. "I'm sure I shall."

"Don't wear yourself out sewing, Miss Brooks."

The concern in her employer's voice unnerved Honor, but Sally was already draping gowns over every available chair — garnet satin, dark blue crêpe, deep green, lovely amber — yards of gorgeous material trimmed with real lace. Some were far too decollete for Honor's taste, but they could be remodeled until even their original owner would not recognize them!

Last of all Laurene ordered Sally to open a satin-lined box.

"Oh!" Honor's dark blue eyes opened wide. Never had she seen such a beautiful frock. The white lace and satin were pearl-beaded — with even a small purse to match.

"You can get married in that one," Heather told her. The next instant her face clouded over. "You aren't going to get married and go away, are you?"

"Hardly." But Honor still fingered the frock, and a rich blush filled her face at the memory of a dark-haired soldier who had once briefly entered her life and then gone away.

When they had all left, Honor sat still, reliving another day when Ben Stone had entered the playroom. She had looked up that day, too — and the world had gone black as she saw the concern in her employer's face and the yellow telegram in his hand.

"Run along downstairs for a little while, please, Heather." He had waited as his daughter scampered out. "Miss Brooks — Honor —"

She had shoved back a lock of golden brown hair and a wave of faintness with one motion. "It's Keith, isn't it?"

Now she bit her lip, feeling the sickening taste of blood, trying to control her shaking hands. She resolutely clamped down the lid on memory of that day, as she had done dozens of times since. Keith was dead. She must go on.

You can't run away from it.

Had the words been whispered by her own heart, or were they merely the remains of the torture she had gone through these last weeks? Automatically her fingers lifted the heavy dresses, fitted them on hangers. One by one she carried them to her own room and placed them in the large wardrobe.

It was no use. All the gowns in the world could not stop her memories. She threw herself on the bed, letting the tears come. Would the pain never end?

There had been no trace of Ben Stone's usual courtroom crispness in his voice that day. But he had not attempted to soften the long-expected blow. "Yes. The War Department has confirmed his death." He had caught her as she swayed, helped her lean against the table. "He fell bravely, fighting for his country."

"That's comforting." Was that her own voice — bitter, harsh? "It's just that — all this time, when there was no word except he was missing — even since the war ended —" She could not go on.

"I know." Mr. Stone's face was sympathetic. "Evidently the War Department found someone who had actually seen Keith killed. There is no doubt." He cleared his throat. "They buried him in France, but if you want his body brought home, I'll see to it. And Honor, don't worry about expense. You've come to be part of our family. Everything will be taken care of."

Another tear fell, splashing against her clenched hands, as she remembered the kindness of the considerate employer for whom she had worked the past two years.

Thinking a walk would help, she tied a heavy hood over the bright brown hair so like her brother Keith's. She caught back a cry of pain. It couldn't be possible Keith had died somewhere in France. When the Armistice Day bells rang on November 11, 1918, she had expected Keith home soon. He hadn't come. Months passed. A War Department telegram informed Honor, his only living relative, that Keith was missing in action.

A fresh wave of torture filled her as she remembered the long days, sleepless nights. Missing in action — dead or alive, no one knew. Yet deep inside was the assurance Keith would return. Surely God wouldn't let Keith die when he was all she had left!

Honor's face darkened. She couldn't think of God, not now. Snatching up a long cape that covered her dress to the hem, she wrapped it around her and fled into the early afternoon. She was unconscious of the stares from passersby. The long cloak was out of place in the late spring softness of San Francisco. Yet huddled in its depths Honor still felt cold, outside and inside.

Memories threatened to drown her: moving to Granny's cottage when both parents were killed in the great earthquake — she had been eleven, Keith six; teaching her little brother to read before he went to school; learning to rely on Granny for warmth and love.

Honor shuddered. Keith would answer her call no more. Why had he lied about his age to serve his country? Had God punished that lie with

death on the battlefield? No! Her inner rebellion could not accept that. Keith had accepted Christ as his Savior when he was small. She could almost see his happy face becoming clouded over as he pleaded, "Honor, you have to accept Jesus, too. You have to be sorry for your sins and believe on the Lord."

She had scoffed in the lofty way her twelve years allowed. "If God really loved us, He wouldn't have let Mama and Daddy die."

Wisdom shone in the little boy's eyes. "The Bible says God loved us enough to send His own Son to die. God must have felt just as bad as we did about Mama and Daddy. Don't you listen when Granny tells us about Jesus and reads the verses?"

It hadn't been the last time Keith worried over her. Through their growing up years he kept on trying to win her to the Lord he loved. But Honor would not give up her stubbornness, even when Granny had died a few days before the Armistice. She clung to the idea Keith would be back. When he came would be time enough to talk about whether God loved her.

Her fingers clenched as a terrible thought crossed her mind: *If I had accepted Christ, would Keith be alive now?*

No! Granny had taught them they were responsible for their own actions. God would hold them accountable for what they did — Honor's lips twisted — or for what they failed to do. Although others could be hurt by their actions, salvation was a one-to-one transaction between God and every person on earth.

Her remembrance left weakness. There had been an unpaid mortgage. The little home had been sold. The day had come when Honor's pocketbook and tiny cupboard in her dingy rented room were empty. She had tried to pray at first, but nothing got better. If God still knew she was alive, it didn't seem to matter to Him. Only the thought of Keith's homecoming had kept her moving down the street looking in every window for a HELP WANTED sign.

It was through an old family friend that Honor had met Ben Stone, a lawyer who wanted someone to give his four-year-old daughter the time and attention his wife was unable to give. Heather walked into the library of the Stones' mansion and into Honor's heart at the same moment.

Laurene Stone seemed glad to be rid of even the minimal care she had been giving the child, and within a week Heather and Honor had become inseparable. The flaxen-haired little girl trotted after Honor eagerly and never argued when told to do something. Was it because of mutual loneliness? Laurene always seemed to have enough energy for balls and parties, but none for Heather. As a result, the child automatically turned to Honor's

welcoming love. Honor believed that Mrs. Stone's only real problem was being spoiled, but she had little contact with her and poured out all the love she had on Heather.

Ben Stone had been as good as his word. It was several weeks before Keith's body could be shipped home, but Mr. Stone had done everything in his power to speed the process.

For Honor the waiting was even worse than when she had waited for Keith to come laughing in the door. Now her waiting was without hope. She was truly alone. Only Heather could reach through her suffering.

One night as she tucked the child in bed, Heather, rosy from splashing in the ornate marble tub, said, "I'm sorry your brother died. Daddy said he was a soldier." The beautiful face was wistful. "I never had a brother. Aren't you glad you did, even though he died?"

It caught Honor unprepared. Thoughts whirled through her feverish brain. Heather's face was turned up, expectantly waiting for an answer. What she said now might be of lasting value or damage to the child.

"Yes, Heather. I am glad I had a brother."

Heather's wide-open eyes indicated she was in the mood for confidences. "Tell me about him, when he was little like me."

Haltingly at first, then buoyed by her listener's interest, Honor uncovered some of the buried memories she had put aside because of their painfulness. It got easier as she went along. When Heather's reluctant eyelids finally stayed closed and Honor had slipped to her adjoining room, she lay awake for a time. It *was* better to remember, even painfully, than to try to forget. Heather's final sleepy comment still hung in the air. "I bet Keith'd be happy now he's gone to know you still have me."

A trickle of comfort touched her. It was true. She had a place to live, the love of Heather, admiration of Mr. Stone. She wasn't totally alone.

The child's love had helped her through the hard memorial service, the final laying of Keith to rest in the soil of the country he loved and for which he had given his life. Yet in the weeks following the burial Honor was unable to pick up the shattered pieces and go on. She grew thin, pale, nervous. Even Heather wanted to know if she was sick. Honor told stories of her own childhood to amuse Heather and comfort herself, but continued to toss restlessly at night.

Alarmed, the Stones sent for a specialist, who checked her over. Honor overheard him tell them, "Shock. She carried on so long, but when hope was taken away, her body rebelled. She needs to get where there is a better climate. I don't like the sound of that cough she's developed."

Nothing more had been said until the Stones had come into the playroom today with the incredible announcement of a vacation to the Grand Canyon.

Honor suddenly realized she was chilly. Afternoon had given way to evening while she journeyed to the past. She hastily returned to the mansion and went in search of Heather.

The little girl was bubbling over with happiness. "Daddy says we're going in a great big car. There's going to be sand and mountains and all kinds of things to see! Aren't you excited, Honor?"

Honor led her small charge to the nursery, where Heather had her meals. "Of course I am. Keith —" her voice faltered, then firmly went on "— Keith and I always thought it would be a good place to visit."

With uncanny insight Heather read the meaning behind Honor's words. "Since your brother can't take you, we will. I heard Mama tell Daddy you needed to go —"

Honor's heart lifted. She wouldn't have thought Laurene cared about even a high-class servant that much. But Heather's continuing monologue shattered her illusions. "— and that we needed a vacation anyway, and this summer was the time to go while everyone thought it so smart."

Yet even those revelations could not completely dim Honor's anticipation. She lay in bed that night staring at the ceiling. She had always wanted to visit the Grand Canyon. She had read every book she could get her hands on, secretly hoping in her childish dreams she could visit a big cattle ranch someday, yet knowing the possibility was slight.

A rich blush crept up from the high ruffled neck of her cambric nightgown, touching her thin cheeks with color. She had even daydreamed of being mistress of such a ranch.

The excitement of the proposed exodus provided Honor with strength. Within a week she was working on the frocks Laurene had discarded. She and Heather took long walks past the great stores of the city, noting a knot of velvet here, a trick of gores there, that set apart the stylish frock from the ordinary. Honor's skillful needle faithfully transposed those tricks into her growing wardrobe. Heather learned to sew along with Honor's alterations, and doll clothes emerged for her favorites.

One evening Honor wore her new dark blue dress down to dinner. Most evenings she had dinner in the nursery with Heather, but on occasion she was pressed into service when an absent dinner guest made an uneven number. Her glowing cheeks were attractive and her eyes shone.

She wasn't prepared for Mrs. Stone's reaction. "Why, Honor, where did you get that lovely dress?" Astonishment narrowed Laurene's eyes. "That can't be —"

"It is." Honor laughed and whirled. "I wondered if you would recognize it."

"You certainly did a nice job!" Laurene peered at her more closely. "That fichu — it's just like the one on the Paris dress I found in a darling shoppe. If you don't mind, I may let you help me with my wardrobe at the canyon. I'd just as soon not bother with Sally."

"I'd be happy to help." Honor's sincere smile brought an answering glimmer to her employer's wife's eyes. Honor treasured the extra sign of friendliness. Laurene wasn't one to praise other women, especially one so insignificant as the governess.

It seemed only a few days passed, and suddenly it was time to leave. The house would be cared for by Sally and Jimson in their absence. Honor had a final glimpse of the mansion as they stowed themselves in the big touring car Mr. Stone had purchased especially for the trip. A strange desire to flee back to the security of the walls that had housed her for so many weeks and months touched Honor briefly and was gone. Ahead lay — what? Why should she suddenly long for her own room?

It was a long trip. By the time they arrived Laurene was tired, and she ordered Honor to see that Heather had a snack and was put to bed. Honor's heart beat quickly as she obeyed, anxious for her first sight of the canyon. She had already thrilled to the massiveness of El Tovar Hotel, built just after the turn of the century. Its native boulders and pine logs were different from anything she could have imagined, yet perfect for the setting. Grateful she could be alone for that all-important first sight of the canyon, she reassured Heather, promising she would get to do all the wonderful things the canyon offered while they were there.

Honor deliberately did not look into the canyon until she found a secluded spot a good distance away from the hotel. She kept her eyes fixed on a distant point of the far wall.

Her trembling fingers caught the twisted trunk of an old tree as she finally peered into a rent that could have been created only by the hand of God. She gazed down on mountaintops — and they were a mile high! No wonder writers described the canyon as indescribable. Nothing on earth could have prepared her for it. It was beautiful, awful, magnificent, terrible.

How long she stood gripping the tree she never knew. She turned away, only to look back at once. Every movement of light and shadow changed the canyon from red to purple, light to dark. It was impossible to grasp with the human mind — a never-ending, shifting panorama.

Honor tottered back, sinking down on the needle-covered ground. The sorrow of the past months had been drawn from her by the sheer force of

what lay before her. She shuddered. God had created all this and still sent His Son to die to save sinners — the God Granny said was waiting for her to accept Him. She tried to laugh and failed miserably. She deliberately brought up her losses: parents, Granny, Keith, home. No. Even such a God could not find place in her life after taking away everything precious. She could stand no more.

Yet after a simple dinner with Heather she again slipped into the evening's dimness. She watched until no light was left to reveal the canyon's secrets, an uneasy peace fighting with something inside clamoring for recognition. What if God really was calling her to accept His Son? Granny had talked time and again of those who were "under conviction" for their sins. Was this what she had meant, this terrible tearing apart inside? Part of her longed to fling herself to the ground and cry for mercy, while her head told her it was insane. More than likely it was just the effect of her illness and shock coupled with the beauty of this place.

Without warning a handsome face laughed in the still night air before her, leaving her drained. "I need someone," she whispered.

She laughed bitterly. First God — then a wraith from the past. If this was what happened when she came to Arizona, she'd better run back to San Francisco and find another job. Still the new idea tormented her. She needed someone to love and honor, to cherish, to fill her life. Overhead the bright Arizona stars seemed close enough to pick.

She had attended many weddings, seeing inner-most feelings and glimpsing what love between man and woman could be. She could even remember how her parents had been. It kept her from being attracted to a cheaper form of excitement. She would not accept second best. *Someday he will come,* she thought.

She caught her breath. Was this the recognition for which she had been brought to Arizona? In her soul, the searing certainty it was not shook her. What of the far greater truth she had so steadfastly denied?

Refusing to answer, she hurried toward the main entrance of El Tovar and dashed across the lobby. She heard a group clattering down the stairs before she saw them. The next instant she lay sprawled on the floor.

Honor looked up into the devastatingly handsome face of a dark-haired, dark-eyed man, who was apologizing and helping her up.

"I say! I've knocked you down with my clumsiness. I should have been watching where I was going."

His face changed. Delight, incredulity, and recognition mingled in rapid succession. "Honor? Honor Brooks?"

From her unladylike position Honor saw what her mind could not accept — the man who had knocked her flat was her soldier from long ago — Phillip Travis.

Phillip! He had come into her life like a whirlwind, appearing with a small group of soldiers who came to church one night. He had made a special point to talk with her afterward.

It was the beginning of a tremulous, butterfly world. Phillip's home was *Casa del Sol,* "House of the Sun," near Flagstaff, Arizona. Dark and handsome, he fit the storybook image of the knight in shining armor who would one day sweep her off her feet and carry her to his ranch to live happily ever after.

Honor's mouth twisted in a slight twinge of the pain she had suffered when he went overseas, promising to write and disappearing as suddenly as he had come. She wondered if he, too, had fallen in France. It seemed inconceivable he would not have written, if he were able, after spending every free moment with her and Granny.

She could still remember his farewell. "Honor, I don't know if I'll be back. But would you wait for me? When I come home, will you marry me?"

Alarm had brushed gentle wings against her spirit and reason. "We hardly know each other!"

His gaze was compelling. Taking both her hands in his, he drew her unwillingly toward him, overriding the strange combination of longing and reluctance she felt.

"You can't tell me you don't care."

Honor had tried, but there was a biding-my-time look in his smile. "We will have time when I come home."

She had felt her heart pound as he promised, "I'll write."

Phillip drew her to her feet. 'I'm sorry. I'm terribly sorry. You aren't hurt, are you?" He held her off with both hands, still clutching her wrists as she mutely shook her head. "Come in for dinner with us. We just arrived, and the dining room is still open."

Some of Honor's composure returned. "I have already eaten, Mr. Travis. Besides" — she glanced down at her white shirtwaist and plain dark skirt — "I'm not dressed for dinner."

"You look fine." He turned to a girl in the party. "Babs, tell Honor — Miss Brooks — she looks fine."

He didn't seem to catch the scowl on the pretty redhead's face as her social breeding forced her to respond. "Of course. Do come in for a cup of coffee, at least."

Phillip led her to a table. "Everyone, this is Honor Brooks." His ardent gaze made her uncomfortable. "She is the girl I told you all about, the one from San Francisco. Or did I? Anyway, now that I've found her again, I won't let her get away so easily!"

In spite of herself, Honor blushed. He made it sound as if she had once escaped him when the opposite had been true. He was the one who had promised to write and never followed through.

The blush didn't escape Phillip. "A girl who blushes in this day and age? Will wonders never cease!" He waved a lazy arm toward his friends. "Mark, Cecile, Jon, Patti; you've already met Babs." There was something in his voice demanding recognition, but Honor had never heard of them before.

Phillip surveyed her with keen eyes. "When did you come? You've never been here before, have you?"

Honor was aware of her position in the split second before answering. She was also aware of how painfully crumpled her shirtwaist must be and how her hair was falling all over the place. "I'm here with Mr. and Mrs. Stone. He is an attorney in San Francisco."

Phillip's eyes widened in admiration. "I'll say he is! Everyone has heard of Ben Stone. I didn't know you knew him."

"I am his daughter's governess." Honor didn't miss the glance of scorn from Babs. Her chin came up. "After Granny died and when Keith didn't come home from France —" Suddenly the cloud of smoke around the

10

table got to her. What was she doing here with this group of people? She had no part in their way of life. Phillip was the only one not smoking. Drinks were being poured.

She stumbled to her feet, throat thick from emotion and smoke. "Thank you for the coffee. I'll excuse myself now."

"Oh, I say, Miss Brooks!" Phillip trailed her to the door. "I'm sorry — about your grandmother and Keith, that is. I didn't know."

His sympathy was so sincere that she found herself smiling up at him through the gathering mist. "Thank you, and good night."

"You aren't going to run off from me, are you?" he demanded. "Not just when we've found each other again?"

Honor's heart leaped in spite of herself. The memory of his charm hadn't done him justice. Phillip Travis held an appeal for her that couldn't be denied. But what was he doing in such a crowd? Evidently he knew them well; they were his friends. He hadn't been like that in San Francisco. There had been no mention of smoking or drinking. He had called at her home and taken her to church. Sometimes they had taken long walks. Had he changed so much, or had she been wrong about him?

Phillip totally misunderstood her silence. "It isn't because you're working, is it?" He grinned. "I always thought I'd try it. They tell me it's fascinating." A hoot of derision came from the table they had just left, and Honor's face flamed. This was no place for her. Evidently Phillip was a member of the "pleasure seekers," or "parasites," as Mr. Stone classified such people.

"Thank you again for the coffee." Before Phillip could detain her she slipped away, but not before overhearing Babs cattily remark, "That girl walks like royalty."

Honor couldn't help smiling grimly to herself. Why not? Her family might not have been rich, but they were honorable. Why shouldn't she walk proudly?

Yet as she prepared for bed with a last glance out the window toward the canyon, her heart beat faster. Phillip was so handsome. There had been gentleness in his touch and voice as he spoke of Granny and Keith. For a moment it overruled the indolent arrogance she had sensed in him, an arrogance that was not in keeping with the long-held image in her heart. Did he still own the ranch, Casa del Sol? Her face cleared a bit. That might explain it. Perhaps he was an important man here in northern Arizona.

She remembered stumbling home, anxious to tell Granny about Phillip's proposal. She could still see the troubled look in the blue eyes, the lined face surrounded by curly white hair.

"Is he a Christian, Honor?"

"Who cares? I'm not, either."

Granny's gnarled hands lay still in her aproned lap. "I pray every day you will be."

Remorse filled her, mingled with anger. "I thought you liked Phillip!"

"He is courteous, charming, and utterly godless."

"That's not fair!" Honor's white face had waved battle flags of color. "After all, I met him in church."

Granny suddenly looked old. "Anyone can go to church, Honor. If he hasn't trusted the Lord Jesus Christ in his heart, his going to church doesn't mean anything." Granny's next words rang like a prophecy. "I believe someday you will accept our Lord, who has waited for you so long. I don't know what it's going to take to make you see you can't outrun God. When you do, if you are married to an unbeliever, your life will be misery." She softly quoted, " 'Be ye not unequally yoked together with unbelievers: for —' "

" '— for what fellowship hath righteousness with unrighteousness? and what communion hath light with darkness?' " Honor finished bitterly, noting the surprise in Granny's eyes. "Oh, yes, Granny, I know Second Corinthians six fourteen — you've made sure I know Scripture well. Too bad it just 'didn't take.' " She ignored the pain in Granny's face. "I'm going to wait for Phillip Travis. Besides, if God does catch up with me, there's no reason He can't catch Phillip, too."

In the following weeks, when no letter had come, Granny never mentioned Phillip. Neither did Honor. A new fear had touched her. If Phillip were dead she would never know. Should she write Casa del Sol? No. Phillip had not gone home before being shipped overseas. They wouldn't know she existed. Phillip had said he had one brother and seemed disinclined to say more, so she hadn't questioned him.

So long ago! Almost another lifetime. In the years since she first met Phillip she had been too busy and harried to meet other eligible men. Since coming to the Stones she had never gone to church. Granny was gone. She would not be a hypocrite. It couldn't be that her half-promise to wait for Phillip had haunted her, could it?

In weakness of spirit, Honor faced it squarely. Ridiculous as it might seem, she had been bound to Phillip Travis. Until she knew for sure he was dead, she had not been able to accept another in his place.

Finally the excitement of the trip and the fresh air did its work. Honor could stay awake no longer.

She was awakened by a broad ray of sunlight crossing her room and Heather standing by her bedside.

"Miss Honor, just see!"

Heather's face was barely visible above the largest bouquet of flowers she had ever seen, eyes sparkling as Honor protested, "There must be a mistake! No one would be sending me flowers."

"It says H-O-N-O-R," Heather pointed out proudly, glad to show off her newly gained ability to recognize letters.

Honor took the flowers from her small charge and put them on the table. American Beauty roses, a wealth of them, catching the sunlight into their depths, filled the room with fragrance.

"Great Scot!" Laurene Stone had wandered into Honor's room. "Where did those come from?" She looked at Honor suspiciously.

"I don't know." Honor's clear gaze met Mrs. Stone's. "Oh, here's a card."

> HAVE BREAKFAST WITH ME, OR I WILL
> THINK YOU HAVEN'T FORGIVEN ME
> FOR RUNNING YOU DOWN. I'LL BE IN
> THE LOBBY WHENEVER YOU'RE READY.
> Phillip

Honor could feel her face heating as she silently passed the note to Mrs. Stone.

"Who is this Phillip?"

"Phillip Travis. He knocked me down when I was coming upstairs last night. I met him a few years ago when he was stationed in San Francisco."

"Philip Travis! Not the one who owns that fabulous ranch here in Arizona — some Spanish name meaning sun?" New respect shone in Mrs. Stone's face. "How did you ever meet *him?*"

"He came to church with a group of soldiers. I suppose they were lonely for home." A reminiscent smile curved Honor's finely carved lips.

"Well, what are you waiting for? Get ready and meet him for breakfast."

Honor's memories faded. "I can't do that! He's here with a group. Besides" — she smiled at Heather — "we have all kinds of things to do today."

"He can join us for breakfast. I'm sure Ben will enjoy meeting him. Get Heather ready, and we'll meet downstairs as soon as possible." Mrs. Stone ended the discussion by sweeping out the door.

Honor stared openmouthed after her employer's wife. Well! It certainly made a difference whom she knew. Mischief briefly touched her face, but she busied herself arraying Heather in a charming red dress, then quickly got ready herself. She hesitated, trying to decide what to wear, then firmly pushed aside the party dresses and settled for another shirtwaist, sparkling white and crisp. Her brown hair had been brushed and shone by the time she and Heather descended the stairs.

The Stones were already there, seated in a sunny corner. So was Phillip. Honor couldn't help the soft color that mounted to her hairline as she joined them.

Laurene Stone showed no traces of ill health this morning. "Honor, as you can see we went ahead and introduced ourselves. It's so important making good contacts right away when one goes into a strange land."

Honor disciplined a laugh at Mrs. Stone's implications. She didn't dare look at Phillip. But a few minutes later she raised her head. "Thank you for the roses, Mr. Travis." In the time since she had learned Phillip really was an important person, she had also decided it had better be "Mr. Travis." She had no right to presume on former friendship.

Phillip would have none of it. "Make it Phillip, all of you." His glance included the Stones but returned to Honor. "Perhaps I'd better introduce myself a little more, Mrs. Stone. My brother and I own a cattle ranch just north of Flagstaff. He actually does most of the work, but I —"

"A real ranch? With cowboys?" Heather broke her usual silence around strangers, with a frankly hero-worshiping look.

"Real cowboys." His smile at the little girl was endearing. The next moment he leaned toward her. "Miss Heather, how would you like to visit that ranch when you leave here?"

"Oh, Daddy, Mother, could we?"

"Really, Mr. Travis — Phillip." Ben Stone's face was dark with annoyance. "We have barely met. Heather shouldn't have hinted."

"I didn't hint, Daddy. He 'vited us." Heather's lip trembled, and her clear eyes filled with tears.

"That's right." Phillip had never been more charming. "I really mean it. Casa del Sol is a sprawling hacienda with room for a dozen people. We love company. Our housekeeper, Mama Rosa, likes nothing better than cooking for a housefull."

Honor was amazed at how quickly Mr. Stone capitulated. "If it isn't an imposition. I really have always wanted to visit a working cattle ranch." He grinned. "My doctor told us to get out of doors. I'm sure he'd approve!"

"Then it's settled. Whenever you're ready to leave the canyon, let me know. I'll go on ahead and get ready for you." He turned back to Heather. "We even have ponies just your size."

She smiled delightedly as he added, "Oh, by the way, you must take the mule trip into the canyon while you're here."

"Not I!" Laurene Stone threw her hands up in mock horror. "I'm going to spend my time right here in this lodge. Some of our San Francisco friends are coming, and we already have bridge games arranged. The rest of you can take care of the outdoor life." She lifted one shoulder daintily. "I'm sure my husband and Honor will want to go. I can keep Heather with me."

"Oh, Mama!" Heather's face fell with disappointment. "Can't I ride a mule?"

Again Honor was impressed by Phillip Travis's quick evaluation of the situation. He leaned across to Heather once more. "Those mules are pretty big, Heather. How about riding down the trail with me? I've been several times, and it's always a little lonely on the mule's back. You can fit in the saddle just in front of me."

Mr. Stone looked worried. "Are these donkeys safe?"

"Not donkeys, sir. Mules. Our donkeys are smaller and known as burros, or 'Arizona Nightingales.'" Phillip laughed. "You won't believe it when you hear them bray. The mules that go down in the canyon are trained beyond belief. The trainers flap slickers at them, do everything in the world to startle them before they are even allowed on the trail.

"You know, the little burros have been given a rather unique legend." An unusual softness crept into his voice. "It is said Jesus put a cross on the back of each burro as a reward for service. The old prospectors believe it. If you look at a burro's shoulders, you'll see that cross. Some are plainer than others, but there is a more or less distinct marking on every burro's back."

He paused, smiling again. "Our burros have saved countless lives. They are not only good pets but the prospector's best friend. They are also sturdy. Now *mules* are different — ornery. Wait until you get on a trail edge and your mule decides to reach over the side to chomp grass. I do believe the good Lord created them with a sense of humor!"

Honor's eyes sparkled. Had she been wrong about Phillip and his friends? He spoke so easily of the legend and the good Lord's creation. He was quite a man. The man for her? The thought was enough to fill her face with a shine and set her heart pounding.

The rest of the meal passed swiftly. Heather's laughter rang out at the witty remarks of Phillip, who seemed to take delight in talking with her. When they finished he said, "I don't want to intrude, but since I do know the canyon, would you consider taking me on as a guide?"

Even Honor was touched by the wistfulness in his question, and the keen glance of Mr. Stone seemed to be weighing Phillip's sincerity.

"I really mean it. My crowd has been here so often the thrill is gone. It will be like seeing it for the first time, showing you everything there is to see."

"We would be happy to have you with us for whatever time you have free," Mr. Stone told him.

"Then I'll be with you all the time!" His dark eyes twinkled. "Just wait and see!"

Phillip became the perfect host. First he introduced Laurene to several avid card players he knew. By the time her San Francisco friends arrived, she was already part of a well-established circle that widened to include them. Her reaction to the Grand Canyon had been a shiver and, "What a terrible hole in the ground!" Then she settled into a daily routine of sleeping late, breakfasting in bed, and meeting with friends for cards, followed by a leisurely preparation and donning of exquisite gowns for dinner each night.

Ben Stone lost his paleness in the hours he spent outdoors. Sometimes with just Heather, more often as part of the foursome with Honor and Phillip, he radiated happiness. Once when Honor found him alone on the canyon rim as sunset threw mocking banners into the sky to reflect on the panorama before them, she tried to thank him.

"I am the one in debt, Honor." He waved into the ever-changing shadows of night creeping toward the canyon. "I didn't realize how I needed to get away — until I used you as an excuse to come!" A look of reverence shown through his level gaze. "No one could look on such a scene and not believe in a Creator, could they?"

"No, Mr. Stone." But he had already turned back to the canyon, now murky in its depths, leaving Honor feeling she had been forgotten.

Honor was free for a time each afternoon when Heather took a nap and after she had gone to bed. Phillip gradually filled those moments until it became a usual thing for him to be waiting when she came down. Several days after they arrived he asked her if she would walk with him. Something in his look stirred her. The afternoon was bright. Birds called, and squirrels ran along the canyon edge, looking for bits of dropped food.

Honor's hand trembled as she dressed carefully and brushed her bright hair into waves. Was the pale blue dress too fussy? When she had told Phillip the clothes were "made over," he had covered his surprise by commenting how clever she was with a needle.

As they skirted the outcroppings of rock to find a quiet place in full view of the canyon but not the hotel, Honor noted how quiet Phillip had grown. Was there some significance in this particular invitation?

"Honor, will you be my girl?"

She was speechless.

"I mean it." He doggedly forced her to look at him, compelling with his eyes. "You know I was in love with you in San Francisco. I even asked you if you would wait for me. Don't you remember?"

She could only remain silent, unspoken words dying on her lips.

"I know I treated you shabbily, going off and not writing after I promised. But Honor, I've had a lot of time since then to consider." He looked deep into her eyes. "I love you, Honor." Without asking permission he caught her close and tried to kiss her.

She sprang back. "Why did you do that? Why did you have to spoil everything?" Vexation steadied her trembling lips. "We barely know each other!"

"Don't you believe in love at first sight?"

She wanted to shout no, but couldn't do it. She remembered the feeling she had had when they first met, the same feeling that had intensified beyond belief since meeting him again at the canyon. "How can I take you seriously? You don't even know me, not really."

"I know you well enough to know I'm going to get ahead of Mark and Jon." His jaw set stubbornly. "I saw how they watched you, even the night you came. I'm putting my bid in first."

"I'm not up for grabs, you know."

His mouth twisted in an odd smile. "You think I don't know that? I'm twenty-nine years old, Honor Brooks. I've known a lot of women. You think I can't tell the difference between real and imitation? You're what my grandmother calls 'a real lady.' There aren't many of them around these days." He pushed back a lock of hair. "I don't want second best."

From the corridors of memory came Honor's own words, *I'll never settle for second best*. It brought hot blood to her face. "I'm sorry, Phillip. You have your friends. I'm here working, a vacation job. I'm not looking for summer romance."

"And you think I am?" A surge of color filled his own face. He gritted his teeth, obviously trying to control anger as he gazed across the canyon,

seeming to find in its depths strength to calm himself. "What right have you to judge me? I've waited all my life for a girl like you — and that's what you are, a girl, in spite of being almost twenty-four, as you told me. I'll wager you haven't lived those twenty-four years without getting some knowledge of human nature. I fell for you when I first met you. Then with the war and all, you slipped back in memory." His voice deepened. "Then I came here — and found you. When I picked you up from the floor I fell for you — hard. I'd begun to think I'd never find the girl I wanted to marry. Sure, I've had all kinds of girls and women, even considered marrying a few of them, but never did. Men have ideal women, too, you know." The mobile mouth curved in a smile. "If you can honestly tell me you felt nothing when I picked you up, I'll apologize and get lost."

Honor couldn't speak. Only the strength of his hold kept her from falling. When he had spoken of wondering if the "right" person would ever appear, she had identified with him in a quick rush of sympathy. Was her heart trying to tell her something? Was she stubbornly refusing to listen? Had Phillip really been searching — for her?

"You can't do it, can you? Then think about this." Gently he drew her to him, kissing her on the lips. Startled, she broke from him like a shy fawn and fled back the way they had come, only to be followed by his exultant cry, "I'm going to marry you, Miss Honor Brooks — and you're going to like it!"

When she reached her room she was breathless. Tears stood in her eyes, brilliant, refusing to fall. Futilely she bathed her hot face, demanding of her image, "How did he dare?" Yet the gentle touch of his kiss stayed on her lips even after she had furiously scrubbed them. The walls of the room she had found so charming now closed in on her. She must get free. She caught up her sweater and slipped out, carefully checking the lobby to make sure she was unseen. In her walks between El Tovar and the canyon rim, Honor had noticed a secluded spot. She headed for it. Would the canyon reach out to her, slow her whirling emotions?

"What if he meant it?" Honor gazed into the chasm, unaware of anything except the lingering pressure of Phillip's lips on her own. "I love him!"

A cloud flitted across the sun, sending a curious mist to the canyon. To Honor's excited fancy Granny's face seemed to float there with accusing eyes. Her warning about marrying any unbeliever rang in Honor's heart. With it came the memory of Phillip as he had been that first night in the dining room — surrounded by smoke and the tangy odor of liquor. Her heart quailed. In spite of not acknowledging Christ as Lord, Honor abhorred cheapness, and to her smoking and drinking fell in that category.

"But Phillip was not smoking or drinking," she protested brokenly. The mist disappeared, and her rebellion burst its bonds. All Honor's accumulated misery during the hard years gathered in one great force, just as the massive clouds overhead mustered forces to batter the earth. She sprang to her feet. "I will not give him up! I know now I loved Phillip even when he told me good-bye. It's been there all the time. That's why I have felt bound."

A crack of lightning followed by a burst of cannonlike thunder halted the words, striking fear into her heart. She would not bow before it. "Where were You when I gave You a chance, God? Where was the love You told of in those verses I learned when I promised to try and know You better if you'd spare Keith? Or when I begged for a job and only got one by chance? Everything I've ever loved has been taken away. I will not give up Philip!"

She raised her face in defiance, as if to challenge the very storm itself. It had increased in intensity, pelting the earth with raindrops the size of hailstones, kicking up dust and turning it to red mud. "If Granny was right, if misery is ahead —" she caught her breath at the possibility and again hardened her voice "— I'll pay the price for the happiness I'll have in between."

She sank to the ground, not heeding the violent storm soaking her, turning her into a muddy, crumpled figure. For better or worse, she had chosen. Why should another verse learned years before haunt her at this moment? It was Joshua 24:15 — *"Choose you this day whom ye will serve . . . but as for me and my house, we will serve the LORD."* She impatiently refused to admit her slight hesitation, replacing it with Phillip's laughing face. He would ask her again to marry him. Next time there would be no hesitation. After all, hadn't he said he'd known all kinds of girls and women?

Some of her triumph faded. Had he kissed those others the way he did her? She would never tell him he was the only one who had kissed her, but she was glad. She had kept her promise and waited; he had come differently than expected. With a smile, she returned to the present. If she had wanted solitude at the canyon, she had it. No one would be out in this storm.

But she had been wrong. A dark shape hurried toward her. "Honor! I've looked everywhere for you." His voice was filled with fear, for her, she knew. Suddenly all her troubles were gone. Phillip had come for her.

"I'm here, Phillip. You've found me."

He peered into her face, seeing the way it was turned to him.

"Honor!" The next moment she was caught close in an embrace that deepened as she sighed and relaxed against him. Surely it must be right when she felt so happy. She lifted her mouth, and in the storm on the canyon's edge, returned Phillip's kiss. She didn't care if the storm never let up. She had fought so long against the fact of her family's death. It was sheer heaven to lean on someone stronger.

This time it was Phillip who broke away. "Honor — you care. To kiss me like that — a girl like you — it must mean you care." He caught her in his arms, carrying her slight frame, running back through the rain as if he would never let her go.

"Put me down, Phillip! What will they all say?" She struggled furiously, but he rained more kisses on her wet mouth and hair.

"Who cares? We'll announce our engagement at dinner tonight." He set her down just inside the door, still with his arms around her, his face lit up with triumph.

"Engagement!" A cold chill went through her. "Phillip, you're mad. We can't announce an engagement now."

Doubt crept into his face, and his reply was cynical. "Then you're like the rest of them? Lead a man on and toss him aside?"

It hit her cruelly. "Phillip! Of course I'm not like that. It's just too soon — no one would ever understand. I'm not sure I understand myself." She blushed. "What would the Stones think?"

His face softened, and he took both her hands in his. "It's all right, Honor. I'm sorry." One lock of wet hair dangled in front of his eyes, making him look like a truant schoolboy. "You're absolutely right. We'll wait and announce it at the end of your vacation here."

"We'll see." She knew her color heightened under his ardent gaze. "Now if you don't mind, I'd like to get into some other clothes."

Phillip threw back his head and laughed. "You look like a drowned squirrel. Run along, my dear, and meet me back down here when you've changed."

The glow and tingle of Honor's skin wasn't all caused by her stinging shower. Phillip loved her. Phillip Travis loved her! She raced through her dressing. She mustn't wait one minute longer than necessary. She wanted every bit of time with him she could find. To think, a few weeks ago she had been a poor, forsaken person feeling sorry for herself. Today she was loved — and loved in return. Memories of her parents' happy years glorified her feeling for Phillip.

"Tell me about your home," she urged as they sat together on a big couch in the lobby later. They had eluded his friends, who were going to a

dance. Phillip had wickedly whispered, "I don't want any man's arms around you but mine." Honor's heart had pounded. Dancing was another thing she didn't do.

Now Phillip relaxed against the couch and stared into the huge fireplace with its dancing flames. "I suppose the story goes back to my great-grandfather. He married a wealthy Spanish girl, and they acquired Casa del Sol."

"House of the Sun," she translated.

"You know Spanish?" He sounded surprised.

"No, I — I remembered." She wouldn't tell him how she had treasured the phrase all the long, lonely months after he went away.

"Funny, I love it even though I'm not there much. Too busy having a good time. Now that you'll be there with me —" His look said volumes.

Honor hastily changed the subject. "Phillip, Babs looked at me tonight as if she hated me."

"Babs and I grew up together, had a lot of fun. I even would have married her a few years ago. She turned me down cold. Now if she wants me back it's just too bad."

She was shocked by his callousness but soothed as he added, "Babs and I are alike — too selfish, demanding. I won't be that way with you." There was an air of humility about him that Honor sensed was foreign to his nature.

"I'm glad you told me, Phillip. Now let's forget it. If she didn't care a few years ago, she probably doesn't care now." But when Honor entered her room that night, lips still tingling from Phillip's goodnight kiss, she gasped in dismay.

Seated in the chair by the window, Babs waited, enmity in every fold of her exquisite green gown.

"Do come in." Her voice was mocking. "It *is* your room."

"What are you doing here?" Honor barely had breath to ask. She had been shaken to turn from Phillip and suddenly meet the girl he had once loved.

"I thought we should perhaps have a little talk. You seem to be occupied during the day and evening, so I came here." She motioned insolently to the bed. "You might as well sit down, I intend to be here for some time."

Honor wondered if her shaking knees would carry her that far. "If you are going to tell me all about you and Phillip, you don't need to bother. I already know. He told me."

"Did he indeed! I doubt that he told you *all* about us." The green eyes glittered like algae in a lake, murky and treacherous. "Did he tell you that we have been engaged for years?" She held out a long white hand with blood-red nails. A huge emerald winked a wicked eye from the third finger.

Honor felt as if she had been stabbed. "Engaged?"

"Of course." Was pity mixed with anger in the other's eyes? "Don't be a little fool. Every time we go on a jaunt Phillip finds a girl. Not always one like you, I'll have to admit. But when vacation's over, he forgets. Didn't he do just that when he left you in San Francisco?" She hardened again. "He knows we will marry when I get ready. Maybe even soon."

"I don't believe you." The sinking feeling in Honor's heart belied her words.

"I suggest you think about it. Don't rush into anything. Once Phillip gets away from the canyon and you, well, he will laugh at his romantic little interlude." Babs rose, magnificently stretching to full height like a sleek cat. "Let him go. It's for your own good."

Strength born of fear flowed through Honor, as she remembered little things about Philip. She must defend herself — and him. "Phillip will be going first. He has asked the Stones and me to visit Casa del Sol. Even if they have to leave, Phillip says Mama Rosa will chaperone me."

"You can bet your sweet life on that!"

Honor ignored the bitter interruption. "We won't get married until we have time to know each other. When we do, I'll be Mrs. Phillip Travis, and nothing can change it!"

"I wouldn't count on it." Babs glided toward the door. "I wonder what Phillip's brother will say about you." Her laugh brought color to Honor's face. "He's a hundred years older than Phillip in outlook."

"That's why Phillip is going first." Honor wished she had bitten her tongue when she saw the triumph on Bab's face. "Phillip is sincere —"

"I thought so." The redhead pounced on the first half of Honor's statement. "As far as sincere — Phillip wouldn't recognize the meaning of the word if it bit him on his handsome nose. If you expect sincerity, you'd better run as far and fast as you can from Phillip Travis." Bab's eyes shifted, then fixed their cold stare on Honor. "You're one of those do-gooders, aren't you? Then don't deliberately walk into a lion's den." She must have caught Honor's look of surprise. "I went to church — a long time ago, before I met Phillip. Don't think you can change him."

Honor felt herself stiffen. "I'm sure your advice is well-meant, but I believe I know what the real Phillip Travis is like. I am going to marry him someday."

Honor could see emotions warring in Babs's face — pity, disgust, hatred, contempt. Pity won. "Then, my dear little governess, may the gods have mercy on you. You'll need it."

The door opened and closed behind her, leaving Honor alone — more alone than she had been even waiting for Keith to come home. The storm in the canyon was as nothing compared to the storm in her heart. Incredible as it seemed, Babs did love Phillip. Then why hadn't she married him when she had the chance? Honor shivered, remembering the callous way Phillip had spoken of Babs. What if he were to say the same about her? No! Her shocked, white face in the mirror denied the traitorous thought. Phillip loved her. Yet hadn't he loved Babs when he once asked her to marry him?

Minutes ticked into hours, and the questions did not cease. Once Honor thought of digging out the Bible Granny had given her so long ago, but discarded the idea. She had made her choice, forfeited her right to expect God's help. She might not be a Christian, but she did know Scripture, and God didn't bless those who deliberately turned away from Him. With the first touch of dawn she slipped to the stairs. She would get away from her accusing walls.

As she descended the stairs she heard the clink of silver and laughter from those who were preparing the dining room for breakfast. For a moment she envied the happy workers who came from all over the United States to work with the summer crowds at the canyon. The next moment she slipped outside and ran to the canyon's edge.

"It's unbelievable!" A small squirrel eyed her in alarm and scuttled away. Honor's eyes were no longer heavy. The early morning canyon mists had driven away need for sleep.

How could it be so different, bathed in the almost-ethereal glow of morning? She had seen it in daylight, darkness, storm. Now it had changed completely. No wonder she had read that she wouldn't see the canyon, but experience it.

Honor pulled her cape closer against the chill morning air, watching lazy patches of mist yield to the insistent sun. A tug within reminded her of the struggle from the night before. Some of the beauty dimmed. Why couldn't she put aside the childhood teachings now she had made her choice? Must they forever haunt her?

The sun burst over the canyon wall after sending heralding streaks to announce its arrival. "If only Keith were here!" she cried to the warming rays. But Keith wasn't here. He would never see the canyon. Her face hardened. If he had come back, perhaps she could have accepted the Lord

he believed in so strongly. But not now. She had her life to live, and the splendor around her showed that the world could still be beautiful. She would find strength for whatever might come, but not through Christ.

"Good morning, my darling."

Honor whirled from the canyon, feeling betraying color flooding her face. Phillip was standing a few feet away. His appearance shocked her. Where was the frightening man Babs had described? This was Phillip, eyes soft, hand outstretched — the same Phillip who had come for her in the storm the day before.

"I thought I would find you here." He led her a little apart from the other sightseers, seeking privacy beneath the spreading branches of a tall, gnarled tree. "You're even more beautiful in the morning sunlight than you are drenched from a storm!"

Relief filled Honor until she would have fallen if he had not held her arm. Still she could not speak. It was the same as coming from the storm into a lighted room — protected, safe, secure. She raised her face to his.

"You're the sweetest girl on earth, Honor." His husky whisper brought her back.

"And you're the most wonderful man." She was rewarded by a look of almost-humility in his face.

"I don't deserve you, you know."

Honor felt a strange surge of power and covered it by agreeing. "Of course not!"

Phillips' expression changed to match her gaiety. "You rascal! Let's get some breakfast. We're signed up for the mule trip into the canyon, and it will be leaving soon."

"We are what?" Honor's eyes filled with horror. "You won't get me on any mule going down there!" Her scornful finger indicated a narrow, winding path leading down along the gigantic rock walls, melting into infinity around a bend.

"Of course I will. Ben and Heather can hardly wait to get started. I thought you were excited about going."

"I was," she confessed in a small voice, "until I saw the trail."

"You'll be fine." Phillip innocently added, "Even Babs went last year, and you know she isn't about to go in any danger."

She eyed him suspiciously, then relented. "If I fall in the canyon it will be on your conscience."

"You don't really think I'd take you where it was unsafe, do you?" Phillip's gaze settled her more than anything else could have done. "You'll

be as safe as home in your rocking chair. Ben will be right behind you; Heather and I will be in front of you.''

But when breakfast was over and they were ready to go she couldn't help trying once more, appealing to Phillip when the others weren't listening. ''Are you sure you want me to go? What if I faint?'' She didn't tell him she had never fainted in her entire life. ''I'd slow down the whole group.''

''Look at me!'' Heather piped up, already seated on the mule Phillip would ride. She looked so tiny Honor had another qualm. ''She'll be all right, won't she?''

''With me here?'' Phillip just smiled. ''Simple as riding a rocker.'' He helped her mount a shaggy beast who turned and looked her over, then disinterestedly went back to cropping the sparse grass by the trail. She found herself patting his shoulders timidly, wishing he were a little burro with a cross, instead of just an ornery mule.

''We won't stay overnight this time,'' Phillip told her. ''Next time, after we're married —''

''Next time!'' Honor glared. ''If you think there will be a —''

''As I was saying.'' He flashed his famous grin. ''They are talking of building a real accommodation in the bottom of the canyon. Phantom Ranch, I think it will be called. But this time we'll just stop for lunch, then climb back out this afternoon. We go down several thousand feet. It will be hot.'' He looked approvingly at her lightweight jacket, which could be removed. ''It's going to be a real pleasure educating you in all the things you've never done before, Honor.''

Honor's face flamed. Would she always blindly follow his lead, trailing along as she was now trailing on her mule? Her natural common sense and good humor took over.

So what if she did? She'd lead him, too — but in more subtle ways. She clutched her reins, eyes sparkling, and looked straight ahead.

''Don't look down,'' the guide warned as they rounded a hairpin curve what seemed like eons later. Honor had slid off her jacket, and the warm sun hit her back with its rays.

''Close your eyes if you like, and don't be scared,'' Phillip called.

What now? Honor had swallowed her heart countless times already. One by one the mules ahead slowed, then doubled back on themselves to disappear around the hairpin bend. Closer and closer Honor came until she reached the edge of eternity. Her eyes were fixed straight ahead as she had been told — until Old Baldy's neck shot downward, over the edge of the rim. Involuntarily Honor glanced down, following the line of ears with

her gaze, and froze. It was terrible. It was grand. It was the worst thing that had ever happened to her.

"You're doin' fine, miss." The guide's brown face split into a white smile. "Forgot to tell you. Old Baldy always likes to crop a little grass right here." He didn't seem to notice how the reins were being held in a death grip that whitened her knuckles. "Just let him eat a bit and he'll make the turn just fine."

Honor couldn't have answered if her life had depended on it — and maybe it did. She just sat. Old Baldy finished his leisurely munching, turned, and followed the others. The weakness seeping through her almost unseated Honor, but with trembling fingers she managed to clutch the reins and smile weakly. She had kept herself from screaming. Now she even managed to smile at Heather.

From that point on, nothing frightened Honor. She had faced the worst with silence. Even the splash of Old Baldy's hooves as he forged through a creek at the bottom of the canyon didn't daunt her. When she fell off her mule into Phillip's arms, it was triumphantly. He need never know the last mile of trail had been managed by sheer determination.

"Well, Honor, wasn't it worth it?"

She gazed around her, really seeing the canyon bottom for the first time. The valley floor lay before her, an oasis of lush greenness. The burbling Colorado River ran red and sluggish. She was glad she had not had to cross that!

"It's —" She couldn't find words.

Phillip tenderly smoothed back clinging tendrils of damp hair from her hot face. "I know. That's why I come here."

Again she was aware of depths within him that did not ordinarily show. Her heart gave a great leap of joy. Surely he would understand and accept the way of life she had chosen, once they were married and she was able to tell him the happiness she had found in it.

"I feel like a glutton," Honor confessed later as she surveyed the shambles of her plate. "I didn't realize anyone could be so hungry!"

"Remarkable how fresh air and exercise can work up an appetite, isn't it?" The grizzled guide had seated himself next to Honor. "Nothing ever tastes so good as outdoor food. Say, if you're going to be around long, you should plan on some of the other canyon trips. You did a good job today. I'd say you could even tackle some of the rough trails."

"Rough trails! You mean this one isn't?" Honor was astonished.

"Of course not. This one's for beginners and tenderfeet." The guide turned away and didn't catch Honor's expression.

Phillip did, and laughed. "Don't look so shocked, Honor. This is Arizona."

All the way through the rest time and back up the canyon she thought of what Phillip had said. Arizona. It was everything she had dreamed of and more. Soft color stole to her hairline. "Phillip, when — when we're married, would you show me Arizona? All of it?"

"Fervently." The meaning in his one word sent a glow through her. What a change it was, being cared for and protected. The contrast between these past few days and her bleak life since the death of her parents brought a quick rush of emotion to Honor. How could she doubt Phillip in any way when he was so ready to please her?

By the time they got back it was growing a bit dusky. This time Honor didn't fall off Old Baldy, she had to be helped off. "What's wrong with my legs?"

"You're going to be pretty stiff young lady," the guide warned her. "Take a hot bath and get to bed early. You'll be hobbling a bit tomorrow."

The dire prediction came true. Not only was she hobbling, but Honor also found it took her three tries to get out of bed! Only Phillip's note telling her he'd wait and have breakfast when she did spurred her on.

"Miss Honor, are you going to marry Mr. Travis?" Heather's face was innocent in front of the huge bow in her blonde hair.

Before Honor could reply, Phillip said, "I certainly hope so."

"Well!" Mrs. Stone looked as if the breath had been knocked from her. "Why haven't you told us, Honor?"

Phillip came to her rescue, adroitly drawing attention away from the scarlet cheeks above her high-necked white shirtwaist. "She was afraid you'd think it a little sudden."

"Isn't it?"

Honor caught Ben Stone's frown and found her tongue. "I knew Phillip years ago — he was in San Francisco —" She sounded incoherent even to herself. "I guess I never forgot him, and —"

Mrs. Stone cut her off by congratulating Phillip. But Mr. Stone whispered. "Are you happy, Honor?"

"Yes." Joy suffused her face with even more color. "He's everything I ever wanted." Was that a disappointed look in her employer's eyes? Honor pushed the thought aside. How could anyone be disappointed with Phillip?

There was something she must determine now the engagement had been announced. In their favorite spot by the canyon Honor watched Phillip teasing a frisky squirrel, wondering how to approach him.

"What are you thinking?" he demanded.

It was the perfect opening. "How glad I am I found you again."

A dark flush stained his face. "Was it you who found me? I thought I found you."

"What difference does it make?"

"None, to me." His arms reached for her, but she leaned back.

"Phillip do —" her voice trembled "— do you care dreadfully for drinking and all that?"

He sat up abruptly and stared at her. "What are you? A preacher?"

It was her turn to flush. "No. I just wondered." She took a deep breath. "I just don't believe in those things." Her voice was small. "I don't know how well I'll fit in your world — or you in mine."

"I'm a heathen, Honor." He didn't catch her involuntary look of dismay. A steel hand seemed to squeeze her heart. She had known he was no Christian and accepted it. But this —

"Do you believe in God?"

"Doesn't everyone?" He waved an indolent hand toward the canyon. "It took a Master Plan to build that."

Honor turned her head to hide her feelings, scarcely able to sort them out. Why did she feel disappointed at his statement? What did she have to lose when she had already put God aside?

"I don't care about drinking when I have you. You can do with me what you like. I'm weak with the crowd. You're seeing the best of me here."

In spite of the heat waves bouncing off the colorful canyon walls Honor felt a chill trickle down her spine. "You have everything, Phillip. Why follow the crowd?"

A somber shadow crossed his face. "Because of my brother. If he weren't so competent maybe I would be stronger. He thinks it's easier to do everything himself than wait for me to do it. He's right." The shadow deepened. "Don't get me wrong. I love him more than anyone on earth except you, but if he would shove me out and tell me to sink or swim I would be better off."

"What a terrible thing to say!"

"Is it?" Phillip's face contorted. "Let's forget it, kiddo. We'll be happy like they are." He pointed to a bird singing his heart out to his mate.

Honor's throat constricted as she matched the change of mood. Now was no time to preach. Deep inside resentment of the way Phillip's brother treated him began to grow. Was he an ogre? Even Babs had

said he was a hundred years older in outlook. He must be an old fogey, set in his ways. She could just see him: burly; a little uncouth, perhaps, in spite of being the charming Phillip's brother.

Her lips set. She would not build up dislike before meeting him. But once she was established at Casa del Sol she intended to have a little talk with Phillip's brother.

Incredible as it seemed, summer was nearly over. Mr. Stone reluctantly told them at breakfast one morning, "My business is piling up back home." He looked across at Phillip. "I don't want to rush you, but if you still want us to visit your ranch, it will have to be soon."

Phillip rose to the occasion gracefully. "Of course I do! I'll go ahead myself, maybe even leave today. We'll be waiting for you when you come." The look he gave Honor brought flags flying in her cheeks. That afternoon while Heather napped, Phillip led Honor to their private spot by the canyon's edge.

"It's only the beginning, you know." He looked deep into her eyes, and she bit back the impulse to deny it. Ever since she had known he was to leave and go ahead without her a strange — was it premonition? — had filled her. Perhaps it was because she had overheard Babs say, "About time we were leaving, old thing. It's getting a little tiresome here this time. I'll ride with you, of course."

Phillip evidently didn't sense how lost Honor felt. He was going on about what a wonderful time they'd have at Casa del Sol and how she would love being mistress of the ranch.

"Phillip —" Must her voice shake? Something terrifying gripped her, as if she stood on a high pinnacle, ready to be swept away forever. "Do you really think I can make you happy?"

His eyes warmed. Taking both her hands in his own he drew her close, forcing her to look directly into his eyes. "I am the one who should be asking that." The humility so strange to his nature surfaced again. "You are everything I ever wanted, and much more than I deserve. Fate has been kind."

Honor's own eyes brimmed. If Phillip felt like that, helping him find happiness away from his wild companions should not be such a mountainous task.

Then he was gone. A final kiss, a careless wave, and Phillip Travis disappeared around the bend, leaving a strangely silent canyon.

At first Honor felt bereft. Then she sternly snapped out of it. She was here to be with Heather and was touched when Heather said, "I like Mr. Travis. He was a'f'ly nice about taking us places." She skipped alongside of Honor on the trail to the rim, and her hand slid confidingly into Honor's. "But it's nice just us, isn't it? Like it was back home."

Compunction filled Honor. Had she neglected her duties to Heather because of Phillip? She silently shook her head. No, her times with Phillip alone had been while Heather slept or was otherwise occupied. She hugged the little girl hard, knowing how much she would miss her. "Yes, it is."

Heather stopped short under a huge pine, feet planted firmly in the needle-carpeted ground. "You won't be going home with us, will you? Mama says you'll stay at that ranch." Her bright little face clouded over. "What am I going to do without you?"

Honor had dreaded the moment but was prepared. "I talked with your mama and daddy. Heather, they've decided to let you go to school this fall. You'll be six, and it's time. You're going to have a wonderful time. You already know your letters so you'll be ahead of some of the others. There will be other boys and girls and —"

"You mean it?" The rainbow back of her tears chased smiles all over Heather's face. "Oh, Miss Honor, that's next best to having you!" She clapped her hands and bounced in glee. "But first we get to go to the ranch and ride ponies. Mr. Travis promised."

But Heather was doomed to disappointment.

Ben Stone's face was filled with distress as he came into the dining room, where the rest of their party waited for him so they could start dinner. "A case is coming up, and I must go back tomorrow. I didn't think it would be until later, but I must get home — right away."

"But the ranch," Heather wailed. "What about our visit — and Honor?"

Mr. Stone sighed. "Honor can go ahead with her plans. I believe it's only a matter of weeks until she is being married. I'll hire a car and driver to take her to Casa del Sol."

"But won't you need me on the way back to San Francisco?"

"My dear!" Ben Stone didn't catch his wife's look at the involuntary endearment. Neither did he see her eyes narrow, noticing how beautiful Honor had grown during her stay at the canyon. He was too intent on expressing gratitude. "We are in your debt. You will be well chaperoned by Mama Rosa. Perhaps we can visit another time."

Laurene's words fell like hard, cold rocks, every trace of former friendliness gone. "My husband," she emphasized the words, "is right. I am perfectly capable of handling Heather on the way home."

Honor was shocked at the fury in her face, then comprehension came. The woman was *jealous!* It was all Honor could do to quietly stand. "I'll start packing right away. I really am not hungry." She escaped with face burning, humiliated by the unjust accusation in Mrs. Stone's eyes.

Her last night at the canyon was filled with troubled dreams, darkness, hands reaching out. She awoke bathed in perspiration, calling out, "Phillip!" Was something wrong at the ranch? Could Phillip have been hurt? She had never given much heed to dreams, but this one left her unnerved.

The driver Mr. Stone hired was taciturn. While the tires nibbled away the miles Honor had time to reflect. Bitterness toward Mrs. Stone gradually was replaced by pity. What a terrible way to live, suspecting even a hired governess of trying to capture a loved one! She determinedly put the thoughts aside. It was a glorious time to be in Arizona. Already the leaves were beginning to show color. She could picture the bold and golden way the land would look later.

"Take the road toward Kendrick Peak," Phillip had instructed. "About five miles out there is a sign pointing north. Just stay on the road to Casa del Sol. We've had it graded."

His casual directions should have prepared her. They hadn't. She saw the turnoff, then the sign boldly blazoned over an arched entrance and cut into a wooden frame, almost as if in a trance. They drove down an endless, tree-lined lane. Honor marveled, even pinching herself to be sure it was real. It was.

Finally they swung around a gentle curve and stopped. The driver unloaded her bags, murmured a quick good-bye and was gone, leaving her staring ahead. Before her lay a mansion, reminiscent of old Spanish dons. Phillip had said it was a Spanish hacienda. He hadn't told her how the warm cream walls and the red tile roof nestled into the hills as if it had been created there. He hadn't told her that it was built around a courtyard. Through an open iron gate, she glimpsed a fountain, flowers, even singing birds. Weakly she leaned against the lacy iron work. It was too much. How could she ever belong to such a kingdom?

Memory of Babs's taunt flashed through her mind. Honor's chin came up. She would fit in. She would show them all. She and Phillip loved each other, and it was all that was important. It steadied her, but as she slowly approached the great carved door her heart fluttered. Would Phillip seem a little unapproachable here in his own setting?

"May I help you?" Liquid brown eyes in a round face above a spotless white apron looked at her curiously as the door opened.

"Mama Rosa!" Honor impulsively held out her hand, taking the older woman's hand in her own.

"You know me?" The puzzle had not left the housekeeper's face.

"Oh, yes. Phillip has told me all about you."

"Oh. Felipe. You are his friend? Come in. You are welcome."

"I am —" What check chained her tongue from adding "his fiancee"? "I am his friend," Honor substituted. "Is Phillip here?" She looked expectantly around the great hall, subconsciously noting the dark wood against cream walls, the high vaulted ceilings.

"No, he has gone —"

Honor felt his presence before he spoke from behind her. "I'll handle this, Mama Rosa."

The Mexican woman opened her lips to protest, but Honor was already whirling toward the doorway behind her. "Phillip!" Her greeting fell to a whisper. *"What has happened to you?"* Her horrified eyes took in the bloodstained bandage around his head, the way he leaned against the wall for support. "Darling, my dream was true. You're hurt!"

"It's all right," he caught her in mid-flight, before she could throw her arms around him. "Mama Rosa, can you get me something for this? That ornery colt Juan and I were working with stumbled and threw me against the corner of the fence."

Mama Rosa came to life and scuttled away, but Honor clung to Phillip. "You must sit down." She spied a blanket-covered couch against the opposite wall and half led him there. "Oh, Phillip, I just knew something terrible had happened. That's why I got here so early."

The man on the couch looked at her wearily. "You call me Phillip. I don't seem to have had the pleasure of meeting you."

Honor stared at him, unable to believe her own ears. "Not know me! You mean you don't remember the canyon — or anything?"

He passed his hand over his eyes. "I don't seem to. Would you mind terribly? Could we talk later?"

Her face reflected how stricken her soul was, but she only said slowly, "You mean the blow on the head has erased everything — you really don't know who I am?"

Her agony must have shown. The dull eyes looked sympathetic. "I'm sorry." He turned toward Mama Rosa, who had come in with basin and antiseptic. "Mama Rosa, give this young lady a room — what did you say your name was?"

"Honor Brooks."

Phillip staggered to his feet. "I'll talk with you later, Miss Brooks. Wait here until Mama finishes with me, and she'll show you where to go." He lurched against her, then with Mama as guide, disappeared into another room, leaving Honor alone.

She sank to the couch, automatically smoothing the blanket. What a horrible thing to have happen! What should she do? Phillip looked so ghastly with that bloody bandage on his head, not at all like the man she had known. Yet a great sympathy went through her. How must he feel, being hurt and entering his home to find a perfect stranger there, one who called him "darling" and insisted he knew her?

She sprang to her feet. Why was she standing there doing nothing? Couldn't she help? But before she could more than take a step in the direction he had gone, Mama Rosa came back. "Come with me, please." She led the way up a curved staircase and into a room at the right. "You will stay here."

"But how is he?"

Mama Rosa'a impassive face widened in a smile. "He is fine. It is nothing for him to be thrown. Now he needs rest. He will see you after siesta." She threw back the covers of the huge carved bed so in keeping with the other decor. "Rest. I will tell you when to come." The smile came again. "But first I bring you a tamale."

"Thank you, Mama Rosa." The door had closed behind her. Honor smiled. Even in his pain Phillip must have thought of her. The plate Mama Rosa brought contained not only tamales, but a taco as well, bearing little resemblance to the pale imitations Honor had eaten in San Francisco. She drank glasses of ice water to get the heat from her mouth, then threw herself on the bed. If siesta was the custom here, she was all for it.

After her sleepless night, the good food and warm room had done its work well. She slept until slanting afternoon sun rays filled the room. She had only stirred enough to torpidly reach for her shoes when Mama Rosa tapped at the partly open door. "Come now."

Honor ran a brush through her hair and followed the Mexican woman down a long hall, carpeted in red, to the open door of a huge room. "You go in there." Mama Rosa stood aside.

Why should she feel strangely unwilling to cross the threshold? For a moment she hesitated, then the rich voice she had learned to love called, "Come in."

She stepped inside, glancing quickly toward Phillip. He was not lying down as she had expected. He was seated behind the most massive desk she had ever seen. This must be the study. It had all the stark necessities of a business office; typewriter, file cabinets, everything needed to proclaim it the utilitarian room it was. Honor bit back her disappointment. Even if he didn't remember her, did he have to fortify himself behind that desk? It

was as she had feared and more. He was not only unapproachable, he was totally remote from anything connected with her.

She could delay looking at him no longer. To her relief the bandage had given way to a smaller patch near his hairline. He still looked pale, but it could be the filtered light through heavy drapes.

Phillip leaned toward her, motioning her to a chair at the end of the desk. "Miss Brooks, this must come as quite a shock to you. You don't know how sorry I am."

"It is a shock, Phillip." Could that strained voice really be hers? "After the past few weeks, all our plans —" she faltered. How could she talk to the stonefaced man across the desk?

The measured glance softened. Abruptly Phillip rose and walked to her. "I believe we should go somewhere a little more relaxed. You were right. I remember nothing of you, but I want to know." His kindness nearly broke her control. She stumbled a bit, and he caught her arm as they walked downstairs and into the courtyard. Blinded by tears, she was only barely aware of its beauty. His strong hold was all that mattered.

"Now." He seated her on a garden bench, pillowed with cushions, sheltered by a great cottonwood tree. "Tell me all about us."

For a moment Honor was speechless. "But — how can I tell you — it's like talking with a stranger! Oh, Phillip, can't you remember any of it?" A new thought struck her. "Not even knowing me in San Francisco?"

"San Francisco!" For a moment hope flared, but died as Phillip shook his head. "No. I remember nothing of the sort." He must have sensed her distress. "Talk to me not as a stranger, but as a friend. I promise not to interrupt."

It was the most bizarre assignment Honor could have been given. To tell Phillip, beloved, yet not knowing her, how they met — everything!

Honor was aware of the strong clasp of his hand as she leaned back on the bench. Hastily she sketched in their meeting and friendship in San Francisco. She skipped over the sorrow during Granny and Keith's deaths and looking for a job, and went into how the Stones hired her and brought her to the Grand Canyon. Now and then he smiled, giving her courage to go on. After all, this man had fallen in love with her and proposed, even inviting her to Casa del Sol. Why should she fear him simply because he could not remember through no fault of his own?

When she reached the part about meeting again at the canyon she was breathless, glad for the lengthening shadows hiding his face and her own. "I ran for the door, crossed the lobby, started upstairs. I could hear laughing voices. The next moment I was on the floor, staring up stupidly.

You had been talking with Babs and the rest of them. You picked me up, recognized me." A soft glow filled her face. "You said, 'I say, I've knocked you down with my clumsiness. I should have been looking where I was going.' "

There was a muffled sound of protest from Phillip. She continued, "It was the beginning of — of an old acquaintance."

"And love?" His stern voice gave her the shivers.

"Yes," she whispered. "What we felt in San Francisco when you asked me to wait for you all came back. As the days passed, and we spent time together at the canyon —" Her voice trailed off. She returned to the present with an effort. "You invited the Stones and me to visit Casa del Sol. You wanted to prepare your brother before we arrived. I have to confess, I am anxious to meet him. He's grown to be something of an ogre in my mind." She laughed nervously.

As if galvanized into action, Phillip leaped to his feet to tower over her. She was instantly contrite. "I'm sorry! It's just that I want him to like me. When will I meet him?"

"Soon enough. Go on. The Stones couldn't make it?"

"No. He was called home. Is this bringing anything back to you?" She could hear him breathing hard. He shook his head and said, "I promised not to interrupt, but I have to tell you I know this isn't easy for you. Believe me, it's the only way."

She gave a little cry and put her other hand over his. "I'm so glad you understand! Last night I dreamed, strange, troubled hands reaching toward me. I woke up feeling something terrible had happened to you. That's why I came early."

He released her hands and drew her closer. "I don't think it's terrible. I think perhaps it's the best thing that ever happened."

"What a strange remark! Are you sure your head is all right?"

"It's fine." He stood, propelled to his feet with almost catlike grace. "Honor, we must have dinner. You can finish telling me the story later. We'll build a fire in the fireplace."

After the delicious dinner Mama Rosa served on a tray in her room, Honor followed the housekeeper downstairs to what evidently was the library. It was all she had pictured, with its blazing fire. Again she was grateful for the darkness.

"Honor, the one thing you haven't told me is how you feel. Are you in love with me? Did you promise to marry me?"

Her shining hair curtained her downcast face. "Yes."

She could hear the sharp intake of breath before Phillip answered. "And you're the kind of girl who would never go back on a promise." It was not a question, but a statement. It brought Honor's eyes to his.

"I am bound by my word." For one frightening moment she was back on the canyon's edge, facing the storm overhead and the tumult in her heart. It was almost as if she were being given a second chance to reconsider. Phillip didn't remember her. What if he never did? What if she was deliberately deluding herself into thinking she could be queen of this near-palace? The immensity of the very room in which they sat increased her doubts. What was she, a child's governess, doing in this place?

"Well?"

Even as she opened her mouth to break the chains binding her to this unknown Phillip, memory of her position came. Granny, Keith, home — all gone.

Even the security of her position with the Stones was gone. She could not go back. What did it matter if he didn't know her now? When he remembered he would still be her beloved, the man who was kind to Heather, who openly confessed a past dark with unsaid choices but who also reached forward to a brighter future here on the ranch with her to strengthen him.

"You really think Phillip Travis is the husband you need?"

Had he divined her thoughts, or was his memory returning? "Yes." Once it was said, it was easier. "We will share our lives, create a home, have children — just as we planned." It was all she could get out for now.

Phillip broke away, turned to the fire and moodily stared into the flames. "Go home, Honor. Back to San Francisco. You will never find happiness here."

His command roused a demon of opposition she hadn't known lay within. "Never! You asked me to marry you. I accepted. Surely you will remember in a few days."

"Have you ever been in love before?" He swung to face her.

"Once." She could feel a reminiscent smile turn to laughter as she confessed, "A certain soldier came to San Francisco — he asked me to wait for him." She sobered. "When he didn't write, I shut my heart and wouldn't admit how it hurt."

"Phillip Travis?"

"Yes."

He gripped her shoulders. "Are you prepared to deal with drinking, sometimes to excess? With other women?"

Her confidence turned to fear. "But — but you said I was the one you'd waited for all your life. You said drinking didn't mean anything when I was with you."

"And you still want to marry me?" Disbelief filled his eyes. "Even knowing those protestations might not be true?" His face slowly iced over. "Or do you expect me to change?"

"I — I hope you will!" Stung by the agony inside she cried, "Why do you downgrade yourself? I know there is a part of you that wants more from life than idleness." She faced him squarely and had the satisfaction of seeing him drop his eyes.

"Did we talk about this at the canyon?"

She had to be honest. "Some. You told me I was seeing the best of you there, alone, away from temptation. I want to help you, Phillip."

"What else did we talk about?"

"Everything. Your desire to be more part of the ranch, to convince your brother —" She broke off.

She wasn't prepared for the fury in the blazing eyes threatening to scorch her or his low reply, "Forget about my brother!"

"Phillip!"

He ignored her cry. His eyes turned to black coals. "If you expect to have all your childish fantasies come true, you better keep moving. Phillip Travis is not a knight on a white horse."

She swayed, unconsciously putting up her hands in protest. "Why do you keep referring to yourself so? Or are you pretending? Maybe you do remember." Horror filled her. "That's it, isn't it? You do remember and are regretting getting entangled with a governess." Her face felt tight, her lips parched. "You have changed. Did Babs convince you I wasn't worthy? When you prate to me of worth, is it me you are thinking of, *or yourself?*"

He sidestepped the question and gripped her shoulders again until she knew there would be bruises in the morning. "Is there nothing I can say that will make you go away?"

"Only that you never want to see me again." One final time she felt on the brink, but she ignored the bridge and plunged in. "Nothing else on earth can make me leave you."

Phillip's face twisted, a groan escaped his tightly clenched lips. "Then stay — and may heaven protect you!"

Even through her victory the bitter drop remained. She had forfeited the right to expect God's protection — for Phillip. Shaken, she pushed down the thought and lightened the atmosphere. "I expect you to show me

Arizona. Not just Casa del Sol, but the White Mountains and the Oak Creek Canyon and —"

"And just when are we getting married in all this?"

Honor caught her breath. "Oh, not until you remember everything, and you will."

"I am already getting a clearer picture of the past from what you have said."

Joy skyrocketed inside her as she lifted her face and put her arms around him in a gesture both loving and protective. "Then let's do as we planned. We can ride and talk and learn to really know each other!" She was amazed at her own boldness and dropped her arms hastily. "Phillip, you seem almost a different person here in your own home, almost a stranger."

She could feel his surprise as he asked. "Which man do you love? The vacationer at the canyon, or the rancher in his home?"

"Since it will be my home, too, it will have to be the rancher —" She never finished. Slowly he crushed her to him, seeking her lips with his own. Her arms crept around his neck as she returned his kiss. "Why, Phillip, you really are a stranger! You have never kissed me like that before." She pulled back and stared at him.

"A man in his castle is a different creature than on any other ground." A curious glint filled his eyes, and the lips that had claimed hers turned upward into a smile she did not understand. But when he held out his arms again, she flew to them like a homing pigeon. Stranger or not, Phillip Travis was the man she loved.

Somewhere in the darkness a horse softly whinnied. Honor turned in the heavily carved bed, then ran to the window. Why would anyone be out now? Moonlight sneaked through her slightly parted drapes to touch a clock on the wall. One-thirty.

Her eyes widened as she pushed the heavy drapes open. A tall rider was swinging easily onto the back of a white horse that gleamed in the moonlight. His upturned face brought a gasp to Honor's lips. Phillip! The prancing horse daintily stepped away from the corral and down the path. Honor could hear the rhythm of hooves as horse and rider gradually increased speed once away from the hacienda.

"How strange! I didn't think Phillip would be the type to go riding at midnight." A thrill shot through Honor as she shivered her way back to bed. The night was crisp, and fresh air streamed through the partially opened window. She breathed deep and hugged her knees. It all smelled so clean, pines and flowers. How could she be so fortunate?

A smile lit her face in the darkness, sending a glow through her. The next instant it vanished in a frown. How different Phillip was in his own home! Why had he ordered her back to San Francisco? She could feel her heartbeat quicken. He could not be the selfish person he had described, or he wouldn't be putting her ahead of himself. Even though he seemed firmer and stronger here at Casa del Sol, he must have been thinking of her happiness, afraid he could not fill her expectations. A protective wave of love for him replaced her other feelings. She would help him be what she believed he could be — in spite of his own protestations. No one could feel about the canyon the way Phillip did and yet be narrowminded enough not to recognize a better way of life than that of his friends.

The weakness of her reasoning hit her immediately. She refused to listen to the voice inside. She had chosen. She would not turn back. She would become mistress of Casa del Sol. The high ceilings of the spacious room echoed her whisper, "Is it all a dream?" She pinched her arm hard, then rubbed the aching spot. No. She really was here. In her wildest dreams she had only imagined visiting a large ranch someday. Now she would be part of it, and when Phillip's brother came — Honor's face flamed in the darkness. Where was he? She hadn't even thought to ask. How could she have blurted out as she had about Phillip's brother being an ogre? Phillip

must think her gauche if not downright rude. She set her chin resolutely. When he did come, she would make him like her. Much of her happiness depended on the unknown stranger.

Now that she had seen Casa del Sol she should be able to conjure up a better image of Phillip's brother than an ogre! He must be industrious. Phillip had confessed indolence, and the ranch still prospered. Her fingers interlaced as she promised the night wind, "Phillip is going to learn to work. He will be happier. I'll start by asking to see the ranch. He can't help learning when he sees how interested I am."

Honor shivered. "Learning! Will I ever learn everything there is to know about this place? Will I ever really be comfortable with Mama Rosa? She will have to teach me." She laughed nervously. "Nothing in my background has fitted me for this!"

Memory of the mule trip and resulting stiffness brought a rueful twist to her good intentions. "I'll have to learn to ride. Not on that magnificent white animal I just saw. Maybe there's a pony."

Her thoughts returned to the absent brother. No picture would come. Sleepy from her mental gymnastics, she turned over, wondering where Phillip had gone.

A gentle tapping roused her. The brilliance of the sun pouring through the drapes she had left open hurt her eyes for a moment.

"Come in." She pulled the sheet up under her chin, stealing a glance at the clock. Ten! She had slept away half the morning of her first day at Casa del Sol.

"I brought your breakfast." Rosa's brown face above the tray was as impassive as it had been the day before.

Honor smiled warmly, noting it brought a response. The muscles in Rosa's face relaxed. "Good morning, Rosa. What a beautiful day!" She slipped from bed and into a robe and slippers, then ran to the window again. She looked down, amazed at the pang that shot through her when she discovered the corral was empty.

"Where are the horses? And Phillip? I heard him ride out last night."

Rosa's gaze was startled and there was a slight breathiness in her reply. "Felipe is not here."

"And his brother?"

"Senor is not here, either."

Honor whirled. "You sound —" She broke off. It was not for her to comment on how Rosa sounded. "This looks delicious, but I can never eat it all!"

For the first time Rosa actually smiled. "You will eat. Casa del Sol makes you hungry." She fussed about, buttering the hot biscuits, rearranging the silver. "The peaches come from our own trees. The bacon is from our hogs. The honey is from our hives."

"Rosa." Honor put her hand on the sturdy brown one. "I'm going to marry Phillip, but I don't know anything about running a place such as this! I can cook, but not like this. Will you teach me all I should know?"

The smile became a beam, then faded. "It will be for Senor to say."

"Senor?" Honor was puzzled, then light broke. "Oh, you mean Phillip's brother." Something of her fear of the unknown Senor showed in her flat voice.

"Si." Rosa moved toward the door. "Call when you have eaten." She indicated an old-fashioned bell pull. Dignified, with no trace of the softer nature she had shown only moments before, Rosa opened the door and glided through.

"Very much the controlling influence of Casa del Sol," Honor told the empty room. "She changed when I mentioned my new brother-to-be. She calls him Senor. He must be *uno grande hombre.*" Honor laughted at her own mixture of Latin and Spanish. "If I'm going to use any Spanish I'd better learn more than I know now!"

The breakfast was delicious, and when she had finished Honor bathed and dressed, this time in a simple blue gown. She would carry her own tray downstairs. Perhaps Rosa would be a little friendlier. But it wasn't Rosa Honor found when she finally located the kitchen after opening three doors to other rooms. Phillip sat at the gleaming white-topped table so out of keeping with the rest of the house.

"Good morning, Phillip." The pleats in her skirt swung as she started toward him.

He motioned her back. "Don't get too close. I've been with the horses and am not fit to be around beautiful ladies."

Color flowed freely into her face. He sounded like a little boy. "I saw you ride out last night. Where did you go?"

"I had a lot to think of." Laughter fled from his voice. His dark eyes held her as he pushed back his chair abruptly. "How about a ride this morning? You have breakfasted, haven't you?"

"So much I probably won't be able to get on a horse!"

Her fears were unfounded. Phillip led out a pinto pony a half hour later. Clad in knickers and boots, with her khaki skirt and a sombrero borrowed from Rosa's daughter, Carlotta, she managed to get in the saddle with one gentle boost from Phillip. Her pony, Jingles, had an easy gait. Phillip said

Jingles was a singlefooter. It was almost like riding a rocking horse!

Honor reined her in at the top of a cedar-covered ridge. "Does it never end?" Her eyes ranged from the red and white shorthorns grazing the valley floor to the already-snowcapped mountains to the north. Casa del Sol's roof shone red in the sunlight, warming the gray sage and green pines and cedars surrounding it.

"It is a responsibility," Phillip said. "A trust from my grandfather and father." Honor sensed he spoke more to himself than to her. "Dozens of families depend on us and the way this ranch is run. Not just our cowboys and other workers. We furnish meat for a lot of Arizona."

"I believe it. It's almost too much for one family."

"That's what my brother says." Phillip's eyes were somber.

A strange feeling dimmed the sun streaming down on them. He couldn't mean his brother was considering selling the ranch! Not just when she had determined to make Phillip part of it. She started to speak, thought better of it, and said, "I just hope I can be —"

She never finished the sentence. A man on a horse was racing toward them, yellow paper in his hand.

Honor looked at Phillip. His face was the color of parchment. He spurred his horse, and the white stallion leaped forward. Flying hooves ate up the distance between the two men. Honor started to follow. She was struck by the rigidity of Phillip's figure as he took the yellow paper and read it. She automatically hesitated, and Phillip turned back toward her. As he shortened the space between them she couldn't help admiring the ease with which he rode.

The parchment color had left his face, replaced by a dark flush. "Honor, would you marry me right away? Before the end of the week?"

"But we agreed —"

"I know. I just don't feel that way any longer. You don't want a big fancy wedding, do you?"

"No, Phillip." She had a terrifying sense of something lurking ahead, some unknown danger. "I just want a simple ceremony. But I wanted more time, time for you to remember —" Her voice gave way.

"I know." He touched his mount's side lightly with his heels, bringing him alongside Jingles. "I'll take care of you, Honor. I'll make sure you don't come to any harm. Won't you do as I ask?"

Honor's eyes dropped to the yellow page still in Phillip's hand. Sudden understanding filled her.

Phillip's eyes followed her gaze. "Yes, it's from my brother. He will be home sometime next week."

Honor couldn't bear the way his head drooped, as if in shame. A great wave of love and understanding again flooded her. Phillip needed her. He dreaded the homecoming, what might happen. Would there be violent objections? The same protective warmth that had stirred the night before crept into her veins. If disappointment mingled with it, she valiantly pushed it back. Did it really matter if she knew this white-faced man weeks, months, or years? Again she squelched the mighty *yes* her conscience was shouting. If Phillip needed her so much, how could she refuse? "The only white dress I have is one I made from a discard of Mrs. Stone's wardrobe."

"You don't think that matters!" He swept her into his arms. It was enough to eliminate any lingering doubt she might have had.

On the way home Honor was quiet. Phillip did not attempt to intrude on her thoughts. It wasn't until he helped her down that he said, "Honor, no matter what happens, you won't ever despise me, will you?"

He knows I know he is weak. Honor bit back a betraying rush of tears. "I will love you as long as I live."

Phillip did not kiss her again. Instead he held her close to his rapidly beating heart. "It's the only way. When you understand, when —"

"I already understand." She placed gloved fingers over his lips.

"Rest a bit before lunch, Honor. This Arizona weather is far different from what you are used to in San Francisco."

"I noticed I had a little trouble breathing."

"We're several thousand feet high. You'll adjust in a few days."

Honor ran upstairs. In just a few days she would be Phillip's wife — for better or worse. Why did that phrase have to pop up? She whirled into her room.

Carlotta, in school skirt and middy blouse, looked up from folding back the bedspread. Her Spanish ancestry shone in her shining dark hair and eyes. "How do you like Casa del Sol?"

"I don't know if I can ever be worthy of it."

She repeated the words later that week to Phillip. They had ridden through the soft twilight to a different knoll above the valley. "This place — can I ever be worthy of it?"

"Worthy — you? It is I —" He broke off, unseeing eyes tracing the pattern of a bubbling stream in the valley that was only a silver thread from their viewpoint.

"You will be worthy, too, Phillip. When your brother comes, we'll tell him you want to really be part of the ranch. He will respect your feelings."

Phillip's dark eyes flashed. "The ogre, as you nicknamed him?"

Honor turned beet red. "I'm sorry for that. I really didn't mean it. It's just that I want us to be happy here —" The wistfulness in her voice brought a squeeze from Phillip's hand that threatened to crush her fingers, even in the sturdy riding gloves Carlotta had furnished.

"I pray you will never be anything here but happy."

"Just to think that a few weeks ago Mr. Stone was telling me not to come down here and marry some Arizonan!" She laughed.

"Would you rather have waited and asked him to the wedding?" Honor felt the tension in the question.

"No. He would never understand how I could be so sure so quickly, when for all my life I've been waiting." Her fiery color intensified until it matched the jutting rocks near where they had stopped. "I'm not sure I understand myself."

"You aren't regretting it?"

There was no hesitation. "No, Phillip. I will never regret marrying you tomorrow."

"You're the sweetest thing on earth." He leaned across from his horse Sol's back to kiss her, almost reverently. "I will do everything in my power to keep you from regretting it." His eyes were like glittering obsidian in a chalky face. "Honor, will you promise to trust me, no matter what?"

"I will."

Even later, as she dressed for her last hours as a single woman, Honor thought of the scene on the little plateau. Tomorrow she would take her wedding vows. But her real vow had been taken on that little plateau overlooking Casa del Sol.

"This time tomorrow I'll be your wife." Honor's eyes were pools of happiness as Phillip walked her to her door that night. The moonlit night threw patterns of fantastic beauty across the upper hall.

"Yes." Why did Phillip seem distracted?

"You — you aren't regretting?"

She felt him start in the dimness. "I regret nothing." He captured her, kissing her the way he had done the first night she arrived at Casa del Sol. Honor's doubts fled before the intensity of his love. It was a long time before she broke away.

"Good night, Phillip." She slipped through the heavy door, closing it behind her. Just before it shut out all sounds, somewhere in the hacienda a bell rang. The telephone? What if Phillip's brother — she laughed at her own fancies. How melodramatic to think a disapproving man would appear on the doorstep at the eleventh hour to stop her wedding!

At last Honor had time to think.

Tomorrow Juan and Rosa and Carlotta would go to Flagstaff for her wedding with Phillip. Carlotta would be her bridesmaid. Phillip had said earlier this evening he had arranged for them to be married by a minister.

Her heart swelled. How thoughtful! He had instinctively known how she would want it. A horrendous thought marred her happiness.

What if Phillip's brother should be in Flagstaff?

She punched her pillow, then buried her face in its cooling depths. She must get over this obsession about the man! All she knew about him was the little Phillip had told her.

Again Honor heard hooves in the night and ran to her window. Again she saw the tall, dark-haired man mount an unsaddled white horse, one she now knew as Sol. Was he nervous about tomorrow? The thought was strangely comforting. She had been so sure she'd never sleep. Now she dove into bed and moments later was unconscious.

"Senorita, you are beautiful!" There was no disapproving silence about Rosa this morning. "Senora Dolores would be proud to have you marry her son!"

Honor's eyes filled. Early this morning a large box had arrived and a note from Phillip:

I KNOW YOU HAVE A WHITE DRESS TO BE MARRIED IN.
I HOPE YOU WILL WEAR THIS WITH IT.

There had been no signature, but inside had been the most exquisitely wrought lace mantilla Honor had ever seen or imagined. Slightly yellowed with age, it only brought out the highlights in her skin.

"I don't know how to wear it," she confessed to Carlotta.

"We will help you," the beautiful bridesmaid promised, dark face picking up color from the soft rosy gown she wore. Now as Honor faced herself in the mirror, it was not only her own image she saw but the joy on the faces of Rosa and Carlotta. Turning impulsively she threw her arms around them both, heedless of the priceless mantilla. "I am so glad I came to Arizona!"

"We are glad, too! You and Senor will be very happy." Carlotta's eyes danced.

"We will help you dress and arrange the mantilla when we get to Flagstaff," Rosa promised as they disrobed her and carefully packed her dress and mantilla in boxes. "Bad luck for bridegroom to see you in dress before wedding."

"Mamacita believes in old customs." Carlotta laughed, but there was genuine respect and love in her voice.

"I think I do, too." Honor danced to the window, still in her long white slip. "Was there ever a more beautiful day for a bride? I'm a fall person. You know, my birthday is next week."

Rosa beamed. "Why did you not wait and be married on your birthday?"

"Phillip didn't want to wait so long." Her voice was muffled in her slip as she quickly drew on a simple dress for the drive into Flagstaff. "I think he's a little bit afraid of his brother coming home and stopping the wedding."

In the absolute silence that fell Honor pulled the top triumphantly over her head and settled it. Only then did she realize how still it had become. She was instantly contrite! "I shouldn't have said that! It is just that I want us all to be happy, and I wish he *would* come!"

Rosa's sober glance reminded Honor of the way she had responded when Honor first came. Quietly she gathered up the slip and packed it, then turned toward the door. "Senor Travis is a fine man." She slipped out, leaving Honor staring.

"It's all right." Carlotta seemed anxious to bridge the uncomfortable moment. "Mamacita thinks the sun doesn't come up or go down without first consulting Senor!"

Honor laughed in spite of feeling guilty, picturing the sun bowing daily before Casa del Sol and asking permission to rise and set! "Just where is he now?" Honor inquired as she ran a brush through her hair.

"Oh, here and there." Carlotta sounded vague, disinclined to discuss his whereabouts. "Where are you going for your honeymoon — or do you know?"

"Right here. Where could there be anything more glorious?" She spun about and frowned. "When we were at the canyon we talked about going back after we were married. Carlotta, it's so strange. He still doesn't seem to remember a lot of what happened at the canyon."

"Why is it important?" The liquid brown eyes shifted.

Honor turned back to the window, noting how the golden leaves fluttered — cottonwood, aspen, birch. She had learned to love them all. "He just seems so much older here. Different. More mature."

The watching eyes reflected breathlessness in Carlotta's question. "Which do you love more? The canyon man, or this one?"

Honor's face glowed. "I love the man who owns Casa del Sol. More than anything in the world."

"Then I suggest you come with me and marry him." The laughing invitation from the doorway brought consternation to Carlotta's face until she saw Honor light up and bow. "I'll do just that."

"You like my invitation, senorita?" The watching dark eyes were suddenly sober.

"I love your invitation, senor." She turned to Carlotta. "Coming?"

"No. Mamacita and Papa and I will take our own car. You will want to come back alone." Her flashing smile added to her beauty.

"That's right, Carlotta. I'm going to want my wife all to myself for a few hours."

Honor could feel a tiny pulse beating in her throat. "You'll bring everything, Carlotta?"

"Everything."

Carlotta was as good as her word. A few hours later she carefully lifted the priceless mantilla to Honor's head. But it was for Rosa to carefully adjust its folds so it cascaded to Honor's shoulders. Something in Honor's eyes seemed to touch the good woman's heart. "Be happy, senorita." She pressed her warm brown cheek to Honor's paler one, feeling the clutch of nervous fingers before Honor laughed.

"It is time." Carlotta threw open the door of the little room next to the chapel.

How could Phillip have arranged so much in such a short time? The small chapel seemed smothered with autumn leaves, dark fir branches. Fall flowers of every color perfumed the room. The measured tones of the Wedding March from *Lohengrin* softly pulsated, keeping time to Honor's beating heart.

Honor clutched her bouquet of old-fashioned flowers. They must have been especially chosen by Phillip from those she admired most in his courtyard. Late roses, even a few tiny forget-me-nots. It was a shame for such a perfect wedding to be seen by so few.

Carlotta's rosy skirt swished to a standstill. It was Honor's turn. Shakily, she started down the long aisle, seeing nothing except Phillip waiting for her.

The wedding ceremony was a little blurred. Only one thing really stood out in the kaleidoscope of Honor's memory. When the minister turned to Phillip he said, "Do you, James Travis, take this woman . . ."

Honor gasped, feeling as if inchworms were measuring her spine. The next moment Phillip's strong hand tightened reassuringly on her own. His face was pale, but the dark eyes were steady. Honor wondered how the minister could have made such a mistake. Obviously it was all right, or

Phillip would have stopped the service for a correction. Her surprise soon settled down. Of course — James must be Phillip's first name and necessary for legal documents. Her unanswered musings were drowned in the "I do" that rang from the arched beams of the little chapel.

Honor's own response was quieter. Two words, so little to signify passing her life into James Phillip Travis's keeping until death did them part. She blinked back mist that hid the scene for a moment, realizing as never before how truly irrevocable that promise was.

"I pronounce you man and wife. What God hath joined together, let no man put asunder." In spite of her joy, Honor shivered. How could any man or woman break promises as solemn as the vows in the wedding service?

Phillip turned to her. His lips found hers, lingering as if loath to let her go. She could feel his resignation when he finally released her. Her heart responded. Their first kiss as man and wife; holy, beautiful. If only everyone would just go away and leave them alone! But it was not to be. From somewhere a photographer appeared.

"I thought you would want pictures," her new husband explained. "But not during the actual ceremony. I've seen too many weddings interrupted by photographers. Would you mind posing with me, Mrs. Travis?"

"Not a bit, Mr. Travis." Excitement like a skyrocket trembled within her as she laughed and smiled. Phillip had even arranged for a wedding cake in a nearby restaurant's private room. "We want pictures for our children." He watched her color rise as she stammered.

"It's a bit hard to talk to a brand new husband, isn't it?" She finally gave up small talk efforts in total honesty.

"It's also time for us to go home."

"Home!" Something golden glowed within Honor. "House of the Sun. May it ever prove to be so for us."

"And when the shadows come?"

She looked resolutely into his face. "We will know the sun is always there. Shadows pass, the sun returns."

"You darling!" The ardent look in his eyes stirred her. But he only said. "Wouldn't you like to change into something else for the drive back? That mantilla must be heavy."

Honor thought for a moment. "I'll take the mantilla off, but leave my gown on. I won't ever have another wedding day, so I want to look beautiful on this one."

He gently lifted the mantilla from her hair and handed it to Mama Rosa, voice sober. "Put it away, Mama. I'm taking Honor home."

"Vaya con Dios." The beautiful Spanish blessing rested on them as Phillip helped her into the big touring car. She waved and smiled as they backed and turned.

"What does it mean, Phillip? Something about God, I know that."

"Go with God."

"How fitting. *Vaya con Dios.*" She repeated the words, then turned back to him. "Phillip, it will take all the days of our lives to learn what there is to know about each other."

The Willys swerved, righted itself, then slowly inched ahead. Honor vaguely noticed and wondered at a honking carload of people next to them, waiting for a wagon ahead to pass, but paid little attention to them. Phillip's hands were white on the wheel. "Honor, there's something I have to tell you, as soon as we get home —"

His sentence was never finished. From the open Stutz next to them a wild whoop went up. Staring across at the other car, Honor was stunned. A tall dark-haired man was wildly waving — and he was an exact replica of Phillip!

She opened her lips to speak, then glanced at Phillip. He had gone a curious color, as if all the blood had drained from his face under the tan. His lips twisted. The pain in his face caught at her heart. Again she tried to speak, but nothing came from her frozen throat. Was Phillip that much afraid of his brother? It must be he in the other car, but why hadn't Philip told her they were twins?

Her calculations, slowed by shock, were shattered when the other man called, his mocking voice clearly audible in the late fall air. "Well, Honor, James — what have you two been up to? And Honor in a white dress, even!"

Honor reeled back against the seat. It was the same voice she had heard on the floor of El Tovar Hotel. There was no mistaking it — the man in that car was Phillip Travis! Arm about Babs, laughing with the others Honor knew from the canyon, he was in curious contrast to the man gripping the steering wheel of the car she was in — the man she had just promised to love, honor, and cherish for as long as she lived.

"That's Phillip." Her voice broke in a sob, pleading for understanding, just as that same something that had haunted her during the wedding magnified. "But then, who, what — he called you James. You aren't, you can't be —" She couldn't get another sound past the mountain that seemed to have closed off her throat.

Her words seemed to release her companion from the trance they had fallen into, almost as if a wicked spell had been called out in that laughing, accusing voice from the other car.

He turned to her for an instance, then shot ahead and around the corner out of sight of the pointing, laughing hecklers. A crooked smile touched his ashen lips, a mocking salute recognized her stumbling question. "Meet James Travis, senora. Once again the lovely princess has married the ogre."

"You? It can't be true." Honor flexed stiff lips, sliding far away from him, as if he really were an ogre. Flecks of memory darted to her. "Then —" Her laugh was slightly hysterical. "Of course. That's why you didn't remember anything from the canyon. *Because you never were there with me!"*

His silence was maddening. Honor swallowed hard. It must be a nightmare. Her perfect wedding, and now this? Imposible! The man beside her who had been so gentle, so loving — an imposter. She could feel herself shrinking into nothingness. In self-defense she lashed out. "How could you do such a thing? Telling me you were Phillip? Making me fall in love with you?"

"But my dear." James seemed grimly amused. *"You* were the one to call me Phillip. If you remember, I never once told you I was Phillip. Why should I? If you will remember a little more, I tried to send you away. I told you the truth. I told you Phillip Travis could never make you happy. I also told you that your childish longing for someone to come along on a white horse did not fit Phillip."

Honor moistened her parched lips with the tip of her tongue. In minutes the companionable man she had known since she arrived at the ranch had changed into a stranger. "Then I was right. You were a stranger when I arrived at Casa del Sol. You were nothing like Phillip."

"Thank you." This time he laughed aloud. "That's the finest compliment you could give me."

"But why?" She had to break through his calm. "Why did you marry me?"

"There was no other choice." His laughing mask slipped. In its place was a deadly serious man. "I had to protect you from my dear brother. I tried to send you away, and you wouldn't go. I tried to tell you about him, and you wouldn't listen. So —"

"So you passed yourself off as Phillip and hurried up the wedding before he came!" She fumbled for the door handle as they neared another corner. "I'm getting out of here and now!"

"You aren't going anywhere." The strong arm she knew so well reached across, pinning her against the seat, infuriating her more. "Don't ever try and run away from me. This world isn't big enough for you to hide in."

52

"Who are you to tell me what I shall and shall not do?" Honor wrenched free and sat trembling as he picked up speed and headed onto the open road, leaving Flagstaff behind.

"I just happen to be your husband."

"Not for long! As soon as I can get help you won't be." Her voice gathered assurance. "Phillip will never stand for this. He will come to Casa del Sol for me."

"He will be welcome — so long as he remembers you are my wife."

"Your wife? Are you insane? Do you think I'd stay with you after what you have done?"

"Of course." Could that really be surprise in his face as he shot a keen glance at her. "You told me you were truthful and steadfast. You told me you never broke a vow. You also promised to love, honor, and cherish me until death parted us. How can you be ready so soon to break those vows?"

If sheer fury could kill, James Travis would have died on the spot. "You don't by any stretch of imagination think those vows are valid under these circumstances! I believe you are insane! I was right. You *are* an ogre!"

To her amazement, James threw his head back and laughed. Didn't any of this bother him at all? She would show him! She would get away at the first opportunity!

The slow, mocking voice went on. "Really, Honor, don't you believe in fate, or God, or something? I would have bet you do. How do you know this wasn't all planned?"

"How dare you? Isn't it enough that you have ruined my life? How can you mock God?" A tiny drum beat in her brain. *Isn't that what you've done?*

James whipped the car into a leafy lane out of sight of the main road, killed the motor, and turned to her. His face was as white as her own. The hands he placed on her shoulders dug in. "Ruined your life! Shall I tell you what your life would be like with your precious Phillip?"

"No! You have no right to malign your brother!"

The steel fingers bit deeper. It was all Honor could do to keep from crying out.

"It is not maligning to tell you the truth. You think you know Phillip Travis. You know nothing of him! You know only the front he puts on when he meets a new girl or woman. Do you think you are the first to be invited to Casa del Sol? No, not the first, nor the last. Babs is the only one he might ever be true to. When she is convinced of that, she will marry him. In the meantime, it is a succession of girls and women; summer, winter, fall, spring — season makes no difference. Phillip has the art of

loving and leaving perfected to the highest degree." He gave her a little shake, his eyes burning like freshly stirred embers.

"Why didn't he meet you as he promised? Why didn't he come? I can tell you. Once he left the Grand Canyon you were only a dim memory." She flinched, and he shook her again. "Wake up, Honor. Do you think a man like Phillip could be true to you? Do you really think a man who loves women and carousing could settle down and make the kind of home you want, the kind of home you will have at Casa del Sol?"

"He promised to stop drinking! He said he didn't even want to drink when he was with me."

Slowly the fingers loosened. Terrible pity filled James's eyes as he pulled a newspaper from his pocket. "I hoped you would never have to see this."

Wordlessly, Honor took it. Blazoned across the front was a picture, unmistakably Phillip. His hair hung in his eyes, his mouth was slack. Underneath was the caption:

LOCAL RANCHER SPENDS NIGHT
IN JAIL FOR DISORDERLY CONDUCT

The newspaper fell from Honor's nerveless fingers. "How could you be so cruel?"

"Is it more cruel to tell you the truth, or to let you marry him and find out for yourself?"

"But what am I to do?" All the old lack of self-confidence, of being totally alone, rushed over her. "You were joking when you said you expected me to stay, weren't you?"

James gripped her again, face chiseled in determination. "I never meant anything so much in my entire life."

She wrenched free. "To make the perfect touch, I suppose you're going to swear by all that's holy to you — or is anything? — that you fell in love with me at first sight and used this excuse to marry me."

Matching color burned in his face. "Why not? Didn't you do much the same with Phillip?" Speechless with fury, Honor couldn't reply. But James was not through. "Since you obviously wouldn't believe it, I won't swear undying love."

She hated him for the laughter underlying his thrust. "I wouldn't believe anything any Travis told me. You certainly planned it well. Why" — a new wave of indignation shot through her — "even Carlotta, Rosa — how could you get them to agree to such a monstrous plot? I should have

known." Her eyes widened. "Rosa — she called Phillip 'Felipe.' She calls you 'Senor.' Why didn't I notice?"

"You were too busy deluding yourself about Phillip."

Honor buried her face in her hands, biting back a sob. She would not show weakness, not now.

"Cheer up, Honor. Things could be worse." James suddenly abandoned his lightness. "Don't hold it against Rosa and Carlotta. They knew you would be better off married to me, even hating me, than facing the inevitable humiliation you would find as Phillip's wife." His laugh sounded strained. "Who knows? We may even learn to love each other in time."

When Honor found her voice it came out in hard syllables, like crystal tears bouncing on a glassy surface. "That has to be the most ridiculous remark I have ever heard in my entire life. Love you? Never!"

"Never is a long time."

"You — you —" Her fury increased to the snapping point. In the midst of it a snatch of conversation with Carlotta burned red-hot in her mind. *Which do you love more? The canyon man, or this one?*

Her own reply now stood to accuse her. *I love the man who owns Casa del Sol — more than anything in the world.*

"I demand you take me to the ranch so I can pack and go."

James laughed outright. "Wives don't leave their husbands so soon after the ceremony, my dear. Besides, I saw Phillip and his bunch pass the main road. They will be there to meet us. No one forced you to marry me, you know. If you remember, you even insisted —" He laughed again. "What a coup! Even Phillip will enjoy my trick. I'm sure the photographer will put our pictures in the paper. Perhaps there can be some more headlines about the Travis family:

YOUNG BEAUTIFUL BRIDE
MARRIES WRONG TWIN

How exciting! Something you can tell our children and grandchildren." Before Honor could find her tongue, he added casually, "It's lucky for me you are such an honorable person. Why, another woman might even do as you threatened and leave me. But not you." His face was blandly innocent as he put his foot on the gas and shot forward. "You are bound. Honor bound." She could have strangeled him for his laugh. "You will go in looking like the bride you are."

Honor turned her back on him.

Never had miles gone by so slowly. All the glory of the day had gone. Even the red streaks heralding sunset failed to rouse Honor. James's laughing words had gone deep. In spite of everything he had done, she had promised, given her word. But how could she stay at Casa del Sol hating James as she now did? The love she had felt for Phillip was gone, obliterated by the sight of his drunken face in the newspaper. Deep inside a question formed — what if the love she had thought was for Phillip had really been for James at the ranch? She stepped on it, hard. She would never forgive him. Better to break her word than to remain where she had known so much happiness that had now turned to bitterness.

James must have read her thoughts. "Until you get over being upset, you needn't worry about my being around. I have work on the range and won't be in. You'll be treated as a special guest, nothing more."

Honor could feel color creeping up from the high neck of her wedding dress.

"I don't want a wife who still fancies herself in love with my twin brother. Until you get us sorted out in your mind you'll be just what I said, a special guest, nothing more."

Honor sank back against the seat, speechless again. What an unpredictable man! Yet his words had given birth to hope. What if she took him up on it? What if she stayed at Casa del Sol, let time help her decide what to do? She was in no condition to make any decisions right now. Too much had happened. She had been taken from joy to despair to disillusionment.

"You give your word?"

"I do." His warm hand shook her icy fingers in a businesslike grip as he swung into the cutoff toward Casa del Sol, as if a corporation merger had just been signed. "Now, let's show everyone what the partnership of Travis and Brooks-Travis can do. If they once find out you didn't know you married the wrong twin, this crowd will never let it be forgotten."

Wonder of wonders, Honor laughed. If she could just concentrate on getting through one thing at a time it would provide what she needed — a quiet place to think. But first she had to face that crowd — including Phillip. Phillip! How could such a terrible thing ever have happened? In love with one man, married to his twin brother who expected her to keep her vows. She shoved the thought aside. Now was not the time to think about it. She had to go in that house and face them all with a smile on her lips. With an involuntary shudder, she braced herself as James came to a stop, vaulted over the side of the low car, and before she knew what was happening scooped her up in her arms.

"Put me down," she ordered furiously, but he only grinned.

"It's what they'll expect! Hold still." With a mighty kick he shoved open the door, which had been left standing ajar, and strode into the big hall. To Honor it seemed there were a million people there.

"Just what are you all doing here on my honeymoon?" There was no welcome in James's voice, just righteous indignation. He set Honor on her feet, but kept a supporting arm around her. Did he know she would have fallen if he had just put her down?

An indolent figure detached itself from the group. "We came to wish the bride and groom all happiness," said Phillip, smiling as only he could smile. For one instant Honor fought the pain of what might have been, only to have it replaced with relief when he lifted high the glass he was holding.

"Get that booze out of here!" Honor wasn't prepared for James's roar. "You know I don't allow it in this house."

"What's all the shouting about, James?" Babs had crossed to them. "It's just a little drink. We brought our own." The emerald on her finger winked wickedly.

"You're welcome to visit for a little while, but you can't bring that stuff in here."

For one long moment brother faced brother. Honor would never forget it. Seen against the clear and cleancut features of James, Phillip was a rather smudged carbon copy. Her heart suddenly knew the truth of her words to Carlotta. She had fallen for the strength in Phillip that belonged to his twin. No wonder she had been so relieved to find him different at his ranch than when with the crowd. It was a good thing they paid no attention to her. Would her face give it away?

I must never let James know. He wouldn't, couldn't say he had fallen in love with me. He must never know how right he was. But determination was born. She would make him love her until he was glad he had married her — not to protect her from Phillip, but because he loved her. Hot color spurted into her face, leaving her breathless.

Honor's attention returned to the brothers. Phillip's eyes fell first. "Oh, all right." He carelessly set his drink down, followed by the others. To create a diversion, Honor deliberately stepped forward. "Hello, Phillip." Her quiet voice turned all eyes toward her, slim, smiling, more beautiful in her white gown than they had seen her. Desire rose in Phillip's face, but this time Honor was prepared. She had seen his falseness. Scales had dropped from her vision. "I'm sorry you weren't able to attend our wedding." Suddenly she knew it was true. She was free forever of Phillip Travis.

Phillip couldn't seem to answer. It was red-haired Babs who mocked, "Some little trick, Miss Honor Brooks. So Phillip wasn't here when you arrived? He had — other things on his mind."

"It didn't matter. James welcomed me."

Babs drew in a sharp breath. "I'll say he did! You pulled a real trick in getting old James to the altar. I wonder what Lucille's going to say?" Yet behind her baiting Honor sensed genuine relief in Babs's face, an almost-approval of what had happened. Did she care for Phillip that much?

James broke the uncomfortable silence. "Now if you really must go, I believe Mrs. Travis would like to change."

"The old here's your hat, what's your hurry routine," Babs mocked. "Come on, Phillip. We aren't wanted — or needed here." But the glance she threw over her shoulder at Honor was one of gratitude. "You'll just have to put up with me since your lady love prefers your twin." Over Phillip's protests she dragged him away, but not before he called back, "I'll be home soon."

Honor sighed with relief as the heavy door closed behind them. Slowly she turned to find James watching.

"You did very well, my dear." He stepped nearer, and her heart pounded. Surely he could hear it! She wouldn't have expected his next comment. "How would you like to go for a short ride?"

Honor stared at him, then said, "Why, I'd like that. Let me get changed." She ran up the stairs thinking to herself, *When I get to bed tonight I'll probably cry or scream. Now all I do is go riding with a husband who married me to protect me!*

By the time she had changed, James had Sol and Jingles ready. Silently he helped her mount. She laughed a little at her awkwardness. "I'll be a tenderfoot for some time, I'm afraid."

"They you'll stay?" Was that restrained eagerness in his voice or her own wishful thinking?

"For a time. It seems a shame to miss out on a real ranch vacation just because of something so trivial as a mistaken identity wedding." Before he could answer she had prodded Jingles with her heels and was racing down the road.

"Honor, wait!"

What imp of perversity caused her to dig in her heels more? "Come on, Jingles, let's go!" Ignoring the pounding of Sol behind them, she urged her pony forward. Faster, faster, until — Jingles stumbled, went down. Honor felt herself sailing through the air, then blackness enveloped her. A sharp pain stabbed her right shoulder. She cried out and knew nothing

more until she lifted heavy lids to find herself cradled in James's arms. She tried to struggle, but the pain in her shoulder was too much.

"Lie still." She felt the swing of a horse. James must have taken her on Sol.

"Jingles threw me. He must have stepped in a hole." She incoherently tried to explain.

"That's why I called. You don't run horses at night or in half-light." His voice was cold and hard. "Jingles hurt his leg pretty bad. I may have to shoot him."

Honor twisted until she could look in his face. "Oh, no!"

Pain crossed the features above her, still visible in the ruby sunset. "I'll call the vet. If it's only sprained, we can use hot compresses to get the swelling down. If it's broken —"

"It's my fault!" The first tears of the whole amazing day slipped from beneath her tightly closed lids. "If you have to shoot Jingles, it's my fault."

He didn't soften the blow. "Yes, it is. If you won't listen to people who know more about ranching than you do, maybe you'd better just stay in the house. Casa del Sol is a beautiful place. It is also a dangerous place. There are wild animals. There are rattlesnakes in the rocks."

Honor shivered, feeling small. "I'm sorry."

He slid to his feet, still carrying her, leaving Sol with reins dragging. "I'll get you in the house and call the vet."

"Senora!" Even through her remorse and pain Honor caught the change in Rosa's greeting. She was Senora now, mistress of Casa del Sol.

"Mrs. Travis has had a bad fall. I'm taking her to her room, Mama Rosa. Bring liniment. Her shoulder is sprained." For all the feeling in James's voice she might have been of less importance than the barn, Honor thought fleetingly. Mama Rosa and Carlotta worked with swift fingers, undressing her, getting her shoulder bathed, and dressed with a stinging liniment.

"You will feel better tomorrow. What a way to start a honeymoon!" Carlotta grinned impishly before slipping out the big door, leaving it slightly ajar.

Honeymoon! Honor tried to sit up and failed. She was just too tired to move, physically and emotionally. She threw herself back on the pillow, heedless of the pain in her shoulder. Had she ever lived through such a day? Her wedding day, the day she had dreamed of since she was a child, and especially since she met Phillip. What a travesty! Slow tears seeped

into her puffy pillow. It might as well have been a rock. She could no longer put off facing what she had done.

Through her pain and misery came Granny's stern, sad voice, "I don't know what it's going to take to make you see you can't outrun God. When you do, if you are married to an unbeliever, your life will be misery."

A final spurt of rebelliousness brought a protest to her lips, but it died before she could even whisper. No. She couldn't blame God any longer. She had insisted on idolizing Phillip Travis even against her own nagging doubts and the repeated warnings she had been given.

The dimly lit room receded to be replaced first by the scene at the canyon, then later here at Casa del Sol; that momentary, on-the-brink warning. It was not the chill evening breeze from her partly opened window that turned Honor cold. It was memory of her response to God's pleadings — and she knew they had been just that. Instead of listening to the Scriptures that had been planted in her brain, she had been swayed by the beauty of the canyon, the thrill of Phillip's attention, the false assurance that all would be well.

Tossing from one side of the great bed to the other, she faced it head-on. God had not done this to her. She had brought it on herself because she refused to listen to God's call. A new, sharper thrust filled her heart. She struggled to pray, to ask forgiveness, help, peace. *My spirit will not always strive with men* — she remembered the words from Genesis. Why did her prayers only ascend to the ceiling? Was she repenting more for the way things had turned out than for being a sinner? Was she really better off married to a man who obviously despised her than to Phillip? And was what she thought love for James really only clutching for security, strength, someone to stand between her and a world grown harsh?

Her weary brain refused to answer. James must have dropped a sleeping powder in the warm milk he had brought. Even if she could find God and be forgiven for a life of rebellion, she would still have the consequences of her mutiny — either a broken marriage relationship or an unbelieving husband.

James Travis kept his promise. In the month following their wedding, Honor saw little of him. Evidently he had meant just what he said. There was no time for leisure. He had a huge ranch to run and did just that.

Honor found she was a special guest as James had promised, nothing more. When he was in for meals, he was quietly courteous, asking if she was enjoying learning to know the ranch. Most of the time he was gone.

Once she curiously asked, "Do you stay in what Mama Rosa calls 'line shacks' when you are out on the range?"

His smile was sardonic, leaving her feeling she had blundered again. "Sometimes. I can't very well stay in the bunkhouse when the hands think this is still our honeymoon."

His thrust had gone home and silenced her.

To Honor, who had been busy all her life, that month was dreamlike. At first it was enough just to rest and sort things out. Yet that very sorting out left her more confused and miserable than ever. It had been as she feared. God's forgiveness would not extend to making everything rosy between James and her. Would they ever be anything except courteous strangers? Neither did she feel God had forgiven her.

She grew thin, worried. In spite of the time she spent with Rosa learning to prepare the spicy Mexican dishes, there wasn't enough to keep her busy. James had forbidden her to ride alone. Sometimes in the evening he took her out, always a stern shadow, an impeccable escort, and as remote as Kendrick Peak.

James unexpectedly appeared at lunch one day. "Would you like to take a drive this afternoon?"

She hid her surprise. "Why, yes. Can you spare the time?" She hadn't meant to sound sarcastic, but it came out that way.

James's expression changed. "I believe it can be arranged."

Nothing more was said until they were seated in the Willys. Honor nervously adjusted a veil. The snowline on the mountains was steadily encroaching upon the valley. No wonder! It was definitely fall. Every leaf flaunted red or gold winter dress in a King Midas world.

"Where are we going?"

"Do you have to ask a question as if I were still an ogre?" James sounded irritated.

"Aren't you?" Instantly repentant, she laid one gloved hand over his strong one on the wheel, her most unselfconscious gesture since their marriage.

"Don't touch me while I'm driving!"

She snatched her hand back as if it had been burned, more hurt than she would admit even to herself, and made herself small against the door on the passenger side, turning her back on James so he could not read her expression.

"We're going to see an old friend of mine. His name is Judge Bell. I call him Daddy, and have since my own father died."

Something in his voice reached even through Honor's misery. "You really care about him, don't you?"

"I love him and his wife. They're real people."

Honor sneaked a glance at the forbidding face behind the wheel. A ghost of a smile had replaced some of the irritation.

"Judge Bell grew up knowing he was going to be a minister. When he got in his teens he was mixed up in some kind of unpleasantness — he never said what. He was innocent, but since his comrades were guilty, it looked as if he would be sentenced along with them. The judge in the case was known to be harsh. He was always fair, but the boys knew there was little hope.

"Evidently the judge listened and was impressed by the boy's sincerity. He dismissed the charges against Daddy. Daddy was so impressed he prayed about it, he said, and decided he could do as much good as a Christian judge as if he became a minister. He did. He spent over fifty years as a judge before he retired. Now his heart isn't strong enough for the grueling hours required in his former work."

"What does he do now?"

James laughed. "If you have a picture of a broken down man, you're in for a shock. He ministers. He gives love and comfort to the poor, the dying, even to —" He broke off suddenly, giving her a piercing glance that brought red to her face.

"And you think he can bring comfort to me?"

"I hope so." James swung the big touring car into a small lane. "Honor, I want to talk to you."

Why should his simple statement send shudders up her spine?

"I know you aren't happy. I can't expect you to be, I suppose. Daddy said I did a terrible thing, marrying you as I did."

"He knows?"

"Of course." James's mouth twisted. "I rode over the night after we were married and told him." Bitterness filled his face. "So you don't have to play any games with him. He can see right through you."

I hope not.

Had she spoken the words aloud?

No, James went on uninterrupted. "You'll like him and his wife. They live what they believe." He shot her another quick glance. "By the way, what does that God you believe in — or do you — think about our marriage?"

She chose to answer his first question first. "Yes, I believe in God. I always have. I just never did anything about it — until now." Her voice trailed off.

"Are you a Christian?"

"No." She swallowed a lump in her throat, feeling constricted almost to the point of being unable to breathe. "But I want to be, James, I want to be!" Forgetting the estrangement between them, she turned to face him directly. "From the time I was small I blamed God for everything that went wrong. Granny tried to tell me everyone who lives on earth is subject to natural consequences, but I wouldn't listen." Her troubled face reflected her struggles. "I'm afraid I waited and rebelled too long."

"Ridiculous! What have you ever done that was so terrible? You haven't killed or anything like that. You have lived a good life."

Honor shook her head. "I've sinned most of all by refusing to listen to the Holy Spirit sent to show me what God wants — and by turning my back on the gift of eternal life and salvation through acceptance of God's only Son." She turned away, eyes desolate.

James cleared his throat. "I can't help you with that, but Judge Bell can." He changed the subject. "You didn't tell me what your God thought of our marriage." His lips curved downward. "You think God punished you for not accepting Him by letting you marry an ogre?"

"I can't blame God for what I insisted on." Her lips quivered.

With a muttered imprecation James started the car and drove in silence to a small white cottage with a picket fence, leaving Honor to stare at the blurring countryside they passed.

If ever there was a case of love at first sight it was between Honor and the Bells. "Why, you remind me of my father!" Honor's spontaneous remark was met with warmth like flames of an open fire.

"Come in, come in, children." Motherly Mrs. Bell and the equally welcoming judge threw wide the door, but after only a few moments the Judge said, "Run along, James. I'll be wanting to talk with your lassie alone."

"Well!" Mrs. Bell's crinkling eyes belied her pretended hurt. "We've been dismissed, James, my boy. We'll go get our doughnuts ready for when they've finished."

Honor waited for Judge Bell to speak. When he did it was to ask her to call him Daddy.

"You know what happened?" She couldn't hide her trembling fingers.

"Aye. But I wonder if you do?"

It was the last thing Honor had expected. "Wh-what do you mean?"

"Did the laddie tell you why?"

A shake of the head was all she could manage.

"I thought not." The soft burr in Daddy Bell's Scottish voice soothed her as nothing had done for weeks. She leaned forward.

"Did — did he tell *you* why?"

"He told me more than he realized. After you had mistaken him for Phillip and went upstairs he paced his library for hours. He ran the gamut of emotions from wanting to horsewhip Phillip to wishing he had never been born twin to such a philanderer.

"He had tried to send you away. He had tried to warn you what Phillip was and you refused to believe. If he told you he was Phillip's brother, you would have more reason to distrust him."

Honor flushed, remembering how she had referred to the absent brother as the ogre.

"Early in life James and Phillip's father had given James charge over his brother, a brother's-keeper responsibility. When Phillip refused direction, James became bitter. When you appeared, it was the last bit of evidence of Phillip's nature to convict him.

"James could see you would never break your vow. He decided to marry you. It had taken an entire night to decide, and he could no longer stand the confines of the library. He saddled Sol, rode here, and caught me just as I was coming in from a call. He —"

Honor could stand no more. Her eyes flew open. "He *told* you what he was going to do?"

"Of course not. Much as I love the laddie, he knew I'd not stand by for such a thing."

The crisp tone brought a wave of color to Honor's face. "I'm sorry. It's just that it's all been such a shock."

"I understand. Lassie" — Daddy Bell's eyes were kind — "did you not know down in your heart Phillip Travis was no man for you?"

It was the final touch. Honor put her face in her hands. "I knew. God even tried to warn me."

A light came to the old man's eyes. "You are a follower?"

"Any following I've done is after my own way."

"And now you're sorry."

"With all my heart." Honor slipped to the handbraided rug at his feet. "Not just for choosing Phillip over God, but for everything. For not listening to Granny and my brother and —" her voice dropped until it was barely audible "— and the Holy Spirit."

She heard grave concern in his voice as he asked, "Lassie, did you not know the Spirit's calling?"

"That's what is so terrible. I deliberately chose Phillip Travis over God!" She scarcely heard his quick intake of breath. "Now when I try to pray, it's as if God has turned His back on me — just as I did on Him."

"Look at me."

There was something magnificent in Daddy Bell's voice reminiscent of days when he tempered justice with mercy. Honor fixed her gaze on his face.

"Do you recognize now how much of a sinner you are? Do you freely acknowledge it, and believe Jesus died to save you from those sins? Do you accept Him into your heart and life forever?"

"Yes!"

The soft cry in the still room seemed magnified in Honor's ears. Daddy Bell's admonition, "Tell Him so," brought a rush of feeling as Honor stammered, "I'm a sinner, God. Forgive me. I accept the gift of your Son and salvation through Him." She could not go on. The month of sleepless nights had taken their toll, but the next instant she felt weariness leave. In its place was peace — not the false assurance that she could work things out, but the knowledge that no matter what came, God was there to strengthen her. Along with the peace was knowledge — she was free, forgiven. But it did not mean every trouble was over. She was just what Granny had said she would be — wedded to one who scorned the Christ, or at best ignored Him, just as she had done.

Another memory found its way to her lips. "I said, when Granny warned me, that if God ever caught up to me, there was no reason He couldn't catch Phillip, too." Her regret struck deep. "How blind, willful, sinful I was!"

Daddy Bell's hands were warm on her own. "It's over, lassie. I won't try and excuse you in any way for what you have done. You must live with it. Neither will I excuse James." His shrewd eyes searched her. "I will say I doubt the laddie married you entirely to save you from Phillip."

"He despises me as a weakling." Honor couldn't hold back tears. "How can you say he might care?"

"It has been my business to know men."

Daddy Bell's words echoed in Honor's mind as James and Mrs. Bell came in, to be told the news of Honor's acceptance of Christ. Mrs. Bell appeared delighted. James did not. On the way home he spoke of it. "I suppose now you're a Christian you'll be even more bitter about me." He didn't give her a chance to reply, but quickly added, "What does God say about Christian wives with husbands like me?"

She sought sarcasm and found none. Was he serious? She would respond as if he was. "First Corinthians seven fourteen says, 'For the unbelieving husband is sanctified by the wife, and —"

"The Bible doesn't say that!" James shot her a glance that was totally unreadable.

"See for yourself. It's right there."

"If I had a Bible, I might just do that."

Honor rode quietly all the way home. When they reached the sprawling hacienda she climbed from the car without waiting for his assistance, only saying, "Thank you for taking me." She dashed upstairs, threw open the big trunk she had brought from San Francisco, and delved clear to the bottom. For a moment she held close the precious Book she unearthed. She would need it now more than ever. As a child of God, she must study.

With a sigh she touched the worn cover regretfully, then lifted her chin. Daddy Bell would get her another Bible. In the meantime —

James looked shocked when she appeared, out of breath, at the bottom of the stairs. "What on earth —"

"Here." She steadied her voice, forcing casualness into it she did not feel. "I have been wondering what to give you — whether to give you this —" She held it out.

"A Bible?"

The trancelike state he seemed to have gone into released a spirit she hadn't known existed. "It's perfectly proper to accept, Mr. Travis. Even if we weren't married, a Bible is always considered an acceptable gift."

She retreated up two steps, away from the disturbing dark eyes. "Don't forget to read it — especially First Corinthians." Her sense of mischief faded. "And John, especially three sixteen —" She could not go on, so blindly ran upstairs, remembering how he stood staring at her. She gently closed her door and dropped to her knees by the side of the bed. How easy it was to tell someone else to read the best-know of all verses, "For God so loved the world, that he gave his only begotten Son, that whosoever

believeth in him should not perish, but have everlasting life." But how hard it had been to accept it!

Tears drenched the beautiful spread. If only she had accepted that verse and invited Jesus into her heart, asking for forgiveness for her sins long ago when Keith did, how different things would be now! She would not be in love with a husband who cared nothing for her and even less for the Lord she had suddenly discovered was more precious to her than anything else on earth.

That was only the first of Honor's visits to the Bell cottage. James took time from his duties on the ranch to teach Honor to drive, and once she was competent, she traveled to the little home near Kendrick Peak often. Each visit produced growth in her Christian walk.

One particularly beautiful afternoon she said, "Daddy, all the Scriptures I have known practically forever mean something now. Is it because I am reading with my heart?"

"Aye, lassie." The wise eyes lit with an inner glow. "Faith is the key to unlock the mysteries of the universe."

Inevitably their talks included James. Daddy was firm in the belief James would come to know God as other than a Master Mind. "He's a pantheist, you know." He intercepted Honor's questioning glance. "One who equates God with nature and the laws of the universe."

"Is it wrong to see God in nature? At the canyon I felt something of this." Honor's face was wistful, remembering the beauty and magnificence of the place.

"There is nothing wrong with seeing God as Creator of this earth's glory so long as you don't lose sight of God — the Father, the Son, and the Holy Spirit, who brought salvation to this world."

"And James only sees the creating force." A shadow crossed her face. "Daddy, who is Lucille Lawson?"

The old man looked surprised at the change of subject. "Why, she's a twice-divorced woman who —" he looked a bit shamefaced, and Honor could see him carefully choosing words "— who had designs on James and his ranch." He peered at her more closely. "How did you hear of her?"

"Her name was mentioned by Babs and the crowd the day I was married. I also saw it on an envelope in the library."

"She's not your kind — or James's."

Honor spread her hands wide. "Who is?" Her honest eyes met Daddy's. "He is such a mass of contradictions. Laughing one moment, locked behind a granite wall the next. I know he doesn't drink or go in for that sort of thing." Her face shadowed. "Because of my stubbornness here I am married to him. I'm learning the terrible results of sin. If I hadn't insisted on my own way, James would be free."

"Are you sure he wants to be?" The quiet voice cut through her depression.

"How can he help it? He laughed when he told me how he even arranged with Juan to come dashing out with the telegram supposedly telling Phillip was coming. It did say that, but James had already known Phillip was due soon." She stopped, trouble chasing away the joy that always came through her learning sessions with Daddy. "Such a quixotic gesture! He seems honorable enough, except for that —"

"Would you have thought of yourself as honorable before meeting Phillip Travis?"

"I would have then."

"Yet you chose not only to marry Phillip but to deny every teaching you have been given," Daddy gently reminded. "I cannot say why James did such a thing. When he came to me after the wedding and told me, I was stunned. I cried out in protest, asked how he could deliberately plot and arrange this marriage."

Honor held her breath in the little pause that followed.

The judge's face was stern. "He told me that even though you persisted in believing nothing but the best of Phillip, he couldn't stand to see you crushed under his brother's boots like a frail flower."

"I really thought Phillip would change, especially after coming to Casa del Sol."

She couldn't believe the way Daddy's big hand balled into a fist and struck the shining edge of a piecrust table. "Lassie, any girl or woman who marries a man in hopes of reforming him is doomed to a living hell on earth! If it is not in a man to live clean and honorably before marriage, only rarely will he do it after."

"Yet you refuse to see my marriage to James as a tragedy." Honor regretted the words as soon as they came out.

Daddy Bell's face settled into deep lines. "I would have given anything on earth to prevent it. Now it is done, you can only go on from here."

"I know." She stood and restlessly walked toward the window. "Even when I was being married I sensed something wrong. I refused to admit how weak Phillip was. He needed me. Since accepting Christ I have begun to see the awfulness of what God saved me from, and it is from my own actions."

"It always is."

Honor turned back toward him. "It's just that I don't know how to

approach him. I don't know if he reads the Bible I gave him. Even if he does, he never mentions it."

"You've stayed in spite of everything. Are you going to continue to honor your vows?"

Honor looked deep into the searching eyes. "I must. I promised before God and man, gave my word." She bit her lips to steady them. "Unless he sends me away."

"And do you want to stay, lassie?" Before she could answer, his face crimsoned. "Forgive me." He held out both hands to Honor. "I have no right to ask such a thing."

He deliberately changed the subject. "The only good whatsoever I can see coming from such a beginning lies in your heart, and in the life James has led since childhood. He hates anything smacking of cheapness."

Honor nodded, and Daddy continued, "He also believes in God but has not yet met Him face to face. He cannot admit he is a sinner and claim forgiveness through Jesus' death on Calvary."

"Will he ever?"

"He must!" Daddy dropped her hands to bring his fist down against the arm of the chair. "He knows the way. But it may take a long, hard road of traveling before James Travis accepts the gift of salvation through our Lord Jesus."

"Just as it was a long, hard road for me."

Daddy sighed. "Yes. I cannot condone in any way what the two of you have done. Neither is there any time for crying over the past. You must go forward and leave what will be in God's hands."

"You will pray for us?" It was through a blur that Honor saw his benedictory smile.

"I have been — since James came with the news. Live your faith so he can see it is real. Your refusing to break your vows will be a witness."

Mrs. Bell's round, smiling face appeared in the doorway. "Honor, one of these days I'll teach you to make some of my special recipes. James loves them." In the general conversation following, Honor's depression could not help vanishing. She laughed. "It will be a real accomplishment when I can equal your doughnuts!"

"Anything worth knowing is worth working at," Daddy reminded, leaving Honor with a parting word. She knew it was not to doughnuts, but to her own life and walk with God that he referred.

Several days later she told Rosa, "It's good to be back in the kitchen." Her floury hands stilled on the big board where whe was practicing making

tortillas. "I haven't had a chance since Granny died, and I'm really a homemaker at heart."

"It is good. Senor's woman should be home, not off working for others." Rosa snorted. "Flagstaff women are leaving homes and children. Pah! They should stay home where they belong."

Honor hid a smile. What would Rosa, happy with her pots and pans, think of San Francisco, where women were flocking to offices! "Where do the cowhands eat?" she asked.

"The cookhouse." Rosa's white smile widened. "I show you when everyone is gone. Cookie likes my pies, but no visitors."

It took weeks for Honor to discover how big her new home really was. James began to take her around more, as if she were a special guest. She could almost forget their unusual marriage at the sight of the birds, coyotes, a startled deer.

"Honor," he asked on one of the expeditions, "are you unhappy here?"

"No." Before he could reply, she remounted the pony who had replaced Jingles. Although her favorite pinto would recover, he wasn't to be ridden for a time. When she was in the saddle she looked down. "When I forget about — about that ceremony, I am not unhappy."

"I'm glad." He covered her rapidly tanning hands with his own. Something in the dark eyes flickered, making her wonder if Daddy Bell could be right. Was her husband beginning to care for her? It was the first time he had touched her since their wedding day.

Breathless, unwilling to acknowledge what she either saw or imagined, Honor touched her horse with her heels. "Race you back to the ranch!" The spell was broken. She felt the wind in her face and, exulting, cried out encouragement to her pony. She felt rather than saw when James caught up with her. The longer stride of Sol easily overtook her pony.

"Faster, faster," she urged, but always he was there beside them, laughing above the wind she created with her momentum. Neck and neck they raced to the corral. At the last moment Sol leaped ahead and left Honor and her mount to come in second.

"You could at least have let me win," she complained as she slid from the saddle, refusing his help. "Seems it would be the polite thing to do!" Her disheveled hair surrounded the hat that had slid back until it was only held by the cord around her throat. Strangely stirred inside, she felt the need to pick a quarrel of some kind to relieve the tension, even if it was only over a silly race.

"Is that what you want — to be let to win?"

If the quizzical question had a hidden meaning, she chose to ignore it. Stepping close, hands on hips in an easy Western pose, she glared at him. "I intend to beat you fair and square, Mr. Man. And I'll do it with honor."

Her pretended indignation slipped at what she saw in his face. The combination of tenderness and kindness almost proved her undoing. Quickly she turned back to her horse. "I'm going to begin by showing you how well I can unsaddle my horse and rub him down." Her deft hands that had practiced hours in secret for this very moment made short work of lifting the heavy saddle. She staggered a bit, but triumphantly got it where it belonged and went on to groom down her horse in the best way possible.

"Say, you're going to make a pretty good rancher's wife after all!" He took one step toward her, a new admiration showing.

Honor's heart flipped over. The intensity of her own emotion almost overwhelmed her, but the feeling was interrupted.

"Really, darling, it takes more than being able to rub down a horse to be wife of the heir of Casa del Sol!"

Honor whirled toward the speaker. Soignee, every shining blonde hair in place, green eyes smiling maliciously, the woman was everything Honor was not at that moment! Acutely aware of her own appearance. Honor flushed deeply. Who was this woman?

"Hello, Lucille." James's voice was flat, unemotional.

So this is Lucille! Honor boiled as the woman tucked her hand in James's arm and smiled up into his face. "I understand congratulations are in order. This must be the little bride?" She lifted highly painted lips and kissed James square on the mouth. Honor had the satisfaction of seeing him recoil.

"Always dramatic, aren't you, Lucille? What brings you out here?"

"Curiosity." The boldness of her statement left Honor speechless. "I ran into Phillip. He told me he was carefully staying away from the ranch for a while — until the honeymoon was over."

So that was why Phillip hadn't come as promised. Honor's mind ran double track, wondering why Lucille had come.

"Mrs. Lawson is an old friend," James explained. "Lucille, my wife, Honor."

"Honor!" The heavily-made-up eyes widened. "How quaint!"

It was too much. Honor's good nature had been strained. "Yes, isn't it? But then, I'm a bit quaint myself. Perhaps that is why James married me." She saw his jaw drop, and smiled sweetly at their guest. "I must excuse myself and tell Mama Rosa there will be a guest for dinner. You will stay, won't you?"

"I'll stay." With the tables turned, Lucille sounded grim.

"Then I'll see you later."

"Do you dress for dinner?"

Honor thought rapidly, then disarmingly touched her rumpled clothing. "Doesn't it look like we need to dress for dinner?" She walked steadily toward the house before Lucille could answer. This was one time she felt she needed to dress for dinner. The horrible truth dawned on her — she had no evening gown except the white dress she had been married in!

Giggling nervously at the hastily contrived trap that had caught her, she burst into the house. "Mama Rosa! Come quick!"

"Senora, what is it?" An alarmed brown face peered from the doorway, closely followed by Carlotta's anxious one.

"A Mrs. Lawson has arrived —"

"Her!" Carlotta's sniff was a masterpiece. "Mrs. La-De-Dah in person!"

"Exactly." Honor felt herself relaxing under their understanding. "She was hateful, wondered about dressing for dinner. I told her yes. But I don't have anything except my wedding gown!"

"Wear it," Carlotta advised. "Wait!" She dashed into the open courtyard and returned triumphantly with a handful of late roses. "Mama can put up your hair and tuck a flower in it." Her skillful fingers were twining the flowers even as she spoke, carefully removing thorns, fashioning a beautiful corsage. "This goes on your left shoulder."

When Honor was dressed, her two faithful friends stepped back in admiration. "Beautiful!" Carlotta clapped her hands, but Mama Rosa only smiled and said, "Senor will be proud."

He was. Honor could see it in his eyes when she descended the curving staircase. Lucille Lawson stood close, shivering in a backless ice-green gown.

"Why, Mrs. Lawson, come in where it's warm! That hall of ours does stay cold." Honor threw open the door to the library. "James, why did you leave her standing out there?" She didn't wait for an answer. "Tell me, are you here for long?"

Slightly disconcerted, but unwilling to allow anyone else to steal the stage for even a minute, the green eyes matching her gown hardened. "I really don't know. That is, when I came back to Phoenix — I've been shopping in New Yawk, you know — well, I just heard about the wedding and rushed right out here with a gift." She handed a heavy box to Honor.

For one moment Honor felt like throwing it into the fireplace, then her

own breeding replaced the urge with a quiet smile. "It was kind of you to think of us. James, will you open it, or shall I?"

"Go ahead." If the tone of his voice was an indication, they were in for cold weather during Mrs. Lawson's stay.

Honor hesitated, noting the expensive label on the box. She wanted nothing from this woman, especially her gifts. Why had she come, just when things might have improved with James? Keeping her face bland she lifted the contents of the package. "Oh!" She dropped it back in its wrappings, unable to conceal her distaste. James came to her rescue, holding up the platter surrounded with heavily carved silver snakes.

"Lucille, that has to be the ugliest thing I have ever seen."

"Why, Jimmy!" She pouted. "It's solid silver. I thought you'd like it — to remember me by."

His voice was grimmer than Honor had ever heard it. "Then if it's solid silver I'm afraid we'll have to say thank you and return it. We couldn't possibly accept a present so valuable. *Or inappropriate,*" he muttered just loud enough for Honor to catch.

"Sorry, darling." Steel blades unsheathed themselves in her green eyes. "Just thought I'd bring you a reminder of all our past — associations."

"What is that supposed to mean?" James Travis caught her by the shoulders, swinging her around to face him. "You know there's never been anything between us."

"Oh?" She pointed a woman-to-woman glance at Honor, who stood frozen in place. "Of course, darling, if you say so."

"I do say so. To be brutally frank, you've been a nightmare. There hasn't been a time you haven't followed me and tried to give the impression of some hidden relationship between us."

"Poor boy." She stroked his cheek with a white hand she had managed to free. Honor stood like a statue, wondering. *How can she do it? I would be scared to death if James looked at me like that! There's almost murder in his eyes!*

"Don't touch me!" James loosened her so she nearly fell. He jerked the bell rope nearby. Honor could hear it pealing in the distance. Time stood suspended until Juan appeared, almost running. "Senor?"

"Mrs. Lawson won't be staying for dinner. Please show her out, Juan."

Honor gasped as Lucille Lawson went a dull, murderous red. It was her turn to shoot hateful sparks into the air. "So, it's true! This baby-faced little thing has you snared. You think she'll ever have brains enough to be mistress of Casa del Sol? The way I hear it, she fell in Phillip's arms like an overripe apple, got herself invited down here." She spun back to Honor.

"What happened? Did you find bigger game?"

"That's enough!" James seized her by the arm and propelled her to the door, only stopping to scoop up the offending silver gift. The eyes of the carved snakes glittered in the dim light. "Get out and take your snakes with you!"

Honor heard their footsteps across the tiled floor of the hall then the dull thud as the heavy door banged into place. She dropped in a chair, exhausted by the scene, frantically searching for something to say when James returned.

He came back, breathing hard. Without a word he crossed to the fireplace and poked its already blazing contents into a minor inferno.

"Well?" She hadn't known her voice could be so weak and trembly.

"Well, what?" The anger in his eyes were directed at her now.

"Well, Mrs. Lawson — she —" Honor was unable to go on.

"She's a troublemaker and always has been."

Honor waited, but he didn't go on. How could he so casually dismiss that vicious woman? Gnawing doubt crept into her heart. "She must have had something to base all that on. It's hard to imagine any woman bursting into a honeymoon —" She turned fiery, but forced herself to continue. "Unless she had been given some kind of reason to expect —"

James towered over her, tall, terrible, as she had seen him earlier. "She has never been given any reason to expect anything!" Honor's sigh of relief was lost in his fury. "The only mistake I ever made was in treating her as a human being and not telling her to get lost every time she hung around." He laughed bitterly. "You're my wife. In spite of everything I shouldn't have had to tell you that. Do you believe me?"

She was so startled by his abrupt question she could only stammer, "I — I —"

His laugh was even more bitter. "It doesn't really matter. Think what you like. I don't care either way."

"Then since you don't care, I won't bother to answer." Honor rose, her heart dropping like lead. He didn't care, at all. She managed a dignified exit until she got just to the doorway of the library. "Why did she have to come? This afternoon I thought maybe we could be friends —" Her words died on her lips.

"Friends?" James looked at her as if she had dropped in from outer space. "I'm afraid not. Friends are people who trust you." He brushed past her, arrogantly striding toward the door. "I don't believe I care for any dinner. I'm going out on Sol."

Again she heard footsteps cross the tile floor, the same thud of the big door closing. This time she did not try to think of something to say. She was seething with fury.

"You come to dinner now?" Mama Rosa peered into the library. "Juan say Mrs. Lawson is gone. But where is Senor?"

The innocent question brought even more fury to Honor. "I don't know and don't care. I don't want any dinner." She ran for the staircase, trailing the white dress she had put on so eagerly such a short time before. "Senor can go where he pleases. I don't care what he does!" Passing Mama with her shocked face, Honor pelted up the stairs, bolted her door, and fell on the bed.

"Let him go! Let him go riding. I don't care if he never comes back. Why should he take it out on me? Just because I couldn't instantly say I had full trust in him! How could he expect me to trust him, after what he pulled about our wedding?" The next instant she was on her knees, crying her heart out. "Oh, God, what am I going to do?"

Hours later she heard Sol's rhythmic gait. She had learned to distinguish it from that of the other horses. Carefully she slipped to the window, watching as she had watched other times. Even from this distance she could see James's restrained fury. Angry with her? Or Lucille? Or both? Did he regret the mad impulse that had caused him to marry her in a quixotic plan to save her from his brother?

Cold air struck her the same time fear hit. Perhaps now he would realize how insane it had all been and send her away. The new thought paralyzed her and sent her shivering back to the big bed. Wave after wave of fear went through her. He would send her away. She would never see him again. Too numb to pray, still her heart pleaded, "No, don't let it happen! I love him." But only the cold night wind answered by its frosty breath. Half-frozen, she finally stumbled from bed and closed the window. No use trying to sleep. She touched a match to the always-laid fire in her tiny fireplace and cuddled in front of it wrapped in a robe and the comforter from the bed. Gradually the little fire warmed her.

As the heaviest frost of the season turned every branch and twig into a carrier of white rime that sparkled in the first rays of dawn, she wrestled with her problem. Body warm, heart still a chunk of ice, she at last slipped into bed, too worn out to think any more.

The next day Phillip Travis came home.

" 'Home is the sailor, home from the sea,' and all that." Phillip Travis's debonair manner disappeared as he slumped into a chair. Honor had been trying to read in the library without much success. Every footstep on the tiled hall floor brought her heart to her throat. She expected James to come in, look at her coldly, and order her to go.

Her relief was so great that she welcomed Phillip more warmly than she would have thought possible. "Hello! We've been wondering when you would come."

"Oh?" The dark eyes were wary. "Wouldn't have thought you'd care one way or the other now that you're all hitched up with James."

Choosing her words carefully, Honor insisted, "We will always care about you, Phillip." Her gentle voice attested to the truth of her words.

"Sure you will. That's why you came down here and married James within a week of the time we were engaged."

"I can explain that —" But Honor stopped short. She couldn't explain. It would be too humiliating.

Phillip didn't seem to notice. He was staring moodily into the roaring fire that was always kept going now that the weather had turned colder. "I might have known. You were always too good for me. It's really better this way." He grinned crookedly at her shocked expression. "I mean it. I'm a rotten guy. James can make you happy."

It was the last thing on earth she would have expected from him. "You — you really mean that."

"Sure." He looked surprised. "Even at the canyon I knew it wouldn't last." He caught her disillusionment and leaned forward. "I'm just no good, Honor. At least not for a girl like you. I even wish I could be, but not all the time."

From somewhere deep inside Honor was given insight, as she had at the canyon. "Phillip, if you have even a desire to change, God will help you if you will only —"

"Don't preach, Honor." But there was no anger in his voice. "Funny, I'm James's twin, and *he* isn't always drunk or gambling." Again there was a note of wistfulness. "But of course, he has the ranch to look after."

"And you? What do you have to look after?"

For one moment she thought she had probed too deeply, but Phillip only stared at her, then lazily yawned. "Me, I guess." He yawned again. "A long time ago I thought I'd have Babs to look after, but she had other ideas."

Eyes steady, forcing him to look at her, Honor said, "I believe Babs cares for you more than you know."

There was a quick flare of hope in his eyes, replaced by dullness. "Too late. I don't care about her."

"Don't you, Phillip?" Without giving him a chance to answer, Honor stood. "Why don't you invite Babs for a visit? Give her a chance to be something other than your 'good-time' date. You might be surprised."

"At least it would be something different. I'm about fed up with the social whirl. Maybe I will give her a call." He slumped back and closed his eyes, but Honor thoughtfully went to her room. Did she dare? She did. She would dare anything to help that troubled man downstairs. Her original love for him had died, but there was another reason to help him now. He was James's brother, weak, perhaps foolish, but still James's brother — and hers, if she stayed.

Gently she picked up the phone and rang. "Operator? Please give me the number of Barbara Merrill in Flagstaff." She didn't want to let Phillip see her searching for the number. "Babs, this is Honor Brooks Travis." She could hear unfriendliness and suspicion in the other woman's voice, but rushed on, "I believe Phillip may be going to call and invite you here. You will be welcome. Phillip needs you." There was a long pause, along with the thudding of Honor's heart, then Babs's slightly thawed voice said, "Thanks." Was that a husky note?

Honor cradled the phone. Had James been right when he said Babs was waiting for Phillip to prove he could be true? It was odd, out of keeping with her own sheltered life. Such games and social ploys were out of her sphere. Babs seemed to be sophisticated — was it possible she wanted a lasting marriage? Honor would have judged her as someone to try again if the first time didn't work.

Soberly Honor donned her riding outfit. It didn't pay to judge. But how strange it would be if it turned out Babs was one of the first she would be called to witness to about her recent experience in acceptance of Christ! Her heart sank. What a task! Yet if God gave her the task, He would send strength to do it.

Babs had sounded almost thunderstruck when she hung up. The next few days might be quite interesting!

When Honor got downstairs, Phillip was waiting. This time his lazy manner failed to hide his eagerness. "I called Babs. She's coming and will be here for dinner." Suddenly he dropped his pose. "I don't blame you for throwing me down after you met James. We can at least be friends, can't we?"

Without her own volition Honor parroted James's words to her from the afternoon before. "Friends are people who trust you."

"I trust you, Honor." Phillip stepped closer, looking up to her on the second stair above him. "I don't know why you married James in such a hurry, but it's all right."

"Oh, Phillip." Blindly she reached out a hand to be caught in the white ones shaped like James's hands but so different in color and texture from the working hands she had learned to love!

"What a touching scene." The sarcasm in James's voice effectively separated the two on the stairs. "Welcoming the prodigal home, Honor? Don't overdo it." He brushed past them rudely. Honor clung to the banister rail in order to keep from being upset.

"Just a minute!"

Honor had never seen such determination in Phillip's eyes. It must have startled James. He swung around, looking back down with intense dislike in his face.

"Honor was kind enough to suggest that I ask Babs for a visit. I told her Babs was coming and asked Honor to be my friend. That's why she gave me her hand."

"My wife needs no explanation of her actions to me by you or anyone — especially by you." James's face was granite, his eyes flint. "If Babs is coming I would suggest you remember she is your guest. My wife will make her welcome, of course." Had there been the slightest emphasis on the words *my wife?*

Phillip started up the stairs. "Why, you —"

"Phillip, no!" With a horror of scenes, Honor caught his arm. He mustn't fight his own brother on her account! She had longed to bring peace to this house, not contention. "You must not fight! Either of you." She scornfully looked at James. "Phillip told you the truth. If you don't want to believe him, that's your problem."

"Then since it doesn't matter, I won't commit myself. We'll be dressing for dinner, I suppose, in Babs's honor?"

Tears of fury stung Honor's eyes. He had parried her plea for trust as effectively as she had done the day before. "Yes, we will dress for dinner." She turned her back squarely on him. "Phillip, I don't seem to have the

proper clothing for Casa del Sol and its visitors. Perhaps you and Babs will drive in with me to Flagstaff one day this week. I'm sure Babs can tell me where to buy."

Only the sneaking admiration in Phillip's eyes held her together. Had she been expected to knuckle under? Perhaps as Phillip had done — too often? With a weaker personality it must have been much easier just to take the line of least resistance.

"I'll give you a check when you want to go shopping."

Resisting an impulse to kick him in the shins or say something even more sarcastic than he had done, Honor counted to ten and turned. She would not lose her belief in a soft answer's turning away wrath simply because this man infuriated and goaded her beyond belief. Her voice was low and even. "That won't be necessary." She even managed a smile. "After all, brides provide their own trousseaus."

She thought he would protest. His face had thunderclouded to a scowl. At the last moment he changed tactics, stepping aside and sweeping her a low bow. "As you say, my dear." For the first time since the wedding he turned and caught her to him, kissing her lightly on the forehead. "Sorry I was cross. Why don't you have a ride before dinner? There's plenty of time." As if forgetting why he had been going upstairs, James trod heavily down and across the hall, leaving the door ajar behind him.

Phillip smiled. "You've got him befuddled, Honor. He wants to believe in you but isn't too sure about me." He grinned, yet an anxious look crept into his face. "I suppose I should be flattered, but I really don't want to cause trouble between you two. He's the biggest thing in my life. I've always wanted to be more like him."

Honor again caught the cry for help. "There's no reason you can't, Phillip. If you would only believe in yourself — and in God."

"I really can't see myself in that role." He shook his head.

"I can — with all my heart." Her fervent exclamation scored, and a bit awkwardly Phillip asked, "How about that ride? We certainly have James's blessing."

Honor swallowed a lump in her throat. James's change of direction had been superb showmanship, nothing more. The kiss had not held tenderness, as had his kisses before their wedding. It had all been for Phillip's benefit. Dashing back disappointment, she forced gaiety. "Of course! How long has it been since you've really ridden here? I bet I know more about Casa del Sol than you do!"

"We'll see about that!"

But an hour later Phillip had to admit defeat. "You're right. You really do know more. I guess I've been too busy indoors to remember how grand it is." His sweeping hand took in the still-yellow aspens, towering firs and pines, and distance-softened rolling hills leading to mountains dusted by early snow. "You think Babs will like it?"

Honor whirled toward him. "Phillip, I want to know right now — why did you pay all that attention to me — build up promises? You know you've never really loved anyone but Babs!"

She didn't think he would answer, and when he did it was in a shamed voice. "I know. But you were different, sweet. When Babs turned me down I made up my mind I'd never let her hurt me again. She —" He stopped, forced himself to look at Honor. "When I was at the canyon I really did think maybe I could make it with you."

"It was a terrible thing to do, Phillip."

Her gently accusing voice brought color even to his ears. "I know — now. But it all turned out all right. You married James. You could have searched the world over and never found a better man."

"Does your brother know how much you care about him?"

"Don't be ridiculous!" The mood was broken. "Men don't go around telling each other stuff like that."

"You're the one who is ridiculous. He's your brother. If you had let him know a long time ago how you feel, a lot of the trouble between you could have been solved before it began."

"Maybe you're right." But it was too serious for Phillip. "Come on — race you to the ranch!"

"Didn't think you could do it," he teased as he reined in beside her. "A tenderfoot like you beating an old hand like me?"

"An old hand like you had better do more riding. You're getting rusty. Next time I'll beat you worse!" Honor swung from the saddle and prepared to remove it.

"Hey, let one of the hands do that."

"What? A good rancher takes care of his own, or her own, horse. Get that saddle off and your mount rubbed down."

"That's telling him," a soft voice applauded. Babs Merrill leaned against the door laughing at them, even more beautiful than when Honor had seen her before.

"Babs, welcome!" Honor stepped toward her, a smile lighting her face. "I won't offer to shake hands — they're pretty dirty!"

"That won't stop me." Phillip took the well-groomed hands in his own grimy ones. Honor saw the look in his eyes and turned her back. Who

would have thought she wouldn't have minded? She busied herself with her horse, glad for the activity to keep pace with her galloping thoughts. She really didn't mind. She only hoped Phillip could find happiness. Would Babs ever be interested in learning about God? How much happier they could be if they knew Him! She closed her lips tight. She wouldn't preach.

She didn't have to. After the leisurely dinner interspersed with laughter, Babs excused herself and went upstairs. Wondering, Honor followed to see if there was anything needed in the ornate guest suite. Babs's room door was open, but she wasn't there. Strange. Honor glanced in the open door of the guest suite bathroom. No Babs. Her own door stood open. Had Babs gone there?

Babs was sitting on Honor's bed when Honor entered. "Why did you invite me here? Another of your do-gooder deeds?" But her voice held only a flick of her usual sarcasm. "Why did you say Phillip needed me?"

"Because it's true." Honor saw the doubt mixed with hope in green eyes gone suddenly soft. The long, slender fingers trembled. Honor knew what she must do. "Babs, you were right at the canyon. Phillip saw me as a summer romance."

"And you?"

"Much more." She could be candid, open, without fear of hurt. "I was lonely. I saw everything in Phillip I'd ever wanted. Yet I also knew it would take a miracle for us to ever be happy. I wanted to believe Phillip had a longing inside for something more than his present way of life. I felt I had something to offer him." She fell silent for a moment. "Babs, I still do."

Honor saw Babs stiffen, resentment oozing from every pore.

"Wait! Not what you think, Babs! I'm married to James. I have no love for Phillip at all."

"So you didn't marry James for his money!" Babs had the grace to flush. "Maybe I've misjudged you. You're really in love with him, aren't you?"

Honor was speechless — that this woman of the world could so easily shatter her defenses.

"Honor, forgive me. But what did you mean, you still have something to offer Phillip?"

Honor's tongue was released. "I have the Lord Jesus Christ to offer Phillip. A better friend, a finer companion than anyone on earth could ever be. He's there for the taking."

Babs looked disappointed. "Oh, you mean religion."

"Not exactly." Honor's face glowed with determination. She had been given a chance to witness without preaching. She would do just that. "Religion encompasses many things. But the belief in and acceptance of Jesus Christ as your Savior is much more! God sent His only Son to earth that we might know Him and have eternal life."

"You really believe that? Why?"

Honor thought for a moment. "Babs, I was only a child when my parents were killed in the San Francisco earthquake. But I had my brother, Keith, to look after and Granny to lean on. Then Keith died somewhere in France. Granny followed. I was left alone, so alone I wished I could die, too." Tears glittered but did not fall. "For a time I was numb, uncaring. Then I knew my life had to count for something. Their work was over, mine was not."

"You mean this God of yours took away the pain?" Babs was frankly disbelieving, but at least she was listening.

"No, Babs." Honor faced her guest steadily. "The pain is there, but God has given me extra strength so I can live with it." She was encouraged by Babs's face, the almost reluctant fascination.

"Haven't you ever stayed awake at night, Babs, wondering what life is all about? Haven't you ever been so lonely you would have gladly traded everything you have to have one friend close enough to share your deepest feelings with? Haven't you ever been let down so badly, even by Phillip, you wondered if life was worth living?" She could see her shot had struck home. "God doesn't let people down. I know that now. He sent His Son to show us the best and only way to live." She broke off. What she said could be crucial at this point. She prayed silently for guidance.

Babs was no longer cynical or laughing. "Then you believe God controls everything in your life and that it's all for a purpose?"

Honor hesitated, choosing her words carefully. "Only when we accept that we are under God's control. So long as we go our way, feeling we are in charge, we step out from under His protection —" She searched for a parable. "If we were walking together down the street under an umbrella and I deliberately chose to step out from under it, I would be subject to the storm."

"But Christians still have storms in their lives." Babs's green eyes were more speculative than antagonistic. "Why doesn't God take better care of those who worship Him?"

For an instant Honor thought of James's lightly asking how she knew it wasn't God's will for her to marry him instead of Phillip. A spasm of regret chased shadows into her eyes. "Sometimes God does send trials,

Judge Bell says. I really think, though, that most of the time we bring them to ourselves when we refuse to follow Him.''

Babs slowly rose. "Glad I came." So few words in response to the message of salvation. Honor's heart sank as she hesitated, then said, "Babs, it wasn't until after my wedding I stopped rebelling against God and accepted Christ. I can honestly say it's made all the difference in the world. If you want real happiness you will seek God and help Phillip do the same." There! It was out.

Babs looked amazed. "I'd have thought you were —" Her face flushed. "I won't say it. I'll think about it, Honor."

"Don't wait too long." Honor could feel the strain in her voice. "Goodnight, Babs." Prey to her own emotions, Honor still rejoiced. At least some of the bitterness and suspicion Babs carried for her had gone. Would she consider what Honor had said? Troubled by her own flippant remarks to James, desiring to share the Lord she had ignored so long, and concerned over wondering if she could ever become the kind of witness she wanted to be, she restlessly wandered around her room, then donned her riding habit for the second time that day. Jingles was much better now. Maybe she could either lead him or ride a little on the path near the house.

Cautiously she slipped downstairs and out the door, noting it was ajar. How strange Juan had not locked it as usual! Was someone else prowling? She laughed at her groundless fears. Why get panicky over an unlocked door?

The moon was bright as she walked toward the corral, keeping her head turned back over her shoulder. Why should she feel as if she had been observed slipping from the house? Intent on watching the front door she ran smack into a solid, tall figure in riding clothes.

"Phillip!"

There was slight sound, then the man pushed back his sombrero and grinned sardonically. "Sorry to disappoint you, Mrs. Travis. Not Phillip. Just your husband." James Travis stood bareheaded before her.

How maddening! Now what did he believe about her? Honor wasn't long in finding out.

"Why did you invite Babs here? As a cover? Seems like you could wait a bit before sneaking out to meet Phillip."

"I did not come out to meet Phillip!"

"Oh?" She could see his lip curl even in the moonlight. "Then what, may I ask, are you doing running around the ranch in the middle of the night?"

Her voice quivered. "Maybe you can't understand how hard it is for me to be here." Mistaking his silence for disbelief, she stumbled on. "How would you like to live in a place where you were watched, mistrusted? How would you like to have someone spying on you all the time, waiting for you to make a mistake?"

"I was not spying. I have every right to be here. I live at Casa del Sol — or haven't you noticed?"

"I've noticed. I've noticed how everyone around here jumps without even asking how high when you speak. Phillip —"

"So you're still in love with him!"

She ignored the savage way he cut the air with his riding crop. "I am not in love with him! That doesn't mean I can't see what you are too blind to notice. Phillip worships you, wishes with all his heart and soul he could be like you! He envies your strength, longs to be able to take control as you do —"

"And covets my wife."

"He does not! You were right. He never loved anyone but Babs. I was a passing fancy, like all the rest." She paused for breath. "I hope Phillip and Babs marry and get as far away from you as possible. You don't know how to love anyone but yourself!"

It was curious what strange tricks moonlight could play. For an instant she could have sworn a shadow of terrible pain crossed the face above her. There was something deadly in his voice as he softly asked, "Oh? Have you so soon forgotten?" She was inexorably being drawn to him. Her cry of protest was smothered by his kiss, gentle at first, then demanding. When he lifted his face from hers she was exhausted.

"Good night, Mrs. Travis." With giant strides he was at the corral. Before Honor could move he had cut out Sol, leaped to his bare back, and had disappeared around the bend in the moonlight.

As she had done so many times before, Honor stood by her window, gazing down with unseeing eyes. The autumn leaves that used to greet her were gone. They had been replaced with a soft white mantle that had come during the night. She had seldom seen snow in San Francisco. Even if it did fall, the shining veil soon melted, leaving no trace of its coming. Here it meant stillness beyond belief. Every twig proudly bore its new winter garb, shining in the sun that had come out to beam on the scene.

Two laughing figures ran into view, hand in hand. Babs's scarlet coat was a brilliant spot against the all-white background. Honor smiled in sympathy as Babs's silvery laugh rang out. The change in their red-headed guest in the weeks since she had come to visit Casa del Sol was incredible. And Phillip! Honor couldn't stem the tide of warmth flooding her. Gradually Phillip Travis was growing up after all the years of childish self-indulgence.

"Come on out, Honor!"

She shook her head but called from her window. "I have something else to do. Maybe later."

"Sissy!" Babs's upturned, laughing face glowed. She snatched a handful of snow and threw it upward as Honor slammed down the window. If only she could be out there with them! If only James — but her husband was more unapproachable than ever. She had thought after the night by the corral things might get better. He was courteous, nothing more. He treated her exactly the way he treated Babs. If he noticed Phillip's and Babs's speculative gazes he ignored them.

Only once had he unbent. Phillip had insisted on being given more responsibility around the ranch. Reluctantly James had assigned him work, and it had been done well. James had sought out Honor.

"I just wanted to say I appreciate your telling me how Phillip feels." His voice was husky. "I believe he and Babs will marry and live on the ranch. I also believe they can be happy here." James had wheeled and left the room before Honor could reply.

"Hey, Honor!" Phillip's call drew her back to the window. He was lugging a huge old-fashioned sled that he must have discovered in the barn. "We're going to the big hill out back. Want to come?"

Honor's determination not to be a third party weakened. Babs was smiling and beckoning. It was too much. In a spirit of gay recklessness she threw wide her window. "Be right down!" In moments she was bundled into a heavy winter coat James had brought home from a trip to Flagstaff and sent to her by Carlotta. She snuggled in its warmth. Dark green evergreen spires tipped with snow enticed. Why worry on a day like this?

It was the most glorious day she could remember. The snow was perfect, packing down the way it had on sled hills when she was a child. Each time she raced downhill was a thrill. Sometimes alone, or with Babs; sometimes all three of them. The great *whoosh!* across the surface, growing speed, pelting down, and the final slowing and long uphill climb.

"I've never been happier," Babs confided as she and Honor pulled the big sled up the long hill after a particularly exhilarating slide. Her cheeks were redder than her coat, with no need for paint.

"It shows." Honor smiled at the other girl.

"I know." Babs's teeth gleamed. "Phillip asked me last night to marry him — on one condition." Honor could feel herself begin to tense as Babs continued. "He wants to live on the ranch. No more playboy stuff. He certainly has changed since we came here."

"What about you, Babs?"

"Me, too." She grinned impishly at Honor. "Thanks to you. When I saw how much Phillip appreciated your simplicity I decided to take stock of myself. That's why I spent so many hours alone at the South Rim."

Honor scarcely dared breathe. "And?"

"And I decided you weren't for real." She laughed at the disappointment in Honor's face. "Don't look so shocked. That was then. Since I've been here I know it's real. Someday maybe I'll even have you introduce me to your Friend." There was no mistaking her meaning.

Honor's heart swelled. It was worth all the pain and trouble she had gone through to hear Babs say that. "Don't wait too long."

"I won't." Babs twisted the emerald, now worn on her left hand. "I want to talk to Phillip about some things, and —"

"Hurry with the sled, you two! Winter will be over before you get here!" Further confidences were broken, but Babs's warm smile as she broke free and ran the few remaining steps up the hill promised other talks.

Honor trudged slowly, filled with her own thoughts. So Babs and Phillip would marry. A flick of pain at the thought of her own shadowy romance brought a lump to her throat, but she pushed it back. Phillip and Babs were arguing when she reached them.

"Aw, Babs, it's nothing. I've gone down that other side a hundred times when I was a kid." He pointed opposite the well-beaten path they had been using to a sharper decline, dotted with green trees.

"You aren't a kid. You don't know what might be under all that snow." Babs looked worried.

"I just want one trip down there."

"Please, Phillip, don't go." Honor added her entreaty to Babs's. "James has warned me so many times of the dangers on the ranch —"

"Dangers!" Phillip drew himself up in a ridiculous pose. "I know this ranch as well as I know my own bedroom." He flung himself to the awkward sled and with his feet pushed the conveyance toward the edge of the bank.

"*Stop!*" The hail came from a tall man running toward them, his face a thundercloud in its command. "Don't push off that sled!"

Honor saw the opposition roused in Phillip by James's curt order.

"Sorry, brother! I get first ride." With a mighty shove he pushed over the edge and started down before James could reach him. "This is the life!" His voice floated back to them, only to be drowned out. The sled must have hit a hidden snag. For one terrible moment it seemed to stand on end. Phillip was thrown downhill, sliding, arms flailing in a vain effort to stop his momentum. To the horrified gaze of the onlookers he gathered speed in spite of his efforts, smashed into a great tree, and crumpled into a heap.

"Phillip!" Heedless of his own safety, James started down the hill. His great boots sank into the snow as he went, leaving giant stride marks. Clutching at every outstretched branch, he slipped, slid, and by sheer determination stopped where Phillip lay horribly crumpled.

Babs was the first to come to her senses. "Quick! We'll get help!" She grabbed Honor's arm, shaking her back to reality. "We've got to get back to the house and call a doctor. Or at least get Juan and Rosa. They'll know what to do." Cupping her hands around her mouth she called to James, "We're going for help."

Fear lent wings to their feet as they raced back to the house. They burst into the kitchen. "Rosa, Phillip's hurt. Where's Juan?"

Concern didn't detract from Rosa's swift actions. "Out shoveling." She threw open the door and called to him, waving her arms imperatively. "Juan! Quickly, Felipe is hurt!"

In moments Juan, Babs, and Honor were huddled in the big Willys as it

churned through the snow down a little-used road that would bring them out only a few hundred feet below the brothers. "I'm so thankful for this heavy car," Honor breathed.

Juan braked, stopped, and was out of the car and up the separating distance, closely followed by the two girls. James looked up to answer the unspoken question trembling on their lips. "He's hurt — badly." He pressed his scarf against Phillip's head. Honor could see bright bloodstains on the snow. "We've got to get him to a doctor."

"Rosa is calling one now." Honor found her voice, but James shook his head. "We can't wait for a doctor. We'll take him to Flagstaff immediately."

Honor's involuntary protest died under the look of anguish in James's eyes. "But how —" she faltered.

"The roads are clear." Already Juan and James were lifting Phillip carefully, inching their way down to the car. "We'll get him in the back where he can lie down. Mama Rosa will know what to do until we get to Flagstaff."

It was a nightmare Honor would never forget. The seemingly endless procession to the house, the fitting in all of them and still leaving room for Phillip to half lie down.

"Can you drive?" James whirled toward Honor. "I want Juan to help me steady Phillip."

"Not in snow and ice." She shivered. "I only learned here this fall."

"I can." Babs's lips were white but determined. Already she was slipping into the driver's seat. Mama Rosa stayed with the two men, pressing compresses hard on the wound spurting blood. Carlotta huddled between Babs and Honor in the front seat. There had been no question but that they would all go. *It's a family,* Honor thought. *My family.* But there was no time to explore such thoughts.

The road to Flagstaff was icy and had not been sanded. In spite of Babs's skillful handling of the car, it still slid now and then.

Once Babs looked across at Honor. "Now's the time to call on that God you told me about." There was no mockery in her words.

"I am." Honor's lips moved silently.

Mile after mile they traveled as fast as Babs dared. When they reached the outskirts of Flagstaff, Honor breathed normally again, but it wasn't until they were in the emergency waiting room with Phillip on his way to surgery that some of the tenseness left her.

"He's cut badly on his head," the doctor had told them after the first cursory examination. "He doesn't appear to have lost too much blood. No

bones appear to be broken but —" he hesitated "— there is always the danger of internal bleeding."

If James Travis's face could have gone whiter it did. Babs stifled a little moan, and Honor reached for her hand to grip it hard. "Don't, Babs. God will take care of Phillip. I know He will." Something in her level look steadied Babs, who clung to her.

But James couldn't hold back bitter words. "If there really is a God, why did He let Phillip get hurt in the first place?"

Honor's heart sank. James would never understand. "God didn't force Phillip to go down that hill." James didn't speak but turned away, leaving Honor shaken. In spite of everything, she had hoped they could make their marriage work. But if James had no use for God, how could it ever be?

It seemed hours before the doctor returned. His face was grave. "He will live." His words were almost lost in the gasps of relief, but the doctor's face didn't lighten. "He will live, but —" He looked around the little group, at James last of all. "The head wound is close to his eyes. We found a piece of bone depressed into the brain. The surgeons are working with it now. Until it is over and he wakens we just won't know."

"Just won't know what?" James's face blazed.

The doctor's face wrinkled in sympathy. "Whether he will ever see again."

Honor felt the shock ripple around the circle.

"Blind!" James repeated stupidly.

"There is that possibility." The doctor gripped James's arm. "We are doing everything humanly possible, and —"

"You said humanly possible. What else could be done?" James's ashen face frightened Honor.

The doctor didn't waver. "There is a power higher than man." With another strong pressure on James's arm he turned and left them. This time there was no mockery in James's voice. "Honor?" He turned toward her, stumbling a bit. "Honor? You know that higher power. Will you do something?" The pleading in his eyes hurt Honor.

"I have been praying ever since the accident."

Babs seemed to come to life. "Honor, if I promised God to live as He wants, would He save Phillip's sight?"

Honor's lips felt stiff. "You can't bargain with God. All we can do is pray — and wait."

"She's right." Judge Bell stood in the doorway, panting as if he had been running. Babs instinctively turned toward the kindness in his face.

"There, lassie, we must trust our Father in heaven —"

"Trust Him! I don't even know Him!" James's face contorted in agony. "All this time, you tried to tell me, and I wouldn't listen. Daddy — is Phillip's accident a punishment because I haven't believed?"

Honor stood rooted in sorrow. She remembered asking the same question.

"No." There was something magnificent about the judge. "God punishes us for our own sins, not those of others."

James's face was chalky. He went on as if he had not heard. "I should have been an example. Why haven't I been what I should have been? Phillip is weak, and I knew it." He raised dull eyes toward Honor. "If I had believed in Christ and told Philip how important it was, maybe he wouldn't be such a mess. Maybe he wouldn't even be lying there now." His harsh laugh grated in the shocked silence. "I contributed to his weakness."

Honor could not bear his suffering. She turned away.

James looked at Daddy Bell. "You told me I would have to face God, to answer for laughing at the idea I wasn't in total control. But did it have to come this way? Did anyone ever sin as I have, deliberately choosing to ignore everything that really matters in life?"

"Come, laddie." Daddy Bell placed his arm around James as if he had been a child. "We'll fight this out together."

Honor and Babs stood frozen as the two men, one bent with the ministry of years, the other from his growing recognition of sin and careless ignorance of sacred things, slowly walked down the long hall and disappeared behind a door marked CHAPEL.

Honor could not speak. Even when Babs moaned and sank into a chair, Honor remained standing straight, looking down the hall. It suddenly seemed a great gulf separating her from James. What happened now would literally save her husband's life or leave him empty, unfulfilled, bitter.

"Oh, God, let him accept Your Son that he might be forgiven." It was all she could whisper. If only she could be at his side! She could not. It would be for Judge Bell to make clear the only path that did not lead to spiritual death. Then James must make the decision, not to attempt a bargain with God for his brother's sight, but to seal himself as God's child, forgiven and willing to obey.

Was all of life a fight? Sickness, health — good, evil — God, Satan — in spite of her studies the thoughts left Honor helpless.

What was happening in the little chapel? Was James listening with his heart instead of with his head, as so many educated minds seemed to do?

Could the prejudices and false images he had built be shattered? Yes! Hadn't God done exactly that for her?

A little cry from Babs snapped Honor from her trancelike state. There was work to do here. God would help James. She would cling to that hope and silently pray. Her other prayers for Phillip and Babs mingled together in one great plea to God.

For hours she and Babs sat together. The waiting room was mercifully empty of others. Only fear kept them company, and after a time, even it was blunted by sheer exhaustion. At first Honor tried to keep up a conversation with Babs, but it was useless. Babs's eyes were fixed on the door to the emergency room. Was she remembering all the laughing days they had spent carelessly going their pleasure-mad way? Was she remembering moments at the canyon when she had gone away from the others to evaluate? Or was she even remembering days long ago before Phillip, days when she said she had gone to Sunday school?

Honor's brain whirled. The broken woman next to her was a far cry from the worldly creature who had once infuriated a rebellious girl by telling her the truth about Phillip. Impulsively Honor laid her hand over Babs's clenched ones.

The green eyes swung to her briefly. A small tremor of her lips betrayed tightly held emotion, and her hands opened to clasp the one extended in friendship. There was a gentle pressure of the cold fingers that slowly warmed, then the icy face gave way to pain, unashamed.

An eon of time seemed to have passed before the chapel door swung open. Honor held her breath. What would be the results of what had happened in the little room?

"James has found his God." Daddy's tired face still radiated.

With a little cry Honor ran to them. "It wasn't just to save Phillip?"

James went white to the lips, and Honor wished fervently she had bitten her tongue to hold back the words.

"No. It wasn't for Phillip." He looked past her, eyes dulled instead of expectant as they had been before. "I read your Bible, Honor. At first, it was with scorn. How could anyone believe any tale so simple?" His dark eyes were almost black in their intensity. "You had circled a place." He fumbled in the Bible she knew so well, found the marked passage. "John three sixteen: 'For God so loved the world, that he gave his only begotten Son, that whosoever believeth in him should not perish, but have everlasting life.'" He closed the Book, almost reverently. "I still wouldn't admit the feeling I had when I read it." A spasm of pain crossed his face. "Daddy Bell made me reread it. Then I knew. *Whosoever* meant me, and

everyone. Every man, woman, and child on earth must bow before God, admit they are sinners, and realize the fact of the Lord Jesus Christ's death in their place so that they might have forgiveness, mercy, salvation. I only wish I had listened and accepted it all years ago." The last words were almost a whisper.

For an ecstatic moment Honor felt faint from joy and relief. Her prayers had been answered — James was saved! Now there was nothing to stand between them! Now they could — the thought died. Just because James had accepted Christ didn't mean he loved the woman he'd married under such bizarre circumstances.

"I intend to set straight everything I have done to wrong others." James's voice broke into her mind.

Honor bit her lip. He must mean her. He would feel the only way to make things right was to release her. Could she stand the pain still ahead? Would she never stop paying for her rebellion and willfulness, even though she was forgiven?

And James — he would carry forever the memory of the way he had married his twin's fiancee in an underhanded way. Both would pay in being freed by law from unfulfilled vows, bound in God's sight — and in their own. Granny's warning, Keith's pleadings — all had led to this, and there was no one to blame but herself.

She breathed raggedly. It was not the time to explore their relationship, with Phillip still in danger, nor was it in days following. Babs haunted the hospital. For even though the doctors were hopeful, there was nothing to do but wait.

One thing that came about from all the trouble was a new closeness between Babs and Honor. From distrust to wariness, at last to the acceptance of Honor's hand at the hospital that terrible night, Babs took slow steps toward trusting another woman. Honor sensed the struggle. How terrible to have lived among those where self-preservation ruled out real friendship!

One evening Babs said, "Honor, the hardest thing in the world for me is to admit I'm wrong, but if I'd admitted to myself at the canyon what I knew you were, I'd never have said all those terrible things."

Honor looked up from mending a blouse she'd brought to the hospital. "They were all true. I didn't realize how true until I came here and accepted Christ. I'm glad you said what you did, although it made me angry. Even though I couldn't accept it at the time, I thought of it later and admitted you were right."

"Even if Phillip is blind, I'm going to marry him."

Honor dropped her mending. "Will he?"

"I'm not letting him go again — ever." There was nothing of the sophisticate in the determination in Babs's face. "It's not from pity. I've always loved him. I just couldn't trust him not to find another pretty face, and now he may not be able to even see those faces."

"Stop it!" Honor dropped the blouse and shook Babs hard. "The doctor says he has every reason to believe Phillip will be all right."

"Then why doesn't he regain total consciousness?" The cry echoed doubts in Honor's own mind. "Honor, I have to have something to hang on to, like you have. Would God really forgive me and send peace?"

"If you confess youself a sinner."

"You'll never know how great a sinner." The admission was low.

"I don't want to. It's between you and God. That's why Jesus died on the cross, to save you forever from all that. He took your place, Babs."

"But what do I do?"

"Just repent and then accept it. Salvation is a free gift. You gain eternal life. You gain Christ and the Holy Spirit and peace from God. You are free, Babs, free from every ugly thing in your past." Honor breathed a prayer and took Babs's ice-cold hands in her own. "Just tell Him you are sorry for all your sins and accept the gift of His Son and salvation."

"I —" The opening of the door from Phillip's room cut her short.

"He is awake." The doctor's smile warmed Honor's heart.

Babs remained frozen in place for one second, then gave a low cry and ran into the room.

"It's all right," the doctor told Honor. "The first thing he said was, 'Where's Babs?' "

Babs didn't stay long in Phillip's room. When she came back she was radiant. "He complained of a headache, but he can see!"

Honor felt as if the strain that had been holding her up suddenly gave way. She stumbled into a chair, trying to form words for the praise and gladness in her heart. Phillip would not be blind! *Please,* her heart whispered, *cure Phillip and Babs of a different kind of blindness and help them find You.* What would Babs have said if the door had not opened just when it did? She had been close, so close!

The question haunted Honor for the next week. During that week Phillip was pronounced fit and sent home. What a far cry from that terrible trip they had made taking him to the hospital!

The touring car with James, Honor, Phillip, and Babs swung into the driveway to be greeted with Christmas garnish. Decorations were everywhere. The Hernandez family had spread sweet-smelling boughs, bright ribbons, every kind of decoration they could imagine.

"Some welcome home." Phillip sounded subdued. "I could have been —"

"Thank God you aren't." James spoke softly.

"You? Thanking God?"

But the old, mocking light died from Phillip's face as James replied, "I have discovered what a fool I have been in discounting the only thing in the world that really matters."

Phillip swung to Babs, standing close in the lightly falling snow. "I suppose next you'll be telling me you feel the same."

Honor's fingers clenched until they were white, even under their warm wool mitten covering. The group of four stood motionless. Could Babs sense she was at a crossroads?

"I —" her pleading gaze at Honor lifted to Phillip's handsome face "— I am glad to be home." She broke free of the group and hurried through the massive front door.

Honor's disappointment spilled over. She had to turn away from the two men to hide her telltale face. Babs had been so close! It was all she could do to pretend gaiety at the Mexican meal Rosa and Carlotta had prepared to welcome Phillip home. Once she met James's searching eyes, and a faltering smile hovered on her lips. Later he whispered, "Don't forget — God reached even me."

In the library before the fire after dinner Phillip paced restlessly and finally whirled toward Babs. "Well, are you going to marry me on Christmas Eve?"

Babs gasped, then recovered something of her old haughtiness. "I am not." Before anyone could move she added, "But I will marry you on Christmas Day."

"This is our cue for an exit." James motioned Honor out of the room.

"Well, it looks as if things are going to work out for Phillip and Babs." Honor stopped at the foot of the great staircase and smiled at James.

His face didn't light up the way she had expected. For one moment he seemed to be looking over her head and into the future. Somber, brooding, his answer chilled her. "Yes, things have turned out for them. But what about us?"

Before she could speak, he was gone.

As she slowly mounted the stairs to her room, again she felt alone — only this time God was there to help her bear the pain. Yet even that pain gave way before another disappointment the same night. After tossing and turning for what seemed like hours she was startled to hear her door slowly opening.

"Honor?" Babs glided to the bed.

"Babs!" Surprise choked off Honor's voice. "Are you ill?"

"No."

The snow outside had stopped earlier. Now a pale moon targeted the red-haired woman through Honor's partly uncurtained window. Yet even the dim light failed to hide her agitation. Her hands were icy as one brushed against Honor's face.

"Honor? I have to talk with you."

Sleep fled. "What is wrong, Babs?"

"I tried to tell Phillip what you said about God."

"And?" Honor held her breath.

"He laughed. Not so much as he would have done before the accident, but he still laughed."

Honor's heart ached for the desolate sound in her friend's voice. "What about you, Babs? You know it's all true, don't you?"

"Yes." Babs's face turned even paler. "But I can't accept it." As if she felt Honor's shock she brokenly added, "I've waited years for Phillip to notice me in a real way. Nothing must spoil that!"

Her cry echoed in Honor's heart, a duplicate of her own cry at the canyon's edge what seemed like eons ago. "You are choosing Phillip instead of God?"

"I must." The icy hands clutched the warm one Honor held out. "Phillip has already changed more than I ever thought possible. We're going to make our home here. He's going to give up drinking and all that. Isn't it enough?" Her voice was anguished.

"No, Babs." The inflexibility of the two words wilted Babs.

Honor couldn't keep despair from her voice as she cried out, "The greatest sin in the world is not accepting the free gift of salavation through the Lord Jesus Christ. All the being good in the world, all the good deeds won't save you or anyone. Please, Babs." Her voice rose. "Don't turn your back on Him. Don't crucify the Lord again by your refusal to accept Him!"

Babs slowly withdrew her hands from Honor's desperate clutch. Her eyes held fear, regret, pain. She rose from the bed where she'd been seated to tower over Honor. "I have no choice. I can never give up Phillip."

For one wild moment Honor wondered — should she tell Babs she, too, had once made that same choice and with what tragic results? Slowly she shook her head. Now was not the time for that. Instead she said, "Babs, I once demanded my own way and have gone through agony because of it. I had to come to Christ just as I would have done before. But instead of it being easy and natural, there were years of pain and bitterness in between. We have to learn the same lessons, whether we do it God's way — or our own, and our way is hard."

"Someday, if Phillip can accept — I will, too." Babs slipped out.

The tears on Honor's pillow that night were not for herself.

Christmas and the wedding rushed toward them. Soon it was Christmas Eve. Babs had not mentioned her decision since that night. Neither had Honor, who now lay sleepless. When God directed her to speak she would. Until then, she could only pray.

At least she could be thankful for the change in Phillip. He was becoming more like his brother every day. He had accepted his future at Casa del Sol, relishing it. The brothers spent time planning how to make it more efficient. Phillip had come up with some surprisingly good ideas. "Just because I wasn't running this place doesn't mean I never thought about it." The casual remark didn't hide his pleasure at their compliments.

Suddenly Honor could stand the confines of her room no longer. James's inscrutable eyes watched her from every corner. She would slip down to the library and find something to read. James still had her Bible, but she had noticed a big one downstairs with more references than the small one Daddy Bell had given her.

Before she could reconsider, Honor thrust her arms into a heavy turquoise quilted robe and matching slippers. She ran lightly down the stairs, struggled with the heavy doors, then crept inside. Fumbling for the light switch, she was immobilized by the tall, dark figure rising from the couch, etched against glowing flames in the fireplace.

"James?"

"At least you didn't call me Phillip. Do come into my parlor, dear little fly."

Why did he still have the power to hurt her? Or was it weariness in his voice instead of sarcasm? She ran her hand lightly over her hair. "I couldn't sleep. I came for a book."

He came a step nearer. "And just why couldn't you sleep?"

She could feel it coming — the floods of feeling behind the dam of control she had built so carefully. If she answered, that last line of defense would crumble under the onslaught.

"I asked why you couldn't sleep."

His insistence was the final undoing. "How could you expect me to sleep — under the circumstances?"

"You mean because Phillip is marrying Babs tomorrow?" She had never felt as flayed as she did by his accusation.

"Don't be completely stupid!" She hadn't known she could blaze so. All the long nights of wondering, of loving him hopelessly burst forth. "It's you, James Travis. Are you too insane to see it?"

A disbelieving look crept over his face. "Just what is that supposed to mean?"

The ice in his voice drowned all determination to tell him the truth. Honor fell back on the old, original reason. "You really think any woman in my position could be happy? Married to a man who did it to protect her from his own brother?" She could feel his scrutiny even when she dropped her eyes to study the pattern one nervous, slippered foot was making on the floor.

"Oh, that." His voice went lifeless. For a moment he turned to the fire. The lights from the Christmas tree shone on his face, softening it into vulnerability. Honor knew she would never forget the way he looked. To hide the weakness threatening to paralyze her, she walked to the window, noting the heavy frost patterns and that it had begun to snow again.

"Honor, would you come sit down, please." There was no spark in the request. Slowly she turned and crossed to the fire, carefully avoiding him.

"Honor, when I was in the chapel at the hospital and finally quit trying to outrun God, I made a promise." Something in the gravity of his tone

chilled her. "You had said people couldn't bargain with God. I didn't. I did tell Him that when it was all over I'd do what I could to make up to you for marrying you."

For one wild moment Honor's heart leaped. Did he mean that he had learned to care? She was frozen anew by his next words. Face half in shadow, he poked the fire again. "I have put it off, hoping something would happen to change things. Maybe I was even hoping for a miracle. I planned to wait until after the wedding tomorrow." He threw the poker down with a little crash. "I can't wait any longer."

In spite of the warm room Honor shivered with premonition. Could God hear the silent prayer unconsciously going up for help?

"I can't go on the way things are. It's too hard having you here, knowing you despise me."

Shocked, she opened her mouth to protest, only to have the words die on her lips as he said, "I want you to go away. The day after the wedding I'll take you to Flagstaff. We can get the marriage annulled. I'll settle enough finances on you so you can be independent, but I won't keep you here any longer."

Sheer fury overrode Honor's sense of loss. Very slowly she rose to her feet, glaring up at the man who was her husband yet was not her husband. "So now that you've married me, you'll just pack me off the way you'd discard an old pair of shoes." She failed to understand what was in James's eyes. "Well, let me tell you something, Mr. Travis. I won't be shipped off and have money settled on me! I'm not leaving Casa del Sol. You don't have to like it, but you married me for better or for worse. I'm legally your wife. There's nothing you can do about it unless you want the whole story spread across the front page of every newspaper in Arizona."

She paused for breath, then went on. "Have you ever once considered that I don't want to go?"

"I have considered it." His face was still in shadow, but the words came out individually, like small, hard ice cubes hitting a tile floor. "I know you would rather live in misery than break a promise. Now that I have stopped running from God I appreciate it even more. But the promise you made was made falsely. I can't hold you to it."

"So you intend to dispose of me quite properly."

For one moment she felt she had gone too far. There was a quick flash in the set face. "I told you. I can't go on like we are now." In one stride he came close, gripping her by the shoulders, forcing her to look up at him. "If you stay at Casa del Sol it can no longer be as a guest, Honor Travis. It will be as my wife, living with me in holy matrimony the way God intended

man and woman to live." His look seared her very soul. "Will you stay under those circumstances? Or will you go to Flagstaff day after tomorrow, as I suggested?"

Honor's knees felt weak. "You mean — you mean you want me to stay as your wife?"

"Want you! I have wanted you since the day I looked up to see you standing in the hall of my home." His grip tightened. "If ever a man wanted a woman, I want you. You have brought sunlight and laughter. You have brought healing between Phillip and me. You have brought everything a man could ever want. Most of all, you have brought God into this house." His voice had dropped almost to a whisper. "Yes, I want you here — but not as a guest."

Honor was speechless, shaken by his passion. "Then all the time — even when you married me — it wasn't just because you pitied me?"

"No, Honor. It was because I loved you. I didn't know it myself at first. I tried to tell myself it was to save you from Phillip. It wasn't. I fell in love with you the day you came."

Honor's senses were reeling. "But — the day we were married, when I said you probably would say you'd fallen in love with me —" her voice failed.

"Would you have believed me?"

"Not then."

"And now?" The clock ticked off seconds, repeating his question: *And now? And now?*

She was not quite ready to give in. "You said friends were people who trusted you." She moistened her suddenly dry lips. "You said —"

An amused look cut off her stumbling speech. "I said a lot of things — some in self-defense. What I am telling you now is the truth. I love you, Honor, as I have never loved any other woman. I will never love anyone else, even if you go away."

"Then I had better stay."

"You know my conditions."

"I know."

But James wasn't satisfied. He held her off at arms' length. "Are you staying because you promised — because you don't want to break vows you consider holy, even taken under the circumstances ours were made? Or is it possible that Phillip was right?"

It was becoming increasingly difficult for her to meet his searching gaze. "I don't know what Phillip said."

"Phillip told me weeks ago you had never loved him. You had fallen in love with what you thought he was."

Honor didn't answer. Her mind flashed back to the canyon; her rationalizing what Phillip might someday be; her determination to cling to him even at the expense of her own relationship with God.

"Well?"

Her eyes grew soft, but she bravely faced him. "Phillip was right." She hurried on, disturbed by the light filling his dark face. "Carlotta asked me which man I loved — you heard her — and my answer."

Color crept into James's face. "It is the only hope I had these past weeks."

Honor wasn't finished. Her clear eyes confirmed her truthfulness. "I was attracted to Phillip, you know that. In San Francisco, at the canyon.

"When I came to Casa del Sol I had to revamp my opinion. Where was the charming, idle man I knew? My fiance was no longer the laughing Phillip Travis, but 'Senor' — admired, respected, a big man doing a big job. It was hard to put the two together!

"James, I ran ahead of God, went on with the wedding, hoped for the best." Her throat was thick with unshed tears. "I have paid. Learning to know you, feeling I was a duty —" She felt heat creep into her cheeks. "But at least God didn't allow me to actually marry the wrong man."

She faltered as James gently pulled her closer. "You really care, Honor? You aren't just bound by your vows?"

A flash of mischief crossed her face. "All my childhood heroes rode white horses, just as you do." The hope and disbelief warring in his face were too much. She discarded her pretense. "I am bound, but not only by my vows. I am bound by the love I have for you — love that is second only to my love for the Lord."

Somewhere in the hall the clock struck twelve. Christmas Eve was over; Christmas Day had begun.

Honor closed her eyes and crept closer in her husband's arms, feeling the solid strength of James Travis. For one magnificent moment she seemed to see down the aisle of years — laughing, weeping, loving, sharing, together — loving life with Christ the Son as head of Casa del Sol.

Flip over for another great novel!
**THE CALLING OF
ELIZABETH COURTLAND**